THEY ALL HAD A RECKONING

A vow. A risk. A dilemma. A murder.
(They All Had A Reason. Book 7)

Michele Leathers

EMAR Publishing

ISBN-13: 9798863317540

Cover design by: Michele Leathers
Library of Congress Control Number: 2018675309
Printed in the United States of America

To my posterity.

CHAPTER 1

Victoria

Some people seem to attract trouble everywhere they go. Most of the time, it's plain from their choices and actions that they bring it on themselves. But there is a less common type of person, whom trouble just seems to follow through no fault of their own. I was one of these people. When I was in the third grade, my best friend Lucy died from an allergic reaction to a peanut. In sixth grade, my new best friend Monica drowned in her backyard pool. In eighth grade, another friend, Vivian Drennon, died when she fell off a cliff while hiking. The latest friend to die was Chantel Trainer. She was murdered. I worried that through whatever cosmic force of doom that followed me, anyone who became my friend was sealing their own fate. My current best friend was Bellany Silverfield. She was still alive and well, and I desperately hoped she would stay that way.

Lately, Bellany has been obsessing over a guy from her past named Cory. She wouldn't stop talking about him and claimed that she wanted revenge for whatever hurt he had caused her. But I was starting to wonder if revenge figured into it at all. If she couldn't get over him and move on, it obviously wouldn't end well for her. I spent many restless hours imagining the multitude of ways that Bellany's stalking of an ex-boyfriend could leave me, once again, without a friend.

"Victoria!" Bellany snapped, ripping me from my thoughts. She was holding a scorching hot curling iron dangerously close to my forehead. "Hold still."

"I'm trying," I insisted, watching her through the

reflection in the bathroom mirror. "But you keep pulling my hair."

She rolled her eyes. "You complain way too much."

That was totally untrue. I hardly ever complained. In fact, I hadn't complained once about staying at a vacation home in Costa Maya, Mexico, just so she could be close to Cory.

"Now remember," Bellany said, setting down the curling iron. "Tasha may be fourteen, but cognitively, she's more like a seven year old. She's also the most important person in the world to Cory. She's his only family. So you need to become friends with her too."

I had no idea how I was going to convince Cory and his sister to become friends with me--a total stranger. And honestly, I didn't even want to try. Bellany just assumed that I would go along with her plan. She never once asked me what I wanted to do.

Bellany's icy blue eyes narrowed, pulling me from my thoughts.

"What?" I asked, unsure what I had done to make her mad. Was I breathing too loud?

"You cannot wear that." She gestured to my shorts and striped shirt. Then she walked out of the bathroom, and I followed.

"What's wrong with my outfit?"

"It's too bright and cheerful."

"Really?" I was surprised to hear this. I had no idea that my outfit was too cheerful. I thought it was cute. "What do you want me to wear?"

She rummaged through her closet while I slipped out of my clothes. I stood there in a one piece swimsuit, which I had been wearing underneath. Bellany had picked it out, so I already knew she approved.

I forced a smile as she handed me a pair of distressed denim shorts and a plain white T-shirt. "This is cute," I lied. I thought the outfit was boring and ugly, just like the swimsuit.

I quickly got dressed and winced at my reflection in the

full length mirror. I planned on packing a bag with some extra clothes and a different swimsuit to change into after I left the house. What Bellany doesn't know won't hurt her, right?

She tucked a strand of hair behind her ear, revealing a one carat diamond stud earring. I had a matching pair in my jewelry box, but she wouldn't allow me to wear them today.

"Another word of advice..." she said, picking a piece of lint off my shirt. "Cory might act disinterested, but don't let that stop you from talking to him."

How was I supposed to talk to someone who didn't want to talk to me? That wasn't going to be easy. "What am I supposed to say to him?"

"Just be fun and act casual."

"What if he completely ignores me?" I asked, following her down the hall to the bathroom.

"Don't let him."

Ever since Bellany and I first met, she has been mentoring me and teaching me how to be more assertive and confident. I felt like I had made a lot of progress over these past six months. She wasn't calling me an airhead as much any more. Sometimes she even said nice things and complimented me--she never used to do that before.

But today her advice hasn't been all that helpful. I wanted her to provide me with more direction. "I still don't know what to say to him."

"Talk about anything that pops into your head," she said as she smiled at her reflection in the mirror and ran a brush through her hair. She had recently gotten rid of the purple streaks and dyed her hair chocolate brown. The dark color complimented her tanned skin and made her blue eyes really stand out.

I sometimes still couldn't believe how someone as beautiful and smart as her could be my best friend. I felt unworthy.

Her eyes suddenly widened, shifting to me. "Scratch what I just said. You can talk about anything you want, except podcasts and true crime."

"I wasn't going to bring those things up," I assured her.

On our drive to Mexico, Bellany and I listened to several of Cory's old podcasts, which were all about her. I learned about everything she had done wrong and all of the crimes she had committed. She filled in the gaps of the story that Cory wasn't able to tell, because he didn't have all the information.

She told me that Cory had spent two years tracking her down, and she seemed kind of flattered by his commitment.

When he finally caught up to her in Las Vegas, they became real close. Bellany told me Cory was an amazing kisser-- better than anyone she had ever kissed before.

Then she told me how she manipulated him into being her partner in a kidnapping for ransom scheme. Bellany thought she had complete control over Cory, but she had underestimated him. Cory betrayed her, stole all the money, and left her with nothing.

"Hold still," Bellany said as she began coating my hair with a thick layer of hairspray.

She had dyed my hair the same chocolate brown color as hers, and I loved the way it looked on me. But then she insisted on giving my hair a trim. She chopped it up to my shoulders, and I nearly cried.

I had wanted to keep my hair long like hers. But she claimed that shorter hair made me look older. Bellany didn't want people to know that I had just turned seventeen. She wanted me to tell everyone I was nineteen, like her.

"Have you come up with a backstory about yourself yet?" she asked.

"No." I had no clue what kinds of lies I was going to tell Cory. "Do you have any suggestions?"

Bellany dipped a makeup brush in face powder. "You could tell him that you came to Mexico to escape your abusive parents. Act like you're still afraid of them."

I had not grown up in an abusive household and had no idea what it was like. My parents were kind to me. They loved and adored me, and I missed them more than anything. But I had never admitted any of this to Bellany. She thought I hated my parents and had zero regrets about running away from home.

"Abusive parents? Are you sure that's a good idea?" I asked.

She brushed the powder onto my nose and chin. "Tasha's foster parents abused her, so he'll sympathize with that kind of story."

"Oh," I replied, still unsure if I wanted to use her idea.

She dipped the brush into face powder again, then applied it to my cheeks and forehead. "Cory understands how difficult it can be to escape from an abusive situation. He had to kidnap Tasha in order to rescue her from her foster parents."

"How did you find out about that?" I asked.

"I read about it online." Bellany opened a drawer and rummaged through it. "So what do you think?" She handed me a tube of lip gloss.

The lip gloss was light pink. Did she think I wanted to wear something darker? "Pink is nice."

"No." She made a face. "About the story you're going to tell Cory. Do you like my idea or not?"

"I don't know..." I hesitated, trying to think of what to say. I couldn't just tell her straight out that I hated her idea. "Do you have any other suggestions?" I hoped she would come up with something that didn't involve lying about my parents.

"Why? What's wrong with that story?"

"Nothing, I just... That kind of story is too personal to Cory, so I'm afraid he won't believe me."

She angled her head, brows furrowed. "You're a really convincing liar, Victoria. I've seen you do it plenty of times, so I know what I'm talking about."

I wasn't as good as she was--not even close!

Bellany started to put away the makeup and hair care products that were scattered across the counter. "You're all set," she said.

It was time for me to go. But I wasn't ready--I didn't want

to do this. "Bellany, are you sure getting mixed up in Cory's life again is a good idea?"

She tossed a hair brush into the drawer and it landed with a loud thud. "Of course it's a good idea."

I disagreed. This whole situation made me nervous. "Just how do you plan on getting revenge?" I asked. "Because you still haven't explained it to me. All you said was that you want me to spy on Cory. Why?"

"Because I need more information. I need to find out what's going on in his life." Bellany picked up the can of hair spray and set it in the cupboard. "Cory doesn't have a social media presence, so I have no idea what he's been up to. Find out if he has a girlfriend or if he still has feelings for me. Find out if he misses me."

She looked up, staring at me through the reflection in the mirror, a serious expression on her face. "This kind of information is important."

Why did she want to know whether he still liked her and missed her? Was it because she felt that way about him? "Bellany, be honest with me. What's the real reason we're here?"

Her eyes blinked rapidly, brows furrowed. "I already told you why we're here. To get revenge."

"Are you sure there isn't another reason, like maybe you have feelings for Cory?"

Bellany's mouth dropped open in a mask of shock. "Have you lost your mind? He betrayed me. He left me with nothing!"

My cheeks burned with embarrassment as her words echoed in my ears--*Have you lost your mind?* But I had every reason to believe that she liked Cory. I was her best friend and could sense these kinds of things about her.

"Well, it sure seems like you like him," I said with a shrug. I wasn't trying to fight or argue with Bellany. I just wanted her to recognize her true feelings. "I mean, why else would you want to know if he has a girlfriend or if he misses you?"

A line formed between Bellany's eyebrows, which meant her Botox was wearing off, and she was also furious. I immediately regretted pushing her on this issue. It wasn't my intention to upset her.

"Clearly you don't understand how revenge works," she hissed, "so let me explain it to you. Discovering what matters most to a person and then taking it away from them is the ultimate form of revenge." Her jaw clenched. "Does that make sense, or should I break it down like I'm talking to a five year old?"

I ignored her insult and focused on something way more important: Bellany had just contradicted herself, and I couldn't wait to point it out. "Bellany," I said, calmly. "I don't believe there's anything more we need to find out about Cory. You already told me what matters most to him. Tasha."

Bellany slammed a drawer shut, making me jump. "You're not listening to me!" She threw the curling iron into another drawer. "Tasha might not be the only person that Cory cares about. There might be someone else--that's what I want you to find out!"

My heart sank as I contemplated what she just said. I believed the other person she was referring to was herself. Bellany thought that Cory's love for her rivaled the love he had for his sister. I desperately hoped that wasn't true. If she and Cory got back together, where would that leave me?

"Sorry, I didn't mean to upset you," I said.

"Oh, yes you did!" She slammed another drawer shut. "Do me a favor, Victoria. The next time you want to insult my intelligence and call me stupid, just come right out and say it!"

"I didn't--that's not what I meant--" I stammered, unsure what to say.

"Just get out of here!"

Crashes and bangs continued to erupt from the bathroom as I raced down the hall to my bedroom. I had gotten used to Bellany throwing temper tantrums. She did it often. Normally I just stayed out of her way and kept quiet until it was over with.

I quickly packed a bag for the beach as my mind swirled with thoughts about Cory. I had only seen him from a distance, and as far as I could tell, he wasn't that handsome. Sure, he was cute and everything, but so were a lot of guys. I seriously couldn't figure out what made him so special. Bellany was gorgeous. She could have any guy she wanted. Why him?

With my bag in hand, I tiptoed down the hall toward the door.

"Victoria," Bellany called, startling me.

"Yeah?" I said in a small voice.

She glared at me, arms folded tightly across her chest. "You better not mess this up."

"I won't," I promised. But I had never been good at keeping promises.

CHAPTER 2

Victoria

I dug my toes into the warm sand and stared out at the ocean. Despite the sound of soothing waves rolling in and out, the beautiful view in front of me, and the cool breeze blowing through the air, I couldn't relax. I felt conflicted, unsure what to do.

Any minute now, Tasha would come bounding out of her house with a bag full of shovels and buckets, and Cory would be right behind her. I wondered if I should just leave while I still had the chance.

Then I could lie to Bellany and tell her that I tried to talk to them, but they wouldn't cooperate. I could say that they were rude and dismissive. This new plan of mine seemed way better than Bellany's.

Just as I was about to get up and leave, an alarming thought popped into my head. What if Bellany was watching me? Then she would know if I lied.

As I turned to scan the trees behind me, I saw a gray-haired old lady heading straight toward me. I thought that I was alone and was surprised to see her. She was wearing big sunglasses that covered half her face. Her long sundress was blowing in the breeze, getting wrapped up in her legs as she walked.

"Beautiful isn't it?" The old woman gestured to the ocean. I squinted as the sun reflected off of a thick gold chain around her neck. Two pendants hung from it: a large letter S and a small heart.

That's weird, I thought to myself. Bellany and I had bought ourselves necklaces just like that, except with our own initials. She must have gone to the same jewelry store.

I briefly gazed at the ocean to acknowledge what she had said to me. "Yeah, it is beautiful." Then I shifted my focus to Tasha and Cory's house. There was still no sign of them.

"I just moved here," the old woman said, pointing down the beach. "My house is about a half mile away. It's the big yellow one with white shutters."

I had no idea which house she was referring to. "Sounds nice."

"Are you here on vacation, or are you new to the neighborhood?"

This definitely was not a vacation. "I'm visiting a friend." I turned, searching for Cory and Tasha.

"Where are you from?"

That was none of her business. I reached inside my bag for a book. "I'm kind of from everywhere," I replied, opening it to a random page, hoping she would leave me alone. But she didn't move. She continued to stand there, her shadow blocking the sun.

"You look familiar," she said, and my heart constricted. She couldn't possibly know who I am, could she?

The old lady pushed her sunglasses up on top of her head, her gaze drilling into me. She stepped closer and angled her chin. "Are you sure we haven't met before?"

Her words seemed to linger in the air like a poisonous gas, suffocating me with fear. Had she seen my picture on a missing person's website? "I just have one of those faces." I shrugged, trying to act like I wasn't freaked out. "Excuse me, I've gotta go." I quickly gathered my things and started walking down the beach.

I peered over my shoulder to make sure she wasn't following me. Fortunately she wasn't. But she was still standing there.

I picked up my pace and kept walking until I couldn't see

her anymore.

The sand beneath my feet felt almost foreign as my mind raced with memories of home. Just five months before I fled, I was faced with a heartbreaking tragedy when my best friend Chantel was murdered.

Her devastated parents uncovered chilling evidence of death threats in her diary, which the police confirmed when they searched her phone.

Since I used to be Chantel's closest friend, the police turned to me, looking for answers. They wanted to know if I knew about the death threats.

I denied that I did, fearing I would get blamed. But it didn't matter, they blamed me anyway.

Before long, the cops were accusing me of being jealous of Chantel's relationship with her boyfriend, Xavier. According to Chantel's diary, I was trying to steal Xavier away from her.

The cops made several trips to my house to question me. I knew I needed a lawyer. But my parents couldn't afford one. So I felt like I had no other choice but to run away.

When I picked up Bellany from the side of the road after her car broke down, I had no idea that we would become best friends. I thought I would just give her a ride to the nearest gas station or mechanic. But instead we went to a nearby cafe and talked.

I ended up pouring out my heart to her. I told her about all my problems, which was a risky thing to do. But Bellany made me feel like we were already best friends--like we had known each other our entire lives.

I told her about Chantel being murdered, but I didn't tell her about my other friends' deaths. In a way, Bellany kind of reminded me of my best friend from the eighth grade. Vivian Drennon. They had similar facial features, petite and symmetrical. But Vivian was no longer alive.

She fell off a cliff when she was hiking, and died. I was there when it happened. Actually, I was the only one there. I had dared her to walk close to the edge of the cliff, and I didn't think she would do it. But she did.

I chose that moment to confess to her that I had secretly been seeing her brother, Pete. I knew Vivian wouldn't like hearing this, because her brother was three years older than me.

She got angry. She started yelling and said that she was going to tell her mom. She said I wouldn't be allowed to stay the night at her house anymore. Basically, Vivian was going to make sure Pete and I never had a chance to be together again.

I was furious. I lost my temper. And in hindsight, I knew I overreacted.

Even though Bellany reminded me of Vivian, I didn't hold it against her. She obviously wasn't the same person. She and Vivian only looked similar. I didn't have to worry about Bellany forbidding me from seeing her brother. Bellany's brother wasn't involved in her life anymore. She hadn't spoken to Bridger in years.

As Bellany and I continued to talk at the cafe, she confessed that she was also on the run from the cops, which was a total shock. I thought she was too beautiful and too perfect to be a criminal.

I quickly learned that Bellany was incredibly intelligent, strong, and driven, which were qualities I had always admired in a person. These were also qualities that my parents lacked. I loved my parents dearly, but they frustrated me to no end.

They were content living in poverty and seemed to have no other ambition in life besides hoping to win the lottery one day. I didn't want to turn out to be anything like them. They lived in a single wide trailer and sometimes couldn't afford to pay the electric bill.

My mom didn't work, because she suffered from migraines. But even if she didn't get migraines, I still wondered if she would work a regular job. She was super shy and didn't like being around people.

My dad was a delivery driver for a snack food company. He didn't make much money, and he always complained about it. Yet he never tried to get another job.

Since we were so poor, my dad supplemented our food supply by going hunting, and he frequently took me with him. He had always wanted a son, but all he got was me. I learned everything I knew about guns and hunting from him.

My dad and I had always been really close, and I missed him the most. When I ran away from home, I felt really bad about stealing his car. I hoped he knew that I didn't do it to hurt him.

Since Bellany and I were rich now, I wanted to buy him a brand new car. I also wanted to give my parents some money, maybe even buy them a house.

But Bellany refused to let me do it. She claimed it was too risky and might lead the cops to us. I knew I should listen to her. After all, she has been on the run from the cops for over two years and hadn't got caught yet.

A seagull's raucous cries snapped me from my thoughts, and I started heading back toward Tasha and Cory's house. I figured Bellany was probably wondering where I was.

CHAPTER 3

Tasha

Cory's phone started ringing. So I grabbed it. "Heeeey-lo?"

"Hi, is Cory there?" a girl's voice asked.

I peered at the closed bathroom door down the hall. "He's busy doin' his business."

"Can you tell him that Gemma called?"

"Totally! Hold on one sec."

I raced off to my bedroom and grabbed a paper and pencil. Cory told me that whenever someone calls, I'm supposed to take a message. I already had three other names written down on the paper.

Charlotte was the first name on the list. She was so nice when we talked on the phone. She asked me what my favorite color was, and I said blue! Then I told her what my favorite foods were: cheese pizza, ice cream, and cookies with Hershey Kisses. She liked 'em too!

The next name on the list was Bridger. He was a meanie on the phone! He refused to talk to me. He only wanted to talk to Cory.

I told Cory that Bridger was being super rude, and Cory replied that sometimes boys don't wanna talk to girls. But that's not fair! Boys and girls should want to talk with each other, right?

Anyways, next on the list was Wade. He was actually really nice--not at all like Bridger! We only spoke for a few minutes because Cory took the phone away from me.

I set my pencil and paper down on the kitchen counter

before pushing the button that puts the phone on speaker mode. It was so cool when Cory showed me how to do this--I can take messages and talk at the same time!

I hopped up onto the stool before grabbing my pencil again. "Okay, I'm back. How do you spell your name?"

"It's spelled G-E-M-M-A," the girl quickly replied.

I wasn't so good at spelling names. Cory helped me spell Charlotte's, since I had done it wrong the first time. I didn't want to mess up Gemma's name too.

When I wrote the letter A, it wasn't straight enough. So I erased it and wrote it again.

"Okay, what's your phone number?" I asked.

She spoke, and I jotted down her digits.

I was curious if Gemma lived in North Carolina like Bridger, Wade, and Charlotte. But then I remembered Cory saying it was better to have a two-way conversation instead of just one person talking all the time. So I kept my question quiet.

My pencil was all dull. Where did that sharpener even go?

"You there?" Gemma's voice crackled through the phone. She sounded really nice, like one of 'em good singers on the radio.

"One sec." I finished writing her phone number, then dropped the pencil onto the counter. But I couldn't keep my question quiet any longer. I had to ask. "Where do you live?"

"Smithfield, North Carolina," she replied.

Another person from North Carolina! "Woah, that's awesome! If ya ever need a place to chill, come to Mexico. I live on the beach!"

The bathroom door flew open and Cory appeared.

"Gemma's on the phone!" I said.

"Thanks." He grabbed the phone and took it off speaker. But I didn't care. My mind was already thinking about something else. I wanted to go outside and build a sandcastle.

I ended up waiting for a long time, but Cory still wasn't done talking to Gemma, and I just couldn't be patient any longer.

My bag of buckets and shovels was sitting on the floor by

the back door. I quietly picked it up and tiptoed outside. Then I closed the door softly so he wouldn't hear me.

I knew Cory would be mad at me for leaving without him. But I was only going to do it just this one time!

CHAPTER 4

Victoria

Tasha came barreling down the beach, her hair a mass of wild dark curls, swimsuit strap slipping off her shoulder. She threw a bag to the ground with buckets and shovels spilling out. Instead of building a sandcastle, she stood there, her gaze intently fixed on the backyard of her house. But there was no sign of Cory--not yet anyway.

I started searching for seashells, casually keeping an eye out for Cory. I was also checking to see if Bellany was lingering somewhere nearby, maybe hiding behind one of the trees.

When I turned back around, I realized that I had lost sight of Tasha. Her buckets and shovels were still there, but she was nowhere to be found.

My eyes strained, searching for her bright pink swimsuit. But before I could blink, a sharp intake of air caught in my throat. Tasha was in the ocean! The waves were crashing hard with a vengeance, lifting her off her feet.

Was she allowed to go swimming in the ocean by herself? Did she even know how to swim?

As I imagined the worst case scenario, I looked toward Cory's house. But he still hadn't come out.

Tasha trudged ahead, unfazed by the waves crashing against her body, pulling her towards dangerous depths.

My first instinct was to stop her, but then I hesitated. I wondered if I should just allow the natural consequences of her decision to unfold. Then Bellany would have no means to get revenge, because Cory's most important person would have already been taken from him.

CHAPTER 5

Tahsa

I kicked and kicked with all my might, but I still couldn't seem to reach the surface. Then another wave came crashing over me, like a giant hand flipping me around underwater!

This time the wave was so strong, it knocked my hand away from my nose. My arms and legs were aching, but I kept swimming, desperate to get back up where I could breathe again.

Finally, I made it and sucked in the biggest breath of air ever. But another gigantic wave was coming for me!

Then I saw a hand reach out, trying to grab me, but I was slipping under. My arms felt so tired like they wouldn't work anymore. I tried kicking my legs, but even that was too hard.

My throat and nose burned from the water, and I thought I might die. Then something touched my head. Was Cory trying to help me?

But the hand didn't pull me up. It pushed me down!

CHAPTER 6

Victoria

More waves pounded against the shore. I had to at least appear as though I was trying to save Tasha, so I rushed into the ocean until the surf lapped against my thighs.

My voice created a hollow space between my cupped hands. "Hey!" I shouted. "Are you okay?"

I watched as Tasha stumbled under a large swell, falling beneath the surface. No one else was around to rescue her. It was all up to me.

The waves were raging, rising up with a vengeance. I felt my heart thudding against my ribcage as I watched another enormous wave grow close.

What was Tasha doing out there so deep anyway? Had she no fear of the sea? Did she not realize that she could drown?

I watched her get swept away, her dark locks disappearing below the surface.

My chest heaved as I waded further into the ocean, almost up to my waist. Another monstrous wave descended and nearly knocked me off my feet.

"Tasha!" a deep voice cried, making my heart jump. I spun around and saw Cory, his face twisted with fear.

I opened my mouth to say something to him, but the words caught in my throat as he flew past me. He raced across the water, calling out Tasha's name.

The next wave came crashing, and I saw Tasha floating lifelessly in the water. I surged forward, but Cory beat me to her. He pulled her through the treacherous tide, carrying her ashore.

He laid her down in the sand and began performing CPR, begging and pleading for her to live. "Please, Tasha! Don't die!"

I stood there watching him repeatedly push down on Tasha's chest. With every passing second, the odds were stacking up against her survival. I wished he would let her go. Tasha was gone. There was nothing he could do.

"Come on, Tasha! Breathe!" Cory cried. "Please, breathe!"

I watched her closely. But there were no signs of life. "Is there anything I can do to help?" I asked.

Cory ignored me and continued giving her chest compressions.

I knelt down next to Tasha's body, and when my knees hit the sand, she lurched forward with a gasp. Water came cascading out of her mouth.

Her resurrection felt like a punch to my gut. How could she still be alive? She had been underwater for so long.

Tasha hacked and coughed while Cory scooped her up, cradling her tenderly. "It's all right! You're all right now, Tasha. Everything's going to be fine..."

In an effort to appear helpful, I ran to my bag and grabbed my phone. "Do you want me to call for help?" I asked, my finger hovering over the keypad. But I had no idea what numbers to dial. Did Mexico use 9-1-1?

When Cory's eyes locked onto mine, my breath caught in my throat. His eyes were electric blue! I had never seen eyes like his before.

Now it all made sense. I finally understood why Bellany was so obsessed with him. He was unique. He was gorgeous!

I lowered my phone, my heart hammering in my chest, as I tried to think of something to say. Then an idea popped into my head. My car was parked on the street. "I can give you a ride to the emergency room."

Tasha suddenly twisted in agony.

"I don't need a ride," Cory said, sweeping her off the ground and rising to his feet.

The distance between us grew, and my chest tightened. I

couldn't let him leave without me.

I sprinted after him until our feet moved in sync. "My car isn't that far from here. Please let me help."

Cory shook his head, his pace quickening. "I don't need any help."

I opened my mouth to protest, but then I thought better of it. Cory already declined my help twice. I didn't want there to be a third time. It was better to let him go.

As I headed back to pick up my things, I kept thinking about Cory's eyes, wishing I could look into them again.

When I turned back around, my heart leapt into my throat. Cory was gazing back at me, and Tasha was lying limp in his arms. "Hey!" he called, panic in his voice.

I grabbed my bag and ran toward him as fast as I could.

CHAPTER 7

Victoria

My feet tore through the sand. When I reached Cory, my entire body was trembling. Tasha was still lying limp in his arms. Her eyes were closed, her breath shallow. Just how close to death was she?

"I could use your help," Cory's voice shook. He looked down at me with pleading eyes.

"Do you need me to drive?" I waved toward my car, barely visible from this spot.

"No, I'll drive. I need you to sit with Tasha and keep an eye on her."

I responded with a firm, determined nod. "Of course!"

I trailed behind him as we entered through the back gate of his house and then raced down the driveway towards his convertible Mustang. I opened the door and slid into the leather seat. Cory gently set Tasha down on my lap, and I wrapped my arms around her.

Her eyes were open, but there was a vacant look about them. I wondered if she was going to die in my arms.

The Mustang lurched forward at breakneck speed. Cory's driving was reckless, each sharp turn sending us careening wildly around the road.

When we arrived at the hospital, Cory flung open the door and scooped up Tasha's limp form like a rag doll. Her eyes stared blankly ahead as if searching for something beyond this world.

Tasha's feeble moan echoed off the walls of the hospital as

Cory ushered her into the examination room. He was so focused on her that he didn't seem to notice me skulking in the corner. I figured he must have been consumed with guilt, blaming himself for what happened to her. But it wasn't his fault. It was mine. I could have saved her, but I didn't. And I felt bad about that.

After the doctor and nurses stabilized Tasha, she ended up falling peacefully asleep.

Cory finally seemed to relax a bit too. He thanked me for helping him, and I did my best to act as if I was innocent in all of this.

"It was no trouble at all," I said.

He shoved his hands into the front pockets of his shorts. "We could be here for a while, and I don't want to hijack your entire day. Can I call you a taxi or something?"

"Actually, I don't really have any other plans."

He looked me up and down, which made me feel self-conscious. My hair and makeup were probably a total disaster. All of Bellany's hard work was wasted. "You're not anxious to get back to the beach? Were you meeting friends there?"

No, I was there to meet you. I shook my head. "I was just going to be hanging out by myself. I don't really know anybody here."

His eyes traveled over to my bag that was sitting on the chair. Some of my clothes were spilling out. "Are you here on vacation?"

"No, I came to stay. I'm kind of starting over."

He raised his eyebrows. "Starting over? What does that mean?"

I bit my lip, hesitant to explain. "I'm just looking for a change, and felt like Mexico was the place to be."

"Where are you staying?"

"I'm staying at a house in your neighborhood, not far from yours. I'm renting a room. I have my own private entrance, which is nice, but the room is tiny. It kind of makes me feel claustrophobic." I smiled, sheepishly.

Several beats of silence passed, and I was feeling beyond awkward. Clearly he did not want me to be here. I picked up my bag. "Maybe I should go."

"No, no. You can stay." He shook his head. "I was just thinking about what happened." He gestured to Tasha, then sat down and buried his face in his hands.

His damp shirt clung to the curves of his broad shoulders and tapered back. He was so close to me. I wanted to touch him, but it didn't feel like the right time.

He sighed heavily. "I thought I was going to lose her."

"I know, it was so scary."

Another few beats of silence passed, and I tried to come up with something to say that might cheer him up. Luckily he started talking first, because I couldn't think of anything.

"I should have never bought a house on the beach," he said. "It's too dangerous."

But his house was so amazing--at least it looked like it on the outside, and I couldn't wait to see the inside. "Well, maybe she won't ever go into the ocean without you again. Maybe she learned her lesson."

"I don't know." He shook his head, eyes on the floor. "I still think it's too dangerous."

"The ocean is a dangerous place," I agreed. "But it's so beautiful. Everybody is drawn to it." I felt drawn to Cory, like I was to the ocean. I could feel his body heat radiating off of him and wanted to get closer.

More silence passed, but it didn't feel quite as awkward anymore. It gave me some time to think and figure out what to say to him. "Your house is beautiful. Are you renting, or do you own it?"

"I own it."

"Wow. You must make a lot of money. What do you do for a living?" I couldn't wait to hear Cory's answer. Was he going to mention anything about stealing money from Bellany? I doubted it.

The line in his jaw grew more pronounced as he scratched

the side of his face. Was he stalling and trying to think of a lie? "I came into some money unexpectedly," he said, turning to check Tasha's IV bag, which was mostly full. There was no need to check it.

"Oh, okay," I said, not really satisfied with his answer, but I didn't want to press him on the matter. Clearly he didn't want to talk about Bellany--not yet anyway.

He pulled the blanket over Tasha's shoulders. She was still sound asleep.

"You're really good with her, you know."

The muscles in Cory's jaw relaxed slightly. "Thanks."

My eyes swung between the two of them. Cory's hair was blond. Tasha's was dark brown, almost black. She was petite, probably six inches shorter than me. I was five-four. Cory had to be over six feet, maybe six-two. He was lean and muscular. Tasha had low muscle tone. They were complete opposites. "You two don't look anything alike. Were you adopted?"

The corners of Cory's mouth turned down. "Neither of us were ever adopted. We used to live in the same foster home."

"That explains it," I replied, acting like I was surprised even though I already knew this.

He sat down and placed his arm over the back of an empty chair next to him. I wished I was sitting in that chair. I wanted to be close to him. I sat in the chair on the opposite side. "Is it just you and Tasha, or do you have other siblings living with you too?"

"Just us."

"So is it hard taking care of Tasha by yourself?" I asked, wondering if he regretted bringing her to Mexico. He was going to have to take care of Tasha for the rest of her life. This was a huge commitment.

"I manage just fine."

That wasn't true. If it was, then Tasha wouldn't be in the hospital right now. Cory needed help. "Has she tried to go swimming in the ocean without you before?"

Cory hung his head. "I've warned her a hundred times not

to swim in the ocean without me."

Why hadn't she listened, I wondered. "Is she incapable of feeling fear?"

Cory furrowed his brow. "She's scared of all kinds of things... monsters in her closet, clowns, sour milk, boats. Her grasp of reality is a bit skewed sometimes. She thinks she can do things on her own like drive a car, cross a busy street, cook on the stove... but she needs help with all those things." Cory let out a sigh. He looked and sounded exhausted.

"So she needs constant supervision."

"I don't dare leave her home alone." His eyes drifted over to Tasha as she lay there peacefully sleeping.

Cory had so much compassion and was completely devoted. I could only imagine how perfect a relationship with him would be. I doubted he would ever cheat. He didn't seem like the type. Once he was in, he was in to stay.

My fingers twitched with the impulse to reach out and touch Cory's arm. I knew Bellany would be furious if she found out. But I just couldn't stop myself--I had to touch him.

I rested my hand on his arm and my stomach fluttered at the touch of his warm skin. "What happened today wasn't your fault," I said. "Accidents happen all the time. They can happen to anyone." I bit my lip, feeling stupid for saying something so cliché.

Cory's gaze lowered to my hand on his arm. Did he like me touching him, I wondered.

A nurse walked in, and I wasn't sure if he pulled away, or if I did. Maybe we both did at the same time.

I wiped my hand on my shorts while Cory wasn't looking, making sure it was sweat-free. Then I reached inside my bag and checked my phone while he was talking to the nurse.

The only person who had my phone number was Bellany. She hadn't sent me any text messages, but she had called me six times for some strange reason. I felt confident that whatever she wanted could wait. I planned on calling her back later.

"Hey," Cory said to me, as soon as the nurse left the

room. "I really appreciate your help today. Thank you for waiting around all this time."

Was he going to ask me to leave? "Of course. It's the least I could do."

Cory's eyes suddenly widened. His face full of horror, like he had seen the grim reaper. I followed his gaze through the doorway, but I didn't see anything.

A split second later, he was sprinting out of the room, and I had no idea why.

CHAPTER 8

Victoria

I followed Cory into the hallway, but I didn't go any further than that. He was moving too quickly, leaving me behind.

He raced toward the elevator, running as fast as he could. But he didn't get there in time. The doors shut swiftly, right in front of his face. Cory spun around wildly, careened around the corner, and vanished from sight.

I stood in the doorway of Tasha's room, waiting for him to return. The hospital was incredibly busy, and the hallway was packed.

As I turned to look the other direction, I caught sight of an old lady with gray hair and I practically jumped out of my sandals. Holy crap! It was the same weird old lady from the beach. What was she doing here? Was she following me?

I ducked inside Tasha's room and hid behind the door, waiting for her to pass, my heart racing.

This was just a coincidence, I tried to convince myself. She was an old lady and probably had some kind of medical issue she needed to take care of. And where else would she go besides the hospital? There was really no reason for me to be concerned.

I started to feel kind of foolish about hiding from her. My reaction made no sense. Sure, the old lady thought I looked familiar, but that didn't mean anything. I probably just reminded her of a granddaughter or a family friend. And the necklace she wore, that was just a coincidence. It meant nothing.

Feeling a lot more relaxed now, I checked the hallway again. There was no sign of the old lady or Cory.

Since Tasha was still asleep, I grabbed my phone and called Bellany. It went straight to voicemail. I didn't leave a message. I just hung up. Bellany would see that she missed my call. If she really needed to communicate something to me, she could send me a text.

About five minutes later Cory returned to the room. The color had drained from his face, and he was out of breath. He leaned over the bed to check on Tasha. "Did she wake up while I was gone?"

"No, she's been sleeping the entire time."

"Good." Cory wiped the sweat from his forehead.

I smiled at him, hoping he would tell me why he ran off so suddenly.

He paced the room, peering through the doorway repeatedly.

"Are you okay?"

Cory finally sat down. He raked his fingers through his tousled blond hair. "I thought I saw someone."

"Really? Who?"

His gaze slowly rose from the floor, and he swallowed hard. "Bellany."

My stomach dropped. She was spying on me. She must have followed us here. "Bellany?" I repeated as if I was saying the name for the first time. I wondered if Cory was about to tell me about his relationship with her. I sat on the edge of my chair, anxious to hear more. "Who's Bellany?"

Cory snapped his head in my direction, glaring at me. Why was he looking at me that way? Had I said something wrong?

"Who are you, and why are you here?"

I crossed my legs and sat up straighter. Don't be nervous, I told myself. He has no idea who you really are. "My name's Victoria, and I came to Mexico to get a fresh start in life."

His eyes narrowed. He leaned toward me. "I don't know you. You're a complete stranger."

Crap! He was suspicious of me. Maybe I shouldn't have

asked him about Bellany. Tears flooded my eyes. "I just wanted to help."

"Cory?" Tasha's voice croaked, her eyes now open.

He rushed to her side, reaching for her hand. "How are you feeling?"

"My throat burns," she said in a raspy voice, then she coughed and grabbed her chest. "Ouch!"

While Cory tried to console her, I stood in the doorway with my bag on my shoulder. The tears in my eyes were real. I didn't want to leave--not like this.

"Who are you?" Tasha asked.

I wiped a tear off my cheek. "I'm Victoria."

"I remember you," she said, her dark eyes boring into me. "You were at the beach."

"That's right. I was at the beach." My eyes shifted to Cory. Was he going to tell me to leave? Should I walk out of here before he kicks me out?

Tasha coughed and winced in pain. "My throat hurts."

Cory wrapped his arm around her. "I'm so sorry. I know it hurts."

Then an idea popped into my head. "I'll go get the nurse," I said, rushing into the hallway.

When I returned, I brought the nurse with me. I waited anxiously while she checked on Tasha. Cory hardly even looked at me. Was it best for me to stay, or should I leave? I couldn't decide. All I knew was that my heart ached at the thought of being away from him.

As soon as the nurse left, I moved to the other side of the bed, thinking about something my mom had said to me when I was ten. I had fallen off of a friend's skateboard and broke my arm. I figured I could say the same thing to Tasha that she said to me. "It's gonna hurt for a little while, Tasha. But the pain won't last forever. You will heal. You will get better."

Cory nodded. "That's right. You will get better. Everything's going to be fine."

Tasha soon fell asleep again and Cory's demeanor

changed. He scrutinized my face, towering over me.

"I'm so sorry. I overstayed my welcome," I said, backing away from him. "I should have left a long time ago."

The tension in Cory's jaw released, only slightly. "You can understand how I'd be a little suspicious of you, right?" He shook his head. "I don't know you."

I shrugged, feeling the weight of my bag on my shoulder and the weight of the secret I was keeping from him. "I don't know you either. But I'd like to get to know you."

The corner of his mouth twitched. Was he about to smile or frown? He shoved his hands into his pockets, staring at me.

"Maybe we can talk again sometime," I suggested, hoping he would agree.

"Don't leave," Tasha's voice croaked, and my heart leapt into my throat.

"I wish I could stay, but I gotta go."

"No," she moaned. "You're my new friend. Please stay."

"Well, only if it's okay with Cory." I waited for him to respond, hoping he would invite me to stay.

He rubbed the back of his neck and sighed. There was no hint of a smile on his face.

I took a step back and Tasha reached her hand out. "Victoria."

Cory sighed again. "Please stay," he said in the most unenthusiastic tone I had ever heard.

"Come sit by me," Tasha gestured to the chair beside the bed.

I knew my time was limited, so I had to make the most of it. Bellany had advised me to become friends with Tasha too, and that was exactly what I was going to do.

As I talked with Tasha, I learned that she loved building sandcastles. She loved mermaids and thought they were real. Cory seemed to be warming up to me, probably because Tasha liked me. I had no idea why. Maybe she was just desperate for a friend, and I knew what that felt like.

There were several times in my life when I was desperate

for a friend. I was so lonely. One of those times was when I was in the third grade. None of the other kids wanted to play with me. They made fun of me. They teased me about my pants being too short and my clothes being dirty. They said I was ugly and that I had cooties.

Then a new girl got transferred into class. Her name was Lucy. She sat next to me, and we quickly became best friends. But then the other kids started making fun of her too. They said that my cooties had rubbed off on her.

Lucy cried. I told her she shouldn't cry and that it didn't matter what the other kids thought about her. We didn't need them. We had each other.

The next day at school, the teacher moved Lucy to a different table. And she stopped playing with me during recess. She wouldn't even talk to me anymore.

One day I asked her to sit next to me at lunch. She told me no and said that I had cooties. The other kids laughed at me. She did too.

When a new boy got transferred into class, the teacher sat him next to me, in Lucy's old seat. His name was Tyler. Tyler was friendly. He didn't make fun of me like the other kids. He even hung out with me a couple times during recess. I really liked Tyler, and he liked me too. But then he started hanging out with Lucy and her friends, and she wouldn't let him talk to me anymore. She wanted to keep Tyler to herself.

About a month after Lucy stole Tyler away from me, she had an allergic reaction to a peanut. She was in the bathroom when it happened. I know, because I was there too. Lucy was gasping for air. She couldn't breathe. That was the last time I saw her.

The doctor returned to the room, pulling me from my thoughts. He checked on Tasha and determined that she was well enough to go home.

Tasha insisted on sitting next to me in the car, so Cory invited me to come along. She fell asleep on my shoulder right away. When we arrived at Cory's house, I opened the front door for them and followed them inside. Cory was carrying Tasha in his arms, and she was already starting to fall asleep again.

"Looks like the pain meds are working," Cory said.

I followed him into Tasha's bedroom, pulled down the covers and fluffed the pillow. He laid her down on the bed, and I gently tucked her in, careful not to wake her.

Cory kept her bedroom door cracked open. "Hopefully she'll stay asleep for a while," he whispered.

"Yeah," I agreed, following him down the hallway, a smile on my face. Finally, Cory and I would have some alone time together. I couldn't wait to sit and talk and stare into his mesmerizing eyes. But before we did that, I kind of wondered if I should offer to help clean up a bit.

Tasha's toys were strewn all over the living room floor. Dirty dishes were piled in the kitchen sink and on the counters. Even though the house was a mess, it didn't detract from its beauty, or the million dollar view of the ocean through the back windows.

I loved the kitchen. It was decked out with top-of-the-line appliances, granite countertops, and custom cabinetry. The floors were some kind of expensive-looking tile. Vaulted ceilings made the house feel even more spacious than it already was.

The only thing Cory's house lacked was a sense of style, some coziness and warmth. There were no soft rugs to sink your feet into. The leather furniture in the living room didn't match. The couch was black and the loveseat was brown. Folding metal chairs surrounded a glass table in the dining room. There weren't any pretty things to look at on the walls, just a massive flat screen TV.

Cory offered me something to eat and drink. I followed him into the kitchen and sat at the counter while he grabbed a couple bottles of water, a bowl of grapes, and a box of cold pizza from the fridge.

"Do you want me to warm that up?" he asked, gesturing to the pizza.

"Cold is fine." I reached in and grabbed a slice.

Cory ate three slices, then he went to check on Tasha.

While he was gone, I grabbed my phone and took some pictures of his house. Bellany told me to do this. She wanted to see everything. But I didn't take pictures of anything nice.

I took pictures of Tasha's mermaid drawings that were hanging on the fridge. I took pictures of the messy countertops and the stack of empty pizza boxes on the floor next to the trash can.

When Cory returned to the kitchen, he had a strange look on his face, and I had a sinking feeling in my gut that I knew what he was about to say.

He was going to make some excuse as to why I should leave. But I couldn't let him kick me out. I had to think of a good reason to stick around.

I scanned my surroundings, and my eyes landed on the Kitchen-aid mixer. I remembered Chantel's mom had one just like it in her kitchen. It was the same color too. Black.

"Do you bake?" I gestured to it, remembering all of the delicious cookies and breads that Chantel's mom used to bake.

Cory shook his head. "I've only used that mixer one time."

Why hadn't he used it more often, I wondered. "Oh really. What did you make?"

He chuckled, stroking his chin. "Tasha loves those cookies with the Hershey Kisses on top. I thought maybe I could learn how to make them." A smile played on his lips. "But that was a huge mistake."

Tasha loved cookies? How perfect! "Those cookies are called peanut butter blossoms. I know how to make them. I used to make them all the time with my mom." That was a lie. My mom never had chocolate in the house. We couldn't afford it. But Chantel's mom did. She was the one who taught me how to bake.

He arched an eyebrow. "Really?"

"Yes, they're super easy to make." I walked around the kitchen island and opened up a cupboard, searching for ingredients. But all I found were plates and bowls. I opened another cupboard and found cups.

"Where do you keep the flour and sugar?" I asked, opening another cupboard and still having no luck. "Do you have any Hershey Kisses?" I followed his gaze to the pantry door.

When I walked inside, I couldn't believe how packed it was. There was enough food to last for months. Why did he have so much? Was he afraid the grocery stores would run out?

"Did you find what you're looking for?" he asked.

"Yep!" I grabbed a container of flour and a bag of Hershey Kisses, anxious to get started. Cory was going to be so impressed by my baking. And I couldn't wait to see Tasha's face when she saw all the cookies I was going to bake for her. I just hoped I would still be around when she woke up.

I was going to have to do more than bake cookies. I had to find a way to gain Cory's trust. As I wrestled with this thought, another piece of Bellany's advice entered my mind: the backstory about my parents. Even though I didn't want to lie about them, I felt like I had no other choice. Bellany was probably right. Cory would sympathize with this kind of story. Playing the role of the victim would give him the opportunity to rescue me. I just hoped he would take the bait.

I began pouring my heart out, telling him how I had escaped my abusive parents and all about the terrible things they had done to me. Cory hung on my every word. He asked me questions and the lies flowed freely, so did the tears.

When that ordeal was finally out of the way, I returned my focus to baking cookies. These had to turn out just right. They had to taste delicious.

CHAPTER 9

Cory (Cam Whitmeyer)

All I had said to Victoria was that I wasn't good at baking cookies. I hadn't asked her to bake some for me. But before I could explain this to her, she began gathering together all the ingredients and was starting to give me instructions on how to help.

The last thing I wanted to do today was make cookies. I was exhausted and in no mood to do this. My stomach was a bundle of nerves. I was still in shock over almost losing Tasha. She could have died. And on top of that, I saw Bellany at the hospital. She must have followed us there.

"Cory," Victoria said, staring at the carton of eggs. She seemed upset. Were they broken or something?

I checked the eggs and they were fine, but Victoria certainly wasn't. Her eyes were red and glossy.

I pushed my concerns about Bellany aside to find out what was wrong with Victoria. She began telling me stories about her childhood. The abuse she endured was extreme. It pained me to hear all of the horrific details. Her stories were so similar to Tasha's.

Victoria grabbed a paper towel to wipe her tears. "I'm sorry for dumping all of my problems on you."

"No, don't worry about it. And you didn't dump your problems on me. You've already handled the situation. You got out. You got away and escaped. Hopefully you'll never have to see your parents again."

She dabbed her eyes with the paper towel. "Thanks for

listening." Then she turned to the sink and washed her hands. "Okay," she sighed. "Now I need to finish baking these cookies."

Victoria struggled to unscrew the lid of the sugar container. "I can't open it."

I took it from her. "How much sugar do you want?"

"Just shy of a cup."

I measured out the sugar and poured it into the mixing bowl while she stood there watching me. Her eyes were still glossy. "How long are these supposed to bake?"

"Oh, I forgot to turn on the oven," she said, spinning around. As she pressed the buttons, I caught sight of the clock and realized how late it was.

I grabbed my phone while the mixer was humming and made a beeline to the couch. I began typing out a text to send to Charlotte, Bridger, Gemma and Wade.

I had met all of them in North Carolina, while I was investigating Bellany's disappearance. None of them were surprised to learn that Bellany had fled the United States. She was wanted by the police and the FBI for multiple crimes and murders. She had to leave the country, or risk getting caught.

They already knew that Bellany was up to something devious again. This time her target was me. When I informed them of this, they volunteered to come help.

My fingers skated across the screen of my phone. I wondered if they would get a chance to read this text before boarding their plane.

Me: **I saw her today. She's definitely here!**

I laid my head back and closed my eyes, taking a moment to relax. Then my phone beeped with a reply.

Gemma: **No way! Did you talk to her? What did she say?**

Me: **She ran and jumped into an elevator before I could catch her.**

Charlotte: **She escaped again? Do you think she's going to leave Mexico?**

Me: **I'm sure she's still here--just hiding. I think she was spying and didn't want me to see her.**

Gemma: **She got caught! Hahaha! I bet she feels stupid!**

Wade: **She's either getting bold or careless. I wonder what she's up to.**

Charlotte: **Me too. Be careful, Cory.**

They didn't need to warn me about Bellany. I was well aware of who I was dealing with.

Gemma: **Don't let her rattle your nerves, Cory! She's nothing but a hot mess.**

Charlotte: **We're about to board the plane. We'll see you soon.**

I wondered why I hadn't seen a text from Bridger yet. He was supposed to catch the same flight as them. Was he running late?

Me: **What about Bridger? Is he there?**

Gemma: **He had to switch his flight because he has a test in Philosophy. I told him he should have taken online college courses like the rest of us. But he didn't listen to me. Anyway, he's gonna catch a flight tomorrow.**

For a moment there, I was worried. I thought Bridger wasn't coming. He was the most important one of them all. He was Bellany's twin brother--he had to come! He was probably the only person in the world Bellany would listen to.

When I first reached out to Bridger and informed him that Bellany was here in Mexico, he was in total shock. He had no idea what had happened to her. Despite all of the bad things she had done, he still cared about her.

Charlotte: **We're boarding now. See you soon.**

Me: **See ya.**

As soon as I lowered my phone, I realized I had a problem. Before long I would have to head to the airport to pick them up. But how could I manage it with Tasha? She needed to stay in bed and rest.

Craning my neck, I looked toward the kitchen. Victoria was sitting at the counter unwrapping Hershey Kisses. Should I ask her to watch Tasha?

She looked up and our eyes met. A small smile emerged

on her face. Victoria had told me that she was nineteen, but she looked younger than that. Even if she had lied about her age, I knew she couldn't have lied about the abuse she had endured growing up. The stories she told me were so detailed. Her emotion was so raw. Only a sociopath could lie about something like that.

"You okay?" she asked.

I realized I was still staring at her. "Yeah. I'm fine."

"Good." She smiled again, but this time her smile didn't travel up to her eyes. It looked forced.

I didn't feel comfortable asking her to watch Tasha. But I did need her help. And she seemed like a nice person. Otherwise why would she be here baking Tasha's favorite cookies? Why would she come with me to the hospital?

Victoria giggled. "Why are you staring at me?"

Was I staring again? I didn't even realize. "Sorry. I was just wondering if you could do me a favor."

"Of course." She shrugged, her smile beaming. This time it looked genuine. "What do you need?"

I would rather give her the keys to my car than ask her to babysit Tasha. "Do you think you can pick up three of my friends from the airport?"

"Sure, no problem."

"You can drive my car." I fished the keys out of my pocket.

Victoria shot me a strange look. "I'm not sure your Mustang's big enough for three people and their luggage. I might have to take more than one trip."

I didn't intend for her to drive the Mustang. "You can take the Expedition. It's in the garage."

"Oh, that sounds perfect!"

I sent Victoria's contact information to the group text, letting them know she was going to pick them up. Then I helped Victoria unwrap the Hershey Kisses. I was glad I let her stick around after all.

CHAPTER 10

Bellany

A wave of red hot anger flooded through me as I read Victoria's text.

Victoria: **Things are going absolutely awesome! Don't expect me to come back tonight. I'll be staying at Cory's house! Good thing I packed an overnight bag. Haha!**

Learning that Victoria had packed an overnight bag only fueled my rage.

At no time had I advised her to throw herself at Cory! I just wanted her to get to know him and become his friend. What part of that plan was not clear?

Another text came through.

Victoria: **I'll be picking up a bunch of Cory's friends from the airport. He gave me the keys to his Expedition! But I kind of wished I would be driving his Mustang. It's so amazingly fast!**

She's picking up his friends from the airport and driving his car? What?

My fingers pounded over the screen of my phone at lightning speed, clicking filling the air as I furiously typed out a message. My emotions were spiraling out of control with each passing keystroke.

Me: **Apparently you misunderstood the plan! You were supposed to get to know Cory and gradually become his FRIEND. It takes time to gain a person's trust. You're doing the complete opposite of what I told you to do! You're going to ruin everything!**

Victoria: **I'm sorry! I thought you would want me to do**

this. I thought you'd be happy.

The audacity! She thought I would be happy! Had she lost her mind?

Me: **Did I tell you to pack an overnight bag? NO! Did I tell you to stay the night with Cory? NO! You're only 17. He's 21!**

"Keep your greedy little fingers off of him," I shouted out loud, my voice echoing off the walls of my bedroom.

Victoria: **Oh Bellany! It's not like that. Cory and I are just friends. I'm only staying here because Tasha got hurt today and Cory needs my help. Nothing has gone on between us. I promise!**

"You promise?" I hissed.

Me: **You better not be lying to me! If you are, I swear, you'll regret ever crossing me!**

Victoria kept texting me, swearing that she was being honest and that nothing was going on between her and Cory. But how would I know if she was telling me the truth? I wasn't there to see what was going on.

As time went by, I began to calm down and think about the situation more clearly. Victoria was cute, but she was definitely no beauty queen. She was no match for Cory. He was handsome and she was awkward. Her neck was too long. Her legs weren't straight. Her knees knocked together when she walked. She had no grace or poise.

I, on the other hand, was exactly Cory's equal. We were both strong tens. If a stranger saw the two of us together, they would think we were the perfect couple.

As I took a deep breath to relax, another thought came to my mind. Victoria mentioned picking up Cory's friends from the airport. What friends?

Me: **Who are you picking up from the airport?**

Victoria: **Some of Cory's friends. He said their names are Charlotte, Wade and Gemma.**

This wasn't a harmless social visit with those three. This was a gathering of haters. Who did they hate? Me!

My knuckles whitened as my fingers curled around my

phone. I knocked over the bedside lamp with a crack and sent it crashing to the floor. Rage and adrenaline propelled me around the room. Curtains were ripped from their rods, chairs overturned, shelves emptied, pictures torn from walls...

When I finally calmed back down, I surveyed the damage. Objects lay strewn about everywhere. But I didn't care. I could pay for the damage. I was filthy rich. I had plenty of money.

I picked up my phone and saw a missed text.

Victoria: **Do you know who these people are?**

Of course I did. I knew all three of them, and Charlotte was the worst of them all. First off, she was obsessed with me-- always has been and always will be.

It all began when Charlotte tried to steal my boyfriend. Then she tried to take my place in my family. She became close to Bridger. Then she introduced her mother to my father so they could date. Fortunately, I was able to squash that relationship real quick and humiliate her mother in the process.

Charlotte, of course, never recognized her responsibility for the wrongs she had done. She blamed everything on me. But she wasn't the victim. I was. So I had to get revenge.

I framed her for my supposed murder, and then I convinced my boyfriend, Quentin, to try to kill her... It was a real shame that he failed.

Charlotte should have stayed in North Carolina instead of coming back for more. I was going to have to deal with her once and for all, and her dumb boyfriend Wade, and her sidekick Gemma too.

I swiped the screen of my phone and began typing.

Me: **Yes. I know them. Be careful! Keep your eyes and ears open, because they're not coming here just to visit Cory. They're coming here to get revenge on me.**

Victoria fired back several texts, wanting to know more. I reminded her that I had already told her all about Charlotte, Wade and Gemma. Had she not been listening to me? Did she ever listen?

Victoria: **Oh, right. Now I remember. Those are the same**

people! Wow! Well don't worry. I'll keep an eye on them. I'll find out what they're up to. Hold on. Cory's saying something to me.

Victoria: **Holy crap! Bridger is coming too. But he's not coming till tomorrow. And Cory just told me that Bridger and Gemma are seeing each other. Did you know that?**

I had to reread her text again to make sure I read it right. Bridger was seeing Gemma? I couldn't believe it. I never thought Bridger would stoop so low. Gemma wasn't worthy of him. She was trash. Bridger was so much better than her.

It had been years since I had checked Gemma's social media accounts. I opened up my laptop and logged in to one of my fake accounts. When I saw pictures of her and Bridger together, I felt like I was going to vomit.

About an hour later, I got another text from Victoria.

Victoria: **Tasha almost drowned today. We had to take her to the hospital.**

I already knew this. I had tracked Victoria's phone to the hospital and figured this out on my own. I thought that something had happened to Victoria, which was why I went there to check on her. That was when I inadvertently ran into Cory.

He spotted me through the doorway. As soon as our eyes met, I took off. Luckily the elevator doors were in the process of closing, allowing me to slip inside before he could catch me.

But the damage had been done. Cory now knew for certain that I was spying on him. Sure, I wasn't exactly keeping this a secret. I had sent him roses to plant the seed in his head and had planned on messing with him some more. I just wasn't ready to confirm to him that I was here yet. That took all the fun out of the surprise.

I wasn't prepared for Cory to hatch his own plan and invite Bridger, Gemma, Charlotte and Wade to come help.

Was Cory really that angry at me? Did he despise me that much?

Getting him back on my good side was going to take a

whole lot more effort and time than I anticipated. This wasn't going to be easy.

But at least I had Victoria to be my eyes and ears. I just hoped she wouldn't mess things up.

I typed her another text.

Me: **After Cory and his friends get settled, you should suggest playing a game with them--a getting to know you game. Ask them to reveal their top three deepest fears.**

Victoria: **That sounds like a fun game. I know what my three deepest fears are. Being trapped in small spaces. Going to the dentist. And throwing up.**

This game wasn't for the purpose of having fun. It was to get information.

Me: **This is important, Victoria. I need you to find out their top three deepest fears. Got it?**

Victoria: **Of course! I got it.**

I picked up my laptop and began formulating a new plan. Charlotte, Wade and Gemma had to be dealt with. Bridger too. And I decided to include Cory's little sister on the list as well. Tasha was going to be a nuisance to have around. She'd demand too much of Cory's time and attention. That would get old real quick.

CHAPTER 11

Victoria

All three of them were waiting on the curb when I pulled up to the airport. I already knew what they looked like. Cory had shown me pictures, so I recognized them right away.

I hopped out of the Expedition to greet them with a smile on my face, even though I felt intimidated. How was I going to convince them that I wasn't a fraud?

Gemma didn't even acknowledge me. She was too focused on her phone. The only time she looked up was when she climbed into the front passenger seat.

Charlotte seemed happy to see me. She gave me a hug. "It's so nice to meet you, Victoria."

"You too," I lied. I knew Charlotte wasn't as nice as she was pretending to be. Bellany told me I couldn't trust her.

Wade gave me a quick head nod and then started loading everybody's luggage into the back.

When I climbed into the driver's seat and looked at Gemma, I saw tears streaming down her cheeks. She was busy texting somebody, and I didn't want to interrupt.

I waited until her fingers stopped moving before I said anything to her. "Are you okay?" I asked as I pulled out onto the road.

"Do I look like I'm okay?" she snapped. "My life is falling apart."

Great. This was not the start I was hoping for. Why hadn't Bellany warned me about how mean Gemma was?

"Your life isn't falling apart," Charlotte said from the back seat. "You're gonna get through this, Gemma."

"The love of my life just broke up with me, over a text. A text!" Her hands flailed with each word. "How could he do this to me?" She pulled a tissue from her pocket and blew her nose.

Wow! I couldn't believe it. Bridger broke up with her! Bellany was going to be thrilled to hear this.

"I thought things were going so well," Gemma cried. "This came as a complete shock--totally out of nowhere. He gave me no indication, whatsoever, that he was having second thoughts about us. I don't understand what happened?"

"That is strange," I said, as I merged into the next lane. I glanced over my shoulder. Wade was wearing headphones and staring out the window. He wasn't listening to any of this.

"Gemma, there was some indication that things weren't right," Charlotte corrected her. "You guys have had some rocky times before. This isn't new."

"Yeah, but I've never been this far away from Bridger before when he's broken up with me. What if he starts seeing someone else? I won't be able to stop him."

"He's not coming to Mexico?" I asked, surprised.

"No, he said he's not coming." Gemma pulled down the visor to look at her reflection in the mirror. She wiped away some of the smeared mascara under her eyes. "He said he wants space. Can you believe it? Space! He already has all the space he needs. We live in completely different houses. How much more space does he need?" She flipped up the visor and checked her phone. "And now he won't text me back!"

"He might be busy," Charlotte said.

"Yeah, with another girl." Gemma started typing furiously on her phone.

I looked at the GPS to make sure I was on the right road. I had muted it, because I didn't want it interrupting us.

"Have you tried calling him?" Charlotte asked.

"About fifty times." Gemma exhaled heavily. "His phone just goes straight to voicemail."

"Did you leave a message when you called?" I asked,

wondering if maybe Bridger couldn't receive texts for some reason. Maybe leaving a voicemail was a better option.

"What decade are you living in? Nobody listens to voicemails anymore." Gemma unbuckled her seatbelt to reach for something on the floor in her backpack.

I thought about braking suddenly and smashing her face into the dash, but I hesitated too long and the opportunity passed.

"Turn left here," Charlotte said, pointing.

"Oh, thanks." I took the left turn, grateful for her help. I had no idea Charlotte had her GPS pulled up too. "Would you mind helping me navigate the rest of the way so we don't get lost?"

"Of course."

I needed to change lanes again, and as I took a quick look over my shoulder, I saw Wade with his head back and eyes closed.

"Stay on this road for another three miles," Charlotte said. "Then you'll be making a right turn, and I'll tell you when you get close."

"Thank you so much." I smiled at her in the rearview mirror.

Gemma released the clip from her hair, allowing waves of long blonde locks to cascade over her shoulders. She twisted it back up again, at least five times, before she was satisfied. She checked her reflection again to make sure it looked right.

She was pretty, but her personality definitely diminished her beauty. Maybe Bridger broke up with her, because he was tired of her attitude. I sure was.

"So are you and Cory seeing each other?" Gemma asked.

I glanced into the rearview mirror and saw Charlotte's eyes on me too, waiting for me to respond. "No, we're just friends." Unfortunately.

"Hmm," Gemma said, retrieving some lip gloss from her purse. "So he's single."

Why did she want to know, I wondered. Wasn't she

heartbroken over Bridger? Was she already looking for his replacement? Or maybe she just wanted to make Bridger jealous. "Yeah, I think so."

"Why couldn't Cory come and get us?" Charlotte asked, leaning over the seat.

My fingers squeezed the steering wheel. I didn't know how to say this without being blunt. "Because he had to stay with Tasha. Um... she almost died."

"What?" Wade's voice pricked my ears. I thought he was asleep. "What happened to her?"

Maybe I should have left this story unspoken. It wasn't mine to tell--it was Cory's. But now I had to. I forced tears into my eyes and began to explain how Tasha drowned in the ocean and how Cory saved her. Silence followed for several minutes.

Then Gemma's phone beeped. She typed something and sighed. "Well, I was considering catching a flight back to North Carolina, but Bridger just texted me and said that he's not going to be there. He's going on vacation! Can you believe it? And he won't tell me where he's going, or who he's going with." She shook her fists in the air. "I'm so angry, I could just scream!"

"Wow! The nerve of him," I said, in an effort to gain her friendship.

Wade grumbled something under his breath from the backseat, but I couldn't hear it.

Gemma spun around. "What did you say?"

"I said, *get over it*."

"Get over it?" she repeated, surprised. "Believe me, I would if I could. I don't want to be heartbroken. I don't want to feel betrayed or angry or sad or mad or confused. I don't want to feel any of those things. I want to be happy and with the person I love. Not everybody is fortunate enough to be in a perfect relationship like you and Charlotte. What you guys have is rare. You're lucky."

"It's not luck," Wade corrected her. "It's love."

My heart melted a little hearing that. Dang.

When Gemma turned back around, she leaned toward

me. "They're engaged to be married. Charlotte's got the rock on her finger and everything. I went with Wade to the jewelry store to help pick it out, so the ring's amazing."

"Congratulations." I glanced into the rearview mirror. "When are you getting married?"

"We haven't set a date yet," Charlotte replied. "We've got to call around and check with a few wedding venues to see what dates are available and then coordinate with our families."

Why was I jealous of them? I was way too young to even be thinking about getting married.

Plus, I didn't have a good track record with relationships. My most recent one was rocky and unsustainable, mainly because my boyfriend already had a girlfriend.

Xavier wouldn't break up with Chantel and commit to me. He wanted to keep our relationship a secret. He only wanted me whenever it was convenient for him. I felt like I was his mistress, and I hated it. We had to sneak around all the time.

If only Xavier had the nerve to break up with Chantel, then maybe things could have turned out differently between us. But there was no going back now--that was for sure.

"Take this next turn," Charlotte said, cutting through my thoughts.

I knew Bellany wanted me to glean as much information from them as possible. I just didn't know how to go about getting it. I hoped I wasn't going to make them suspicious of me. "So how long do you plan on staying in Mexico?" I asked.

"As long as it takes," Gemma replied, and then she spun around to look at Charlotte and Wade. "Am I right? Wade, you don't have to get back right away, do you?"

"This is a working trip," he replied. "My mom and stepdad have a couple people who jumped bail and we suspect they might be here. I have a couple addresses to check out."

"I always get so nervous when you go out searching for fugitives," Charlotte said.

"Yeah, well, looks like we're both going to do that now," he replied. "Bellany has no idea what she's in for."

"Wade works as a bounty hunter, just part time while he's in school," Gemma said. "So he's the perfect person to help us track down Bellany. I just wish Bridger would have come, so he could help us too. After all, it's his sister we're trying to track down."

"His sister?" I asked, pretending to be clueless.

"Yeah, she's on the FBI's most wanted list. And after we catch her, we're splitting the reward." Gemma looked over her shoulder, her gaze on Wade. "Equally."

"I never said I wasn't going to split the reward money," Wade said, defensively.

"So is that why you're here? For the money?" I asked to clarify so I would know what to tell Bellany.

"The money has nothing to do with it," Charlotte replied, her voice tense. "This is about revenge. The money is just a nice perk."

"How much is the reward?" I asked.

"Two hundred and fifty thousand," Wade replied.

"You each get that much money?" I asked.

"We're splitting it," Gemma said, a smile spreading across her face. "I know what I'm buying with my share of the reward money. I've got my eye on this amazing Louis Vuitton purse, and it will be mine--no doubt about it. Plus I have to pay for college."

"You could just get a job and pay for it that way," Wade said.

Gemma placed a hand over her heart. "I'm a full time college student. I don't have time for a job."

"I'm a full time college student too," Wade replied. "I still have time for a job and so does Charlotte."

"I don't have a job anymore," Charlotte reminded him. "I got fired."

"You got fired?" I asked, anxious to hear the story. Charlotte didn't strike me as the type of person who would get fired. She didn't seem careless at all. She seemed careful.

"I was working as a receptionist at a dental office, and they wouldn't give me any time off for this trip. When I told them that I was going to go anyway, they fired me."

Gemma pulled the clip out of her hair and started messing with it again. I thought it already looked fine. I didn't know why she was redoing her hair again. "That's why you need the reward money, Charlotte," Gemma said. "Because you don't have a job and you have a wedding to pay for."

"I'm aware of that," Charlotte replied. "But I wouldn't have come here just for the money. I've got a history with Bellany. And I thought I could get past it, but I can't." She sounded like she was going to cry. "I really wish I could."

I glanced in the rearview mirror. Wade had his arm around her. "Babe," he said. "I don't want you to get upset. Just try to relax and have a good time as much as possible while we're here."

Gemma cracked her knuckles. "You two can relax all you want. I'll do the dirty work, and I'll enjoy it."

"What did Bellany do?" I asked, knowing exactly what she had done. But I had to play dumb. What I didn't expect to hear was Gemma complaining about how Bellany ran over her cat with her car--as if Bellany had done it on purpose.

She also complained about how Bellany wouldn't let Bridger go out with her. It wasn't until after Bellany disappeared that they became a couple. But now they're apart again. And Bellany had nothing to do with their breakup. She hadn't talked to her brother in years. So Gemma ruined her relationship all on her own.

Gemma was so selfish. It surprised me that she hadn't brought up what Charlotte went through first. Being framed for murder was way more serious.

Once Gemma was finished talking, Charlotte told me about her history with Bellany. I pretended to be shocked and appalled.

"What did Bellany do to Cory?" I asked, wondering if they knew.

Gemma explained what had happened, and it sounded like Cory had been completely honest with them. He told them everything. He even admitted that he helped kidnap an innocent lady.

It surprised me that they trusted Cory after learning he was a criminal and used to be in a relationship with Bellany.

But then I figured Cory must have done a really good job painting himself as one of Bellany's victims in order to gain their trust. Or maybe he pulled on their heart strings by telling them that he was raising his foster sister who had special needs and he feared for her safety. Or maybe they all just wanted revenge and the reward money, so it didn't matter what Cory had done.

"How do you plan on finding Bellany?" I asked. It kind of made me nervous that Bellany and I were staying in a house that was located in the same neighborhood as Cory. I thought it was too close, but Bellany insisted that it wasn't.

"She's already been messing with Cory, so we're just going to wait for her to come to him," Wade replied. "Like a mouse to the cheese."

"Bellany has been messing with Cory? How?" I asked as if I had no clue.

"She left some roses and a note on his front porch," Wade explained. "And Cory caught her following him. She'll be back again--there's no doubt in my mind. And we'll be ready."

That was their plan? It didn't sound like much of a plan to me. Bellany was probably going to laugh when she heard about this. Or maybe she wouldn't. Maybe she didn't have a plan either, other than sending me to spy on them.

I still had no idea what she was going to do next. And that made me nervous.

When we arrived at Cory's house, I only stayed for about another half hour. I figured Bellany was probably dying to hear an update from me.

I headed back to the rental house and when I pulled into the driveway, I caught sight of the old lady in my rearview mirror. She was walking by the house rather slowly, in my opinion. Her eyes were trained on the house and on my car. I sunk down in my seat and waited for her to pass, hoping she hadn't seen me.

Should I be worried, I wondered. This was the third time I had seen this old lady.

But instead of freaking out, I tried to think about the situation logically. The old lady was wearing tennis shoes just now, so she was probably out walking for exercise. And she was probably just a nosey neighbor, which was why she was walking by so slowly. Old people did weird things like that, didn't they?

Looking up, I noticed Bellany peeking through the curtains of the living room window, her eyes trained on me. I grabbed my bag and immediately got out of the car. As I headed to the front door, I glanced back to see if the old lady was there. Thankfully she wasn't.

CHAPTER 12

Victoria

Over the past couple weeks, I had managed to become an ever-present figure in Cory and Tasha's lives. I had also become friends with Gemma, Charlotte and Wade.

Tasha was like the sweet little sister I never had. She was so innocent and good. I doubted she had a mean bone in her entire body.

Cory was a great host, really laid back, and so dang handsome. I had a huge crush on him. Huge! I had been flirting with him a lot, and so far he hadn't flirted back, unfortunately. But I was considering kicking it up a notch and trying a little harder.

Charlotte and Wade were the cutest couple. I hoped Cory and I would be just like them one day.

Gemma was pleasant, but she was also moody. She claimed it was because she was upset about her breakup with Bridger. But I suspected she was moody regardless.

The six of us spent most of our time on the beach, and I had an awesome tan to show for it. I looked so good in my swimsuit. I hoped Cory noticed.

I was having so much fun at his house that I was starting to dread going back to the rental house at night to see Bellany. She always insisted on receiving a detailed explanation of everything that happened that day. Her questions seemed to never end. I felt like I was being interrogated by a cop, which was something I was familiar with.

I had been questioned by cops a few times before, like

when I was in the sixth grade and my best friend Monica drowned in her backyard pool. I was the last one to see her alive. The cops didn't seem to believe me when I told them that I had already gone home when she drowned. They also thought it was odd that Monica would drown when she was such a good swimmer. I didn't think it was odd. Anybody could drown if they were held underwater for long enough.

Was I sad when Monica drowned? No, not really. We had gotten into a huge fight over a boy in our class. She said that I couldn't like Jimmy, because she liked him. And if I kept being friends with him, then I wasn't going to be invited to come over to her house to swim anymore.

Monica said that Jimmy liked her more anyway, because she had a pool and I didn't. She also said that she was going to invite him to come over to swim, and not me.

I remembered getting so angry at Monica and wishing she was dead. Then it actually happened. But I never told the cops about our fight. I told them that Monica and I never argued or got mad at each other--we were best friends.

The sound of a chair scraping across the tile floor pulled me from my thoughts. Bellany sat down across from me, folding her hands together on top of the table. I took a deep breath, preparing myself for the questioning that was about to begin.

But I couldn't stop myself from feeling anxious. My nerves were shot. Sometimes I felt like I was on the verge of a mental breakdown. I hated living a double life. I wanted to be happy, and I was happiest with Cory, not Bellany.

Bellany picked at her late night snack with her long, bony fingers. She had purchased a vegetable tray from the grocery store. This was her usual snack of choice. I hated eating this stuff. It had no flavor. What I wouldn't give for something delicious, buttery and full of calories.

I watched her snide expressions as she listened to me recount the day's events. There was never any sign of empathy or compassion. Sometimes her twisted smirk just made my skin crawl.

She thought she was so much better than everyone--
especially me. She treated me like garbage. She never said
anything nice; never said thank you, never said that she
appreciated what I was doing for her. She just ordered me
around and told me what to do; told me how to think and how to
act.

Sometimes after she finished interrogating me, she
would share stories from her past; stories I had already heard
before, and I didn't want to hear them again.

Bellany's eyes burned into me as she took a sip of Diet
Pepsi. "Did you finally talk them into revealing their deepest
fears?" she asked. "You know I've been waiting for you to do
this." With a calculated pause, she adjusted the clasp of her
bracelet. "I sure hope you haven't disappointed me again."

Thankfully I did have some information to share with
Bellany tonight. I actually was able to play this game with Cory
and his friends. I would have tried to play it with them sooner,
but the right moment never presented itself. It was important
that I got to know them first, so that they would feel comfortable
sharing.

"Let's see…" I let out a sigh, gathering my thoughts. And
I quickly listed off their fears while Bellany took notes. Then she
went to the bathroom and told me not to go to bed yet. She'd be
right back.

While she was gone, I replayed the memory in my mind
of what had happened. It was only about an hour ago, so the
memory was still fresh.

We were all sitting around the dining room table eating
dinner together at Cory's house, and I finally got up the nerve to
ask them about their fears.

"Hey, I have an idea," I said. "Why don't we play an
icebreaker game so that we can get to know each other better?"

Tasha clapped her hands. "I love games," she squealed in
delight. "How do you play an icebreaker game? Do I have to get
ice from the freezer?"

Cory reached for her hand to stop her from getting up.

"No. There's no ice involved. You don't have to go get any from the freezer. Just stay here."

A confused look crossed her face. "No ice?"

"Let me explain how to play," I said, flashing a smile at her. "How about if we all share our three biggest fears? That way we can learn more about each other."

Wade rose from the table and pointed a thumb over his shoulder. "I've gotta go check on some fugitives for my parents. Sorry I can't play." He bent down and kissed Charlotte goodbye.

She looked worried. "Don't be gone too long. And be careful."

"I'll be fine." He kissed her again.

"Wait!" I blurted out. "Why don't you just tell us your three fears before you leave? It'll just take a second."

He spread apart his hands. "I don't have any fears." Then he turned and walked off, and there was nothing I could do to stop him.

"Let's go around the table," I suggested, gesturing to Gemma first, hoping she would cooperate. She seemed to be in a decent mood, so I was optimistic.

Gemma strummed her fingernails on the table, making a clicking noise, a look of concentration on her face. "My number one fear is sharks. I never swim in the ocean. Ever. I've seen too many movies to feel comfortable doing that."

Tasha giggled, her hand over her mouth.

But Gemma ignored her. "My other fear is being stranded on a deserted island." She raised an eyebrow. "Have you seen the movie *Cast Away*? That movie gave me nightmares." She shuttered.

I hadn't seen the movie, but I made a mental note to watch it.

"What's your third fear?" Cory asked.

Gemma stared down at her hands for several beats. "Saltine crackers."

Tasha started laughing hysterically and Cory reminded her that it wasn't polite to laugh at people.

"Saltine crackers?" Charlotte made a face. "Do explain."

Gemma took a deep breath, a serious look on her face. "I almost choked to death when I was eating saltines, because I didn't have any water to drink." She placed a hand to her neck. "My mouth was super dry, and the crackers got stuck in my throat."

I placed a hand on my neck too, imagining how horrible that must have been. Then I reached for my glass of Diet Pepsi and guzzled it down.

"When did that happen?" Charlotte asked. "When you were a kid?"

"No. Last year."

Tasha laughed again and this time Cory didn't stop her. He was struggling to hold back his laughter too.

Surprisingly, Gemma didn't get mad. She still seemed kind of spooked about the experience and was lost in her own thoughts.

"Where were you when this happened?" Charlotte asked. She didn't seem amused at all. She truly wanted to know what happened.

"I went hiking with my mom. It was just the two of us. I thought she had brought the water. And she thought I brought the water. But apparently neither of us did. So anyway, my mouth was full of saltine crackers--I mean full! I had eaten like twenty, because I was starving. I hadn't had any breakfast that day. So I was totally choking. My mom tried giving me back blows to dislodge the blockage." She shook her head, eyes clamped shut. "It was just this whole ordeal. I almost died."

"I'm so sorry for laughing," Tasha said, solemnly. "I didn't know you almost died." She gave her a hug.

"Well, you're safe here," Cory said, the smile gone from his lips but it was still present in his eyes. "There are no saltine crackers in the house. And there's plenty of water to drink."

Tasha picked up Gemma's glass and went to the kitchen to fill it up with water. When she brought it back, it was overfull and spilled onto the table. Cory had to get a towel to clean it up.

"You're next," I said to Charlotte.

"Um... going to the dentist, but not because I'm afraid of needles. Ever since I found a bag full of teeth in Quentin's car from the girl that Bellany murdered, I've been terrified of dentists. I don't want anybody touching my teeth, except for me."

I set my napkin over my plate. Hearing about the teeth kind of ruined my appetite.

"My other fear is trains. Ever since Quentin pinned me down while a train was barreling down the tracks towards me, I've been terrified of them." Charlotte took a deep breath. "Sometimes even the sound of a train whistle can give me a panic attack."

Bellany's former boyfriend sure did traumatize her. I had no idea that she suffered from panic attacks. I wondered if she took medication for anxiety.

Cory shook his head, his jaw tight. "Does your third fear involve another memory with Quentin?"

"I used to be afraid of fire, because of a childhood trauma. But now I have another fear that's stronger than that. Ever since Quentin held me hostage in his car, I've been terrified of being kidnapped again. I have the worst nightmares."

It was a good thing that Quentin was dead. Otherwise Charlotte would probably be a nervous wreck all the time. She'd probably be afraid that he would come after her again.

"My turn!" Tasha announced, eagerly. She held up a finger. "My first fear is boats. I'm afraid they'll sink. My second fear is sour milk. One time I drank sour milk, and I got really sick. My third fear is not having any toys to play with." She frowned, then reached for her Barbie doll that was sitting on the table next to her plate.

All eyes were on Cory now. I wondered if he was going to open up and be honest with us, or if he was going to dodge the question like Wade.

"Cory doesn't have any fears," Tasha said, stroking Barbie's hair. "He's brave. He's not afraid of anything." She hopped up from the table, Barbie in hand, and ran down the hall. "I gotta pee."

I leaned forward, staring Cory down. "What are your three biggest fears?" He had better answer me.

Cory cast a glance down the hall. "My biggest fear is losing Tasha," he said in a low voice. "My next fear kind of involves her too. I have a fear of combination locks."

"Combination locks?" Charlotte asked, wrinkling her nose. "Those locks that you spin? You have to go right, left, right..." she said, demonstrating with her hand.

"Yes." He nodded. "I have this recurring nightmare, where I can't unlock the lock and open the door."

"Who's behind the door? Tasha?" I asked.

He exhaled heavily, his eyes on his hands. "Tasha's always trapped behind the door and I can't get to her, because I can't unlock the lock."

"What's your third fear?" I asked, wondering if it involved Tasha again, but also hoping it didn't. I wanted to find out something new about him.

"I don't have a third fear."

"Come on, Cory," I said. "There's gotta be another one. I'm sure you can think of something."

He crossed his arms, sitting back in his chair. "No, there's nothing else."

"Nothing at all," I asked, hoping Gemma or Charlotte would help me pressure him into revealing what it was. But they just sat there.

So I began guessing. "Do you have a fear of clowns? A fear of heights? A fear of spiders?"

Gemma placed her elbows on the table, staring into Cory's eyes. "I think I know what it is. You're afraid of falling in love."

The saddest look I had ever seen crossed Cory's face, but only for a brief moment. "You're wrong," he said. Then he got up and took his plate to the kitchen.

Gemma, Charlotte and I exchanged looks. I felt almost certain that Gemma had guessed correctly. Cory was afraid to fall in love. Was that because of Bellany? Had he given her his heart, only for her to rip it out and stomp on it?

Bellany must have done something to him. She had to have betrayed him somehow. I figured that was why Cory stole the money and disappeared. He probably did it, because he found out she was planning on doing the exact same thing to him. He realized he couldn't trust her.

Bellany may have broken Cory's heart. But I was here to put it back together again.

CHAPTER 13

Victoria

Bellany returned from the bathroom, and I hoped we were almost done for the night. Wasn't learning about everybody's biggest fears enough?

"So what did they say about me today? What kinds of names did they call me? What new insults did they come up with?"

Bellany always asked me these kinds of questions. Sometimes I held back information and sometimes I didn't. It depended on her mood. I always tried to gauge that first. If her fuse was short, I tried not to ignite it. She had already destroyed several rooms in this house.

I doubted I could sufficiently describe just how much Charlotte, Wade and Gemma hated and despised Bellany. They trash-talked her all the time. But Cory never did. He always remained silent. Tasha did too.

I took a bite of a carrot stick, thinking about what to say. Bellany seemed like she might be stable enough to handle a slice of reality pie tonight. "Well, Charlotte told the story about how you pushed her down the stairs and locked her in the basement during your seventeenth birthday party. She said she eventually escaped through the crawl space under the house. She complained about how dark and scary it was."

Bellany's brows knitted together. "Did she say why I locked her in the basement?"

"She said you accused her of snooping--"

"She was snooping!" Bellany interrupted, her voice rising.

"Charlotte was hiding inside my closet and listening to my phone conversation." She jabbed a finger in the air. "I'm telling you, Victoria, that girl has a screw loose in her head. She's psychotic! You better watch out for her. Whatever you do, do not trust her."

I acted like I agreed with Bellany, even though I didn't. Charlotte wasn't psychotic. Bellany was.

Charlotte had told me all about how Bellany used to bully her. She bullied her for years. I knew what it was like. Bellany bullied me too.

I glanced up at Bellany and noticed tears in her eyes, which surprised me. Where was this coming from? Had I said something to upset her? "Are you okay?"

A tear rolled down her cheek. I pushed back my chair, arms reaching out. "Oh, Bellany. Can I give you a hug?"

"No!" she snapped, glaring at me. "Stay away from me!"

Bellany never wanted me to touch her, but I thought maybe this time it would be okay. Apparently not. I sat back down, unsure what to do or say. I picked up another carrot stick and swirled it in some fat free ranch dressing, then took a bite.

"Stop chomping!" Bellany snapped.

I wasn't chomping. I was chewing a carrot, and I couldn't help it if it was loud.

She clasped her hands together, staring down at the table.

I wondered if maybe Bellany was upset, because I sounded like I was on Charlotte's side. Was I being too sympathetic? I had better fix this. "Charlotte always acts like the victim," I said. "It's so annoying."

Bellany's eyes flicked up, staring into mine, and a tear rolled down her cheek. "You have no idea what Charlotte has put me through. If she had just stayed down in the basement, then my entire future would have changed."

Her entire future? "Really?"

"Yes, really! If Charlotte would have stayed in the basement, then I wouldn't have had to fake my death. I would have had time to dispose of that girl's dead body and go on living my life like nothing happened."

Bellany didn't even know the name of the girl she killed. She didn't care about her at all. She was too ruthless. I pushed aside that chilling fact to focus on the rest of Bellany's story. "But I thought you had to fake your death, because you killed that girl while driving drunk."

"You're forgetting something important--something that I've already told you." She sighed, irritated. "There were no witnesses until Charlotte showed up!"

I couldn't remember all the details of the story. Maybe I got some of it wrong. I just wasn't sure if Bellany was telling me the truth, though. "Oh, right," I nodded as if I believed her. "Charlotte was searching for you in the woods behind your house, and that's when she found you and Quentin with the dead girl."

Bellany held up a finger, eyes wide. "No! She didn't catch all three of us. She just saw me."

"I'm confused."

"Charlotte almost caught me and Quentin trying to dispose of that girl's dead body. That's why I had to pretend like I was dead, while Quentin hid in the bushes with the dead girl."

"Okay, I get it now."

"If Charlotte had just stayed in the basement, then Quentin and I would have been able to get rid of the body properly. We could have gone on with our lives like nothing ever happened! Do you get it now?"

I clenched a carrot stick in my hand, every muscle in my body tensing at the thought of Bellany's cruelty. None of this was Charlotte's fault. It was Bellany's.

If Bellany had only made the decision not to drive while under the influence, then that innocent girl would still be alive today. But I kept my mouth shut and remained silent, knowing that uttering these words would only make Bellany question my loyalty.

Bellany wiped her tears, then helped herself to a celery stick. "So how big is the diamond on Charlotte's finger?"

To give Bellany an inkling of how magnificent Charlotte's engagement ring was would only ignite the flames of envy that seemed to perpetually smolder in her eyes. "It's probably like one carat. But it's not a real diamond," I lied. It was real. "Charlotte told me it was moissanite. Wade said that one day he was going to buy her a real diamond to replace it."

Bellany bit into the celery stick, seemingly much calmer now.

I was tired and wanted this discussion to be over. I took one last sip of Diet Pepsi, set the can back down and squished it.

Bellany promptly got up to get me another one from the refrigerator, even though I didn't ask for it.

"So is Gemma flirting with Cory?" she asked, handing it to me.

I still suspected Bellany was in love with Cory. I wished she would just admit it. "Yeah, sometimes Gemma flirts with him," I replied, rolling my eyes.

"Does Cory flirt back?"

"No, not really. I mean, he's just nice to everyone in general."

Bellany leaned forward, eyes boring through me. "Does he flirt with you?"

"No, of course not." I wished he did.

This interrogation had been going on for way too long, and I was beyond tired. I glanced back at my bedroom, wondering if I would get any sleep tonight. Probably not, since Bellany felt the need to accuse me of being romantically involved with Cory again.

I wasn't sure how much more of this I could take.

Bellany sat there staring at me. Did she want me to say something else? I already denied her accusation and couldn't think of anything else to say. But she didn't look convinced. I decided to try again.

"I swear, Cory doesn't ever flirt with me." That was the truth. He hadn't flirted with me, unless his idea of flirting was to do the exact opposite and show no interest at all. "Like I said,"

I shrugged, "he's just nice to everyone." Which was one of the many reasons I liked him so much.

Bellany propped her chin on her fist, studying my face. "What else happened today? What about Tasha?"

"Tasha was her normal self. Happy. Friendly. She's really a sweet girl."

"What about Bridger? Have you heard anything about him?"

I suspected that Bellany missed her brother. She looked a little sad whenever she brought him up. "No, nothing new."

A distant look entered her eyes as if she was recalling a long-forgotten memory. But I was too tired to be curious about it.

CHAPTER 14

Victoria

A month had passed, and Bellany's interactions with me had changed drastically. She was slowly growing more distant.

She went from spending hours interrogating me every night, to sometimes completely ignoring me. It wasn't a rare occurrence for her to already be in bed by the time I arrived at the rental house.

At first, her lack of interest was a huge relief. But then it started to concern me.

I had no idea what Bellany was thinking. Was she mad at me? Was she jealous or suspicious? Did she think that Cory and I were together? All of these questions played on my mind every night.

Bellany's appearance remained flawless whenever I saw her. The nail polish color on her fingernails was changed every couple of days. Her hair was shinier than ever, probably from a lot of visits to the salon. Her arms looked more toned and muscular. She must have spent hours at the gym every day. Her clothes were always new and looked expensive.

But despite spending all that time and money on herself, she didn't seem happy. Was she mad at me?

Call it a guilty conscience, but I was starting to feel uneasy. I wondered if Bellany made a habit of spying on me, or if she had done it only that one time, when I was at the hospital with Cory and Tasha. I hoped it was only that once. There were things that I didn't want her to know.

A beep sounded, tearing me from my thoughts. The noise

hadn't come from the TV. It was Bellany's phone.

She picked it up and started typing, a smile on her lips.

I wondered who she was texting so late at night. I was her only friend. Did she meet someone new?

I watched from the corner of my eye, waiting for her to finish, curious about what was going on.

Bellany giggled, and I couldn't keep quiet any longer. I muted the TV. "Who are you texting?"

She flipped her phone around, showing me a picture of a humongous boat. "How do you feel about leaving Mexico and sailing around the world?"

I took the phone from her outstretched hand. "You want to buy a boat?"

"There's more pictures. Swipe right," she said. "And it's not a boat. It's a yacht."

The yacht looked like a towering palace of white and blue with so many levels it appeared to scrape the sky. My eyes danced across the image, picking up every small detail: a helipad on the roof, a hot tub lined with gold tiles, a bar that seemed to stretch on forever. The name **Jenny** was written across the side of the yacht. I couldn't imagine owning something so spectacular. "How much is it?"

Bellany tossed her hand up. "Who cares what it costs. We've got plenty of money."

She was right. We were filthy rich. But I still felt uneasy about this. "I don't know anything about yachts. Do you?"

She shot me a look. "We'll hire a captain and a crew."

I didn't understand why she wanted to do this. It didn't make sense. "What about Cory and his friends? Have you decided that you don't want to get revenge anymore?" I bit my lip, hoping she would say yes. I just wanted her to leave them alone and move on with her life.

"Their day of reckoning is still coming," she said, her voice cold. "The yacht is for after." Bellany got up and headed to the kitchen.

"What are you going to do to them?" I asked, hoping she

would finally give me an answer instead of keeping me in the dark.

"All you need to know is that..." she paused as she rummaged through the refrigerator. "They're going to regret ever crossing me."

I was tired of her cryptic answers. Why wouldn't she just tell me what's going on? My fingers gripped the phone tightly. I looked down at it, surprised. I still had Bellany's phone!

My heart began to race as I realized that the screen was still unlocked, and I had access to everything on it. Maybe I could find out what she was up to. Maybe the answers were right at my fingertips.

While Bellany's back was turned, I pulled up her text messages. There were no names listed, just phone numbers. I clicked on the first number and read through the recent messages.

My stomach dropped. I couldn't believe it! Bellany had already purchased the yacht--it was a done deal! And there was a crew in place too. Why hadn't she told me? Why lie?

"Victoria."

I jumped, fingers squeezing tightly around her phone. Crap!

She walked toward me, hand outstretched. "What are you doing?"

"I was just looking at the pictures of the yacht," I said, trying to act casual. "It's so perfect! When can I see it?"

She snatched the phone from my hand and stared down at the screen.

Sweat beaded on my forehead. I hoped I had closed those text messages, but my fingers moved so quickly, I might have accidentally clicked on the wrong thing.

Bellany was taking too long to respond to my question. Did she know I had read her texts?

She squinted at her phone as I held my breath in anticipation. The room felt like it was shrinking, the walls closing in on me. My heart hammered in my chest. How is she ever going to trust me if she finds out I was snooping?

Her eyes lifted, meeting mine. Her expression was unreadable. Should I apologize now and try to explain?

Bellany slipped the phone into her pocket. "I don't know when you can see the yacht," she finally replied. "I'll have to check with the owner."

She set a plate of vegetables down on the coffee table, then sat next to me on the couch. "Want some?" she asked, picking up a carrot stick.

She must not have known about my snooping, otherwise she probably would have jammed that carrot down my throat.

We sat in silence for a little while, watching TV and eating flavorless vegetables. But I could not stop thinking about the yacht. Why didn't she just admit that she already bought it? What was going on?

I couldn't summon up the courage to confront her and admit that I knew the truth. I just hoped she would tell me on her own. "Hey, Bellany," I said. "Do you think we can go see the yacht tomorrow?"

"I don't know. I'll ask." Her fingers skated across the screen of her phone.

Why was she pretending to text back and forth with the owner of the yacht? She was the owner! I bit the inside of my cheek while I waited.

Bellany shook her head. "He can't show us the yacht tomorrow. He said maybe Saturday. Does that work for you?"

"Okay." Saturday was three days away. Why was she making me wait so long?

Bellany smiled, but it was fake. "I'll let him know."

You do that, I thought to myself, frustrated. I couldn't stand being around her any longer. I got up and headed to the shower.

While I was shampooing my hair, a troubling thought entered my mind. What if there was something more going on with Bellany? What if she planned on betraying me?

My thoughts raced around in my head, each one more

paranoid than the last. I couldn't trust Bellany.

I felt like I should stick around the house to keep tabs on her tomorrow. And then if she went anywhere, I would follow.

After I got out of the shower, I laid in bed wrestling with these thoughts, wondering if I should just confront her. I could prove that she was lying to me without even mentioning the texts on her phone. All it would take was one glance at the bank account balance. Then I'd have all the proof I needed. I would also know how much she spent on that yacht.

But if I confronted Bellany about purchasing it, would that really be wise? She might become angry and defensive, which would lead to a fight, and then what?

Maybe the reason Bellany didn't tell me that she purchased it was because she felt bad about not consulting me first. It was possible she was just covering her tracks and had pure intentions all along. Holding onto that thought, I finally managed to drift off to sleep.

I was jolted awake the next morning by a sudden and violent nightmare. In it, Bellany had absconded with all our money, leaving me behind in a suffocating cloud of fear and betrayal. The events of my dream seemed so real--I couldn't stop thinking about it.

As I laid in bed, my mind took hold of another terrifying thought. What if all the money was gone? What if there was nothing left?

I grabbed my phone to check the bank account balance. I typed in the username and password, then a message popped up: **Incorrect password.** My stomach dropped. I took a deep breath to calm down, hoping I had just typed it wrong.

Trying again, my fingers moved much slower. I made sure I got it correct this time. But the same message popped up on the screen: **Incorrect password.**

My heart hammered in my chest as I tried a third time.

It still didn't work!

I ripped off the covers and jumped out of bed, fear and anger growing inside of me. Bellany should have told me that she changed the password! She should have told me that she bought a yacht! Why did she lie?

Her bedroom door was cracked open. I barged in without even knocking, and what I saw clutched at my heart like a vice. Every hair on my body stood on end as I tried desperately to cling onto hope.

But there was no sign of Bellany anywhere. The room was stripped bare, like an empty tomb. No clothes, no shoes, no makeup... just emptiness, and it chilled me to the bones.

As I stumbled back into the hallway, a cold sweat broke out all over my body. She left me!

CHAPTER 15

Victoria

Hot tears of desperation stung my eyes, and I felt like screaming into the silence as I scrambled to call Bellany's phone. But it was no use--my calls went straight to voicemail.

I collapsed onto the floor, seething in anger, and sent her a flurry of increasingly desperate texts, hoping against hope for an answer.

Me: **What's going on?**

Me: **Where are you?**

Me: **Bellany! Please respond! Please! I'm begging you!**

About a minute later, my phone chimed. My heart pounded with anticipation as the illuminated screen came to life. But when I saw the name appear, all hope vanished inside me. It was just a text from Charlotte.

Charlotte: **Hey, we're going out to lunch around 12. Want to come?**

Tears were flowing, and I couldn't hold them back anymore. Bellany had betrayed me in the worst way imaginable. She took all the money, then abandoned me here. The injustice seared into me like a hot coal.

My fingers trembled while I tried to craft a response to Charlotte, but my brain felt like sludge. I knew I had to escape this place before the air around me suffocated me completely!

My heart dropped into my stomach as I frantically scanned the living room for my car keys. But they were nowhere in sight!

Frantic, I flew to the window and dragged the curtains

aside. The driveway was empty. Both my car and hers were gone! Panic coursed through me as I spun around, pushing furniture aside in desperation.

I texted Bellany again.

Me: I need to talk to you right away! Please come back to the house!

My heart wouldn't slow down. It continued to race so quickly, I felt like I was going to have a heart attack. How was I going to survive on my own without any money or transportation?

I headed to the couch and once again called Bellany's phone. When it went to voicemail, I started crying. "Bellany, I'm really worried about you. Why aren't you returning my texts? Did something happen? Please call me. I'm really worried." A sob rose in my throat, and I couldn't hold it back. I had to hang up.

I was broke. I had no money! She had stolen millions from me!

With no other alternative, I called Cory.

"Victoria, what's wrong?" he asked.

"I messed up," I cried into the phone.

"What do you mean, you messed up?"

"I've been lying to you. I've been pretending like I don't know Bellany, but I do know her. I know exactly who she is," I sobbed. "She betrayed me, just like she betrayed you and everybody else!"

"What?"

"I'm so sorry!" I gasped, crying uncontrollably. I collapsed onto the couch, feeling like such a horrible person. How could I have ever aligned myself with Bellany? How could I have trusted her? "Cory, I'm so, so sorry. Please forgive me!"

"Victoria," he said, his voice tense. "Just tell me what's going on. What happened?"

I didn't know where to start. The words just came tumbling out of my mouth. "Bellany swore that she would share the money with me. But then she changed the password on the bank account. She packed everything up and took my car. She's gone!"

"I'm coming over. Where are you?"

I gave him the address. Then as soon as I hung up, I sobbed like a baby.

When Cory arrived, I discovered that he wasn't alone. He brought everyone with him.

Wade walked right past me, barely acknowledging my existence. He began looking through the house. I didn't know what he was searching for. Bellany was definitely gone. And she had taken everything that belonged to her. There was nothing left.

Gemma shot me a dirty look. "Cry all you want, Victoria. I don't feel the slightest bit sorry for you."

Charlotte gave me a quick hug, which surprised me.

"Don't cry," Tasha said, patting my arm as her eyes swept over the kitchen. "Do you have any chocolate?"

"No," I replied, wiping a finger under my eye. Bellany was too concerned about calories to keep any junk food here.

Gemma propped her feet up on the coffee table and glowered at me from across the room. "Come and sit!" she demanded, her voice laced with venom and contempt. "We need to talk."

Cory sat at my side, his intense gaze boring into me.

The guilt of my betrayal felt like an iron weight pressing down on my chest, crushing the air out of me. I had pretended to be a friend, and yet I hurt them all. I deserved every ounce of hatred. I was a traitor.

"Tell us everything," Charlotte said.

Every word I spoke dripped with guilt. I started by telling them what had happened in West Virginia. I told them how I had shot and killed Lane to protect Bellany. I told them how she had stolen his money.

"You should have just let him kill her!" Gemma snapped.

"Didn't you know she was a serial killer?" Wade asked.

I shook my head. "No, I had no idea," I lied.

"What else happened?" Wade asked.

I explained how Bellany and I came to Mexico to get revenge on Cory. The truth weighed heavily on my conscience. I didn't know how to make things right. "I'm so sorry."

I couldn't bring myself to look in Cory's direction to see his face. I wiped my tears and fumbled for words. "I--I didn't know who she was. I had no idea that wherever Bellany went, she left a trail of destruction behind her. I had no idea that she ruined so many people's lives."

"She killed people," Wade said, his voice tense.

"What do you mean, you didn't know?" Gemma scoffed. "We've been telling you about her for over a month now. You've heard all the horrific details."

Wade narrowed his eyes. "And yet you chose not to tell us that she was using you to spy on us."

My stomach churned with guilt, and my face burned with shame. "I was in too deep. I--I didn't know how to get out."

"Pretty dresses," Tasha said, sitting at the counter, looking through one of Bellany's fashion magazines. She seemed oblivious about what was going on.

Cory's brow furrowed in concentration, his fingers tapping the couch. Then he started asking me a bunch of questions: *Does Bellany have a car? When did you last see her? Has she returned your texts?*

After I answered his questions, I checked my phone to make sure I hadn't missed any texts. But there was still no response from Bellany.

"Try calling her again," Charlotte suggested. "Maybe she'll answer this time."

The call went straight to voicemail again.

Tasha finally set down the magazine and walked across the room. She pushed the curtains aside, looking out the window. "I'm bored. I wish I had some toys to play with. I should have brought my dolls."

"Just how much money does Bellany have?" Wade asked, his eyes wide with curiosity.

I didn't want to say the exact amount, for fear that they

would get even more angry with me. "I'm not sure how much is left, but I can tell you that we stole eight-figures from Lane."

Gemma counted on her fingers silently, then her mouth gaped. "Eight figures!"

Wade cocked his head in interest. "So eight figures...as in what, like ten million? Twenty million? Or more than that?"

I didn't want to tell them. It was an outrageous amount, which was why I was so devastated that Bellany had stolen it all from me. I cleared my throat. "Eighty-five million."

The room fell silent for a few beats. Then Tasha giggled as she fiddled with the drawstring on her shorts. "Bellany's super rich. She's like a millionaire."

Wade muttered something under his breath as he staggered across the room. He leaned heavily against the window frame, looking out with unfocused eyes.

"This isn't fair!" Gemma's eyes flashed with rage, her jaw clenched. "She doesn't deserve that money! She doesn't deserve any of it!"

"How did this happen?" Charlotte stared at nothing. Pain was etched into her face. "I don't understand how a person like Bellany could end up with all that money and go on living her life like she's done nothing wrong. Will justice ever be served?"

The weight of my involvement in Bellany's wicked plans pressed down on me even harder. If only I had teamed up with Cory and his friends and taken Bellany down while I still had the chance.

Cory hung his head and clenched his fists tightly. "She has the resources to disappear, and that's exactly what she's done."

As I considered the scope of Bellany's wealth, my mind raced with the pictures of her shiny new yacht. Then a new realization popped into my head, and my entire body felt as if it had been hit by a jolt of electricity.

Why hadn't I thought of this before?

Bellany hadn't hopped onto a plane. She wasn't flying to some unknown destination in the world. She hadn't driven off, heading down the highway or down some obscure road.

I knew where she was!

My mind conjured up an image of the yacht peacefully floating on the ocean. "Where is the closest marina?"

"Why?" Gemma asked, a look of confusion on her face.

"What's a marina?" Tasha asked.

"Bellany bought a yacht! If we hurry, we might still be able to catch her!"

They searched for the nearest marina on their phones.

Cory jumped up from the couch. "Puerto de Abrigo," he said, reading off his phone. "Bellany's yacht has got to be there."

We raced out of the house and piled into the Expedition. The engine roared to life as Cory backed out of the driveway and took off down the road.

I tried my best to describe what the yacht looked like, but when we arrived at the port, I realized I hadn't done a good enough job. There were so many other yachts and boats. They all seemed to look alike.

"Which one is it?" Cory asked.

I squinted, desperately searching the assortment of yachts for Bellany's. Eventually my eyesight blurred until I could only make out shapes and shadows.

Then finally, something stood out from the rest: a name written across the side of one of the vessels... "Jenny!" I shouted. "The yacht had Jenny written on the side of it. That's its name! There it is!" I pointed.

We all stood on the dock, watching in horror as Bellany's yacht sailed past us.

CHAPTER 16

Victoria

We searched for someone to give us a ride on their boat. I worried that if we didn't find someone soon, Bellany's yacht would disappear forever.

Gemma's face twisted with determination when her gaze landed upon a man with a small boat. She marched forward with purpose, tossing her long blonde hair back. She curled her lips into an alluring smile and looked up at the man through thick lashes. Soon enough he was gesturing for us to join him on his boat.

"Wait!" Cory said, stopping us. "Tasha's afraid of boats. I'm going to have to stay here with her."

"Boats scare me," Tasha said, burying her face into Cory's chest.

"You can't stay behind," Wade said to Cory. "You have to come with us."

"Yeah," Charlotte agreed, her arm linked through Wade's. "Why don't you leave Tasha here with Victoria. I'm sure she won't mind staying behind. Right Victoria?"

I placed a hand over my heart. "You want me to stay behind?"

"Yes," Charlotte said.

Gemma bit her lip, staring at the water. She looked nervous. Then I remembered she was afraid of sharks. It surprised me that she hadn't volunteered to stay behind and babysit.

Cory shook his head. "I can't leave Tasha behind. I have to

stay with her."

Hold on a second. Did he not trust me? "I can watch her. We'll bake cookies. Does that sound fun, Tasha?"

She lifted her head. "I want to bake cookies."

"We don't have time to debate this!" Wade turned his gaze to the gleaming white yacht. "She's getting away!" Then he looked at Gemma. "Why don't you stay and watch Tasha?"

Gemma's mouth gaped open, eyes blinking rapidly. "I don't know how to bake cookies. Cory, just leave Tasha with Victoria. You can trust her. She'll take good care of Tasha."

This was shocking. I couldn't believe Gemma was sticking up for me, even though it was probably for selfish reasons.

"Victoria's just like all the rest of us," Gemma continued. "We've all been taken advantage of by Bellany at one time or another in our lives."

Charlotte reached for Gemma. "But you're afraid of sharks. Are you sure you want to come?"

Gemma shrugged. "I'll be perfectly fine as long as I'm on a boat."

"Guys, come on!" Wade groaned.

Tasha took hold of my hand, and a smile spread across her face. "Can we bake two kinds of cookies? Hershey Kisses and sugar cookies?"

I could feel everybody's collective stare, especially Cory's. "Of course," I smiled at Tasha. "Two different kinds of cookies sound good to me." Staying behind and watching Tasha would give me a chance to regain Cory's trust.

"We gotta go!" Wade said, impatiently. He climbed aboard the boat, then reached back to help Charlotte and Gemma.

But Cory stayed put, his feet firmly planted on the dock.

"Cory, she's getting away!" Wade called. "We have to leave now!"

My heart sank as Cory looked at me with a pained expression on his face. Tasha was his whole world, and I had recklessly violated his trust. His doubts were justified. He couldn't bring himself to rely on me to take care of the one person he loved above everybody else.

I had to say something to ease his fears, because time was running out. He had to go now. Bellany had all my money and she was about to disappear. "I'm sure you'll only be gone for a couple hours. Tasha will be fine. I promise."

Cory handed me his keys. "I'll be back as soon as possible." He reached into his pocket and gave me some cash. "Don't let her go to the beach without you."

"I know," I said, remembering how she almost died. I forced a smile. "We'll see you soon. Everything's going to be fine."

He gave Tasha a quick hug, then climbed aboard the boat.

Tasha and I waved from the dock as the boat cut through the choppy water like a hot knife through butter. I worried they wouldn't catch up to Bellany in time. The offshore yacht was starting to dwindle away and looked almost like a speck on the horizon.

"Let's stop and get some ice cream," Tasha said, walking beside me.

Thankfully Cory gave me money. Otherwise, I'd have to tell her no. "Sure, that sounds great."

After we got ice cream and started heading home, an icy fear settled in the pit of my stomach. What if something bad happens to Cory and the rest of them? What if they never return? I glanced at Tasha, the weight of this possibility pressing heavily on my mind. I wasn't prepared for this kind of responsibility.

CHAPTER 17

Tasha

Victoria made me peel the Hershey Kisses 'cause she didn't wanna get fat. I was munching away like crazy, scarfing down five already! But Cory had always told me that it didn't matter if I stayed skinny or got all chubby-bubby, 'cause I would still be beautiful and awesome no matter what!

The mixer buzzed, and the batter swirled around and around. My tummy gurgled as I daydreamed about what it would taste like. Before I knew it, my finger was already in there!

"No!" Victoria screamed, and I yelped with surprise.

"What did you do that for?" I cried, feeling mad and scared at the same time. I hated it when people tried to startle me or shout at me. My foster parents used to do that all the time. Cory said they yelled because they were abusers. He said yelling was bad!

"Tasha, you can't put your finger in the bowl when the mixer is running. It'll break your finger!"

I looked down at my finger. It wasn't broken. It was just fine. Was she telling me the truth? "Really?"

"Yes," Victoria said with a sigh. "The mixer is really powerful. It could snap your finger right in half."

In half? That was so scary! I put my hands in my lap fast, glad that my finger didn't break! "I'm so sorry."

"It's all right, Tasha. Everything's fine. Just be more careful." Victoria turned off the mixer, stuck a spoon into the bowl, and scooped out some dough. "Here."

I grabbed the giant spoon. "Yay! Thanks!" The batter was

so sweet and amazing. I could barely keep from eating it all up! I couldn't wait for the cookies to be done baking.

All together, I ate ten cookies. Ten! Victoria just let me eat them. She didn't tell me no. Cory would have told me no. He would have told me to eat some vegetables, and then I could have some more cookies.

Victoria sat on the couch drinking a glass of Diet Pepsi. She said it tasted flat--whatever that meant--and she made a face like it was gross but she didn't stop drinking it.

The TV was on. She was watching some show about housewives. I thought it was boring.

The sun was still up outside, so I put my swimsuit on. Before I went out the backdoor, I remembered what Cory had said to me: *Don't go to the beach by yourself.*

I turned back around and walked into the family room. Victoria was asleep on the couch. If I woke her up, she might get mad at me. Cory never liked it when I woke him up.

Maybe I could go to the beach by myself and get back before she woke up. Then I wouldn't get in trouble, because she wouldn't know!

I grabbed my bag of shovels and buckets and quietly opened the backdoor, even though it probably didn't matter. The TV was super loud.

The sand was hot, so I had to go down by the water where it was wet and cool. Plus, that's where the best sand was to make a sandcastle. I dug a hole and then walked into the ocean--not too far--and filled up my bucket with water. I poured the water into the hole, but it wasn't enough to fill it up. I needed a whole lot more.

An old lady walked by and stopped to look at my sandcastle. The mote wasn't done yet. It needed more water. But she liked it anyway.

I scooped some more sand into a bucket and packed it in tight. Cory showed me how to do this. Then I flipped it over and pulled the bucket off.

"You're pretty good at that," the old lady said.

"I practice all the time with my brother." Cory and I built sandcastles almost every day.

The old lady pointed down the beach. "I saw someone building a sandcastle not far from here. It's as tall as I am. Do you want to see it?"

A sandcastle as tall as her? No way! I had never seen a sandcastle so big. "Yes!" I said, standing up. I brushed the sand off my knees and hands.

She motioned for me to come with her. "It's the most amazing sandcastle. I can't wait for you to see it."

"Did an adult build it?" I asked, walking beside her.

"Yes," the old lady nodded. "There are three people working on it."

"I usually build sandcastles with two people."

The old lady smiled and continued to describe the sandcastle. It was hot out, so I was glad that I could let the cold ocean water run over my feet as we walked.

We walked for a long time, and I still hadn't seen a sandcastle. When I turned back around, I couldn't see my house anymore. What if Victoria woke up, I wondered. Would she be mad at me?

The lady pointed. "I think I see it."

I squinted my eyes, but I couldn't see a sandcastle. Then I turned back around, wondering if I would see Victoria.

"Something wrong?" the old lady asked.

I was tired of walking, and I was thirsty. "I'm gonna go back home."

"Why? Don't you want to see the sandcastle?"

I did want to see it, but this was taking too long. "My legs are tired of walking," I said.

The old lady looked at my legs. "Well, I could drive you the rest of the way. My car is parked on the road."

Cory told me never to get in a car with a stranger. "I'm not allowed," I said, shaking my head. My stomach felt weird. It was doing all kinds of flips.

"Are you afraid that Cory won't let you?" the old lady

asked.

I nodded. "He said I can't get in the car with strangers."

The old lady smiled and giggled. "I'm not a stranger. I'm a friend of your brother's."

"You are? How come I've never seen you before?"

"Well, I've seen you."

"You have?" The flips were getting worse in my stomach. My heart was beating fast.

"Yep. I saw you at the hospital when you almost drowned. I was one of the nurses that took care of you. That's how I met your brother."

I couldn't remember seeing this old lady before. But I did go to the hospital when I almost died, so she must have seen me there.

"My name's Jenny," the old lady said with a smile.

If her name was Jenny, then why was she wearing a necklace with the letter S on it? Didn't Jenny start with a J?

She reached for my hand. "Come on. I'll take you to my car, and we'll go see the sandcastle."

I decided that she wasn't a stranger after all. She was a nurse. She helped people. So I followed her to her car and got in.

CHAPTER 18

Victoria

My heart raced uncontrollably, pounding with dread. Three times I had gone out to the beach to look for Tasha, searching desperately among the shoreline. I questioned everyone, but nobody had seen her. My biggest fear was that I'd discover her lifeless body in the surf.

I scoured every corner of the house in a desperate attempt to find her. I didn't stop until I had searched it from top to bottom. I even spoke to the neighbors, pleading for any information on her whereabouts--all the while fearing the worst.

If only I hadn't fallen asleep. If only I had stayed awake and watched Tasha like I was supposed to. I knew better than to leave her unattended, but when I sat down on the couch to relax, I just couldn't keep my eyes open. No matter how hard I tried, I couldn't fight the fatigue.

My eyes landed on the empty glass sitting on the coffee table. The ice had completely melted. I remembered pouring myself some Diet Pepsi. I got it out of the fridge from the two-liter bottle. It had a weird taste, but I just thought it had gone flat. Was it possible that the Diet Pepsi was spiked with some kind of sedative? Could that explain my inability to stay awake earlier?

My mind raced as I pieced together the puzzle of my missing hours. It became increasingly clear that something sinister had happened. I believed the Diet Pepsi had been spiked! My heart sank as I realized I had been a victim of a despicable act, and my body still felt heavy with exhaustion from sleeping for so long.

But who could have spiked the Diet Pepsi? Did Belllany do it?

As I stood in front of the refrigerator, I wondered what else might have been tampered with. Was it only the Diet Pepsi? Was it the juice too? What about the Dr. Pepper? Feeling sick to my stomach, I slammed the refrigerator door shut.

I headed to Tasha's bedroom again, taking a closer look at what was in there. I hoped I would find some kind of clue as to what might have happened to her. That was when I realized her bag of buckets and shovels was missing. She must have gone out to the beach by herself! Did that mean she went swimming in the ocean again? Fear crept up my spine as I imagined her trying to swim against the tides.

I scoured the shoreline again, searching for her, trudging through the water. The sun slowly descended beneath the horizon, its light dimming until the last of it had disappeared. I was left alone in the dark twilight of the evening, but I wasn't about to give up.

There was another place I hadn't searched yet. I grabbed the key to the Expedition and drove straight to the hospital, hoping I'd find her there, alive and well. But how likely was it that she would survive drowning for a second time?

What would I tell Cory? Would he believe that someone had drugged me and that it wasn't my fault his sister was gone? My chest felt so tight, I could hardly breathe.

I found a receptionist who spoke English. She checked the hospital records for a teenage girl, but nobody matching Tasha's description had been admitted today.

As I drove back to Cory's house, a cold dread filled my veins. I feared that I would find Cory there. The knowledge that I had to shatter his world with the news of his sister's disappearance brought tears to my eyes.

I imagined him standing at the door, livid with rage and hatred directed at me for failing him. His words would echo in my ears as he cast me aside like yesterday's garbage. My future flashed before my eyes; no money, no car, no home. No Cory!

Relief washed over me as I entered his silent house. Thankfully he wasn't home yet.

I sat on the couch and dialed Bellany's phone number. It went straight to voicemail. As soon as it beeped, I said, "Bellany, please call me back. I'm desperate. Please! I need your help. I can't find Tasha anywhere…"

Then the thought entered my mind, why was I begging her for help? She probably kidnapped Tasha.

Bellany was the type of person who would do something sick and twisted like that. She faked her death. She framed Charlotte for a murder she didn't commit. Bellany lied to so many people. She betrayed them. She betrayed me.

I dialed her phone again, leaving another message: "I know you took her! Where are you? Where's my money? Don't be a coward, Bellany. Only cowards run away--" I stopped mid-sentence and hung up as tears rolled down my face.

Those last words I had said tore through my heart like a sharp blade, leaving an unbearable ache: *Only cowards run away.*

I had run away from home. I was a coward too.

CHAPTER 19

Victoria

I sat on the couch in the living room, crying uncontrollably. I had no idea what happened to Tasha. Was she still alive? And what about Cory? Would I ever see him again?

I felt like there was a dark void consuming my entire being. My heart and soul were hollowed out, leaving only despair in its place.

My phone chimed with a text, making me jump. Could it be Cory?

When I saw the name pop up on the screen, I almost fell off the couch.

Bellany: **I am at a loss as to why you broke my trust, especially after all I've done for you. Was it out of greed, envy, or were you just born with a heart of ice? Your actions speak louder than words, Victoria, and the truth is crystal clear. You're a certifiable sociopath!**

I was going to surprise you this morning with the announcement that I had acquired the yacht at an amazing price. All I had to do was move our funds into the same bank as the seller, then complete the purchase using an all-cash offer. This allowed me to negotiate a twenty-five percent discount.

Everything was set. I had hired the previous owner's crew to continue serving us. Groceries had been bought. I had already packed my stuff and moved in. The only thing I had left to do was surprise you with the good news and help you pack.

But when I returned to our house, I saw Cory's Expedition parked in the driveway.

My phone battery was dead at the time, so I hadn't seen all your texts and missed calls until after I discovered your betrayal. Clever how you tried to lure me back to the house with all your desperate messages. You sounded like you were panicking and worried about me.

I bet you got nervous when I didn't return your messages. Was that when you discovered that the password to the bank account was invalid and your money supply had been cut off? Was that why you and your loser friends stole my yacht? Did you think you could use it as leverage to negotiate with me?

Think again, my dear. I still have plenty of money, and it's all mine now. If I wanted to, I could buy myself another yacht. I don't need that one anymore. And I certainly don't need a low-life scammer friend like you! Good luck, Victoria. You're gonna need it.

I lowered the phone, Bellany's words repeating in my head. If she had only explained all of this to me sooner, then I wouldn't have overreacted and brought Cory and his friends into this mess!

Was Bellany serious about the yacht being stolen? How could she think that I stole it?

My hands shook as I dialed her phone number. I had to figure out what was going on and make things right!

The call went to voicemail, and a sudden surge of emotion came over me. Tears ran down my face as I formulated the words in my head, desperate to have them heard.

I had to clear up this misunderstanding, otherwise she would never bother to return my call. There were millions of reasons for me to do this--all of them dollars!

But I knew Bellany wouldn't willingly just give me my share of the money, not with our friendship so strained. Somehow I had to make her believe that I was innocent in all of this and that I hadn't betrayed her.

A beep sounded in my ear, and I began speaking...

"Bellany, I didn't steal the yacht--I swear I didn't! We saw it sailing away, and we thought you were on it! So Cory and his friends hopped onto another boat to chase after it. I still haven't heard back from them. I don't even know if they caught up to it."

I sighed. "But If you weren't on the yacht, then who was?" I paused, trying to think of what to say next. I didn't want to lie to Bellany, but it was my only option. I wanted my money back!

"Bellany, I didn't betray you! Cory and his friends showed up at the house this morning on their own--I had nothing to do with it! They followed me home last night and discovered that you were there."

My heart raced as the lies continued to spill out of my mouth... "Cory and his friends freaked out! They ganged up on me, and I'm sorry, but I cracked under the pressure. They made me tell them what you were up to. So I told them about the yacht and how you wanted to sail around the world. But I didn't know you had bought it yet. I just thought that maybe you had gone to see it, because you weren't returning my texts. I thought maybe you were taking it for a test drive at sea and had no cell signal."

I paused, wondering if that was enough to convince her to trust me. No, it probably wasn't. The damage to our friendship was too great--I needed to say more!

"The only reason I agreed to take them to the yacht was because they promised not to hurt you or turn you over to the police," lied. "They promised they wouldn't, Bellany--I swear they did! They told me that they just wanted to confront you. They were afraid that you were going to do something terrible to Cory and Tasha, and they thought they could talk you out of it."

I almost hung up and ended the message, but then another lie popped into my head. If this didn't convince Bellany to trust me, then I didn't know what would.

"Bellany, I'm sorry. I hope you forgive me for this, but I had to lie to them to stop their desire for revenge."

I sighed, trying to sound like I was ashamed.

"I lied and told them that you were in love with Cory. I told them that was the reason you came to Mexico. I told them that at first, you just wanted me to spy on Cory to find out if he was seeing someone. But then Wade, Charlotte and Gemma showed up, so you decided that you wanted me to spy on all of them to find out what they were up to."

I was satisfied with that explanation, but there was still one more thing I needed to bring up before I concluded my message...

"Bellany, I know you're mad at me, but please don't take your anger out on Tasha. She doesn't deserve this. Please bring her back to Cory's house. Please, I'm begging you! She's innocent in all of this. You know as well as I do that she doesn't understand the complexities of what's going on. Please remember that none of this is her fault."

After I ended the call, I laid on the couch, staring up at the ceiling. I hoped Bellany would listen to my message and give me a second chance.

Several minutes ticked by, and I still hadn't heard back from her. Maybe she was more upset than I thought.

Feeling depressed and defeated, I peeled myself off of the couch and headed to the kitchen. I opened the refrigerator and proceeded to dump all the beverages into the sink.

It made perfect sense that Bellany would spike the bottle of Diet Pepsi. She knew it was my favorite and that I would drink it. But I still feared that maybe she had spiked the other beverages too, just to make certain I got knocked out.

My phone began to ring, and my heart jumped into my throat.

It was Bellany! "Hello!" I gasped.

"Open the front door!" she hissed.

CHAPTER 20

Victoria

I sprinted to the door, desperation propelling me forward. When I yanked it open and saw Bellany standing there, I let out a huge sigh of relief. Now all I needed to do was play it cool, make her believe that I was on her side, and wait for the chance to bring up the bank account. Then I would casually ask her what the password was and all the other details I needed to access it.

"Move!" Bellany said, pushing past me.

I opened the door the rest of the way, realizing I had been so caught up in my concerns about money that I almost forgot about Tasha. I stepped outside, looking all around. But I didn't see Tasha anywhere.

Where was Bellany keeping her? I desperately wanted to demand an answer from her, but I had to restrain myself. No matter how much I yearned for the truth, I had to show Bellany respect and gratitude first. The situation between us was too fragile.

"Bellany, I'm so glad to see you!" I reached out to hug her, even though I knew she hated hugs. But I thought I would give it a shot.

She glared at me, like I knew she would, her eyes flicking over every inch of my body as she stalked around me. Then she slammed the door shut and immediately locked it. Without saying another word, she entered the living room and began closing all the curtains.

I couldn't wait any longer. I had to ask her. "What's going on, Bellany?"

"Someone's following me," she replied without turning around. She was too busy shutting all the curtains and blinds on the windows.

Was she talking about Cory and his friends? If she was, then why would she call them *someone*? No, it had to be another person. "Who?"

"Go check all the doors and make sure they're locked," she said, ignoring my question.

I did as she told me. I locked all the doors, still unsure what was going on. She was acting so paranoid.

As I passed by Tasha's bedroom, I wondered if maybe Bellany was keeping her safe somewhere. Was it possible that Tasha's foster parents were looking for her? From what I had heard, they were bad people. In order to rescue Tasha, Cory had to kidnap her in the middle of the night.

I found Bellany in Cory's bedroom rummaging through the drawers. "Can I help you find something?" I asked.

"Does Cory have a gun?"

"I don't know."

She headed over to the closet and began searching through boxes. When she bent over, the back of her shirt lifted, revealing the grip of a gun. I recognized it immediately. It was a Glock 19, the same gun I had used to kill Lane.

I tried to force the image of Lane's dead body out of my mind, but sometimes it was just too difficult. I always saw him staring up at me with those accusatory eyes and blood all over his face.

Bellany dumped a box of clothes onto the floor. I stood there watching her sift through it, doubting she would find a gun in there.

"Where is it?" she grumbled.

Sensing her frustration, I realized I should be more helpful before she got mad at me. I joined in the search and headed to the closet.

She dumped out drawers and flipped over furniture. Then she walked over to the bed, crouched down and looked under it.

Pillows and blankets were tossed onto the floor.

Cory's bedroom looked like a war zone. He was going to be ticked.

"Bingo!" She pulled out a Beretta 92FS from underneath the mattress. My dad used to have a Beretta too. He had a lot of guns.

Bellany checked to see if it was loaded, and it was. Her eyes flicked up to meet mine. "This is for you."

Okay, things just serious, and I needed some answers. I took the Beretta and followed Bellany to the living room.

She stood in front of the window, peeking through the curtains, and I couldn't hold back my questions any longer.

"What's going on? Who's following you?"

She ran her fingers through her hair, sighing. She looked exhausted and worried. "I have no idea who's following me. But they almost ran me off the road. They shot at me! There are bullet holes in the car. Luckily I got away, but I had to ditch the car and take off on foot. I was literally jumping fences, and running through people's backyards. I almost got bit by a dog-- twice!"

I cupped a hand over my mouth, surprised to hear this. "Oh my gosh! I'm so glad you're okay!"

She headed to the kitchen, opened the refrigerator, and pulled out a pitcher of water. The water was fresh. I had just refilled it. "I'm so thirsty," she said as she poured herself a glass.

"There's some Diet Coke and Diet Pepsi in the pantry," I said, trying to be helpful. "There used to be some cold soda in the fridge, but I had to throw it out."

Bellany shot me a look over the rim of the glass. "Why?"

Her question was absolutely ridiculous. "Because it was spiked with a strong sedative. It knocked me out for hours. But you already know all about that."

She tilted her head slightly and raised one eyebrow. "What?"

Really? I wished she would just admit it and stop playing games. "You drugged me so that you could kidnap Tasha."

Bellany slammed the half-empty glass on the counter, sending a spray of water into the air. "No, I didn't! I didn't drug you, Victoria! And I didn't kidnap Tasha! What in the world is wrong with you?"

My throat tightened as I attempted to swallow down the truth. The situation was far more complex than I thought. Bellany was innocent. "I just--I thought you--I'm sorry," I stammered, collapsing onto one of the stools.

I set the Beretta down on the counter and buried my face in my hands, a wave of panic washing over me.

Someone had stolen the yacht. Someone was after Bellany and had already tried to kill her. Someone had kidnapped Tasha. But who?

Bellany had a long list of enemies, almost too many to choose from. I thought back to what had happened in West Virginia before moving here to Mexico.

Lane wasn't our only enemy. There was a cop who gave us a lot of trouble too. He cuffed Bellany and tossed her into the backseat of his patrol car. He held her captive until she told him where I was. He had figured out that I was a runaway and that there was a reward being offered for my return. He wanted the money.

But Bellany outsmarted him. She threatened to blackmail him if he ever dared to mess with us again. I thought he had been taken care of, but maybe he decided he would take the risk. Maybe he was back and wanted revenge.

I looked up and saw one of Tasha's mermaid drawings on the refrigerator. She had drawn the ocean and the sand too. It was full of seashells, all kinds of colors.

Seeing her picture reminded me of something that had happened on the beach. I had met a strange old lady the same day I met Cory and Tasha. Could she be the person responsible for all of this?

"Get up, Victoria," Bellany said, interrupting my thoughts. "We gotta get out of here. This place isn't safe."

The urgency in her voice jolted me to the core. I ran to get my tennis shoes.

Bellany stood in front of me as I tied the laces. "Give me the keys to the Mustang," she demanded.

I got up and headed to the kitchen. "You don't want to take the Expedition?" I asked, as I began searching through the selection of keys hanging on the wall inside the pantry door.

"I don't want to drive a big, bulky SUV," she said, her voice dripping with irritation. "I need something small and quick."

I dropped the keys into the palm of her outstretched hand and followed her down the hallway, the soles of my tennis shoes squeaking across the tile floor. As we headed toward the garage door, a surge of nervous energy raced through my veins. What if I get shot? What if I die?

Bellany glanced back at me before opening the door. "You got the gun, right?"

"Crap!" I spun back around and raced to the kitchen, realizing I had left it sitting on the counter.

With the gun in my hand, I headed to the garage and pushed the door open with my shoulder. My heart jumped into my throat at the sight in front of me. I instinctively pointed the gun at my target, finger over the trigger.

Bellany was standing there with her hands up, while a menacing figure held a gun firmly against her temple. Terror flooded my senses as two other men pointed their guns at me.

I was outnumbered. Not even the skilled shooting I had learned from my father was enough to take out all three of them.

"Drop it!" the man to my right demanded. I had no idea who these men were. But they were big, and they had guns.

"Okay. I'm putting my gun down," I said, slowly releasing my finger from the trigger. I set it down on the floor and then raised my arms in surrender.

The men loomed over me like ominous shadows. Whoever sent them must have found out about Bellany's fortune. She should just volunteer to give it to them so that we could go free. The money wasn't worth dying over. But before I could say anything, they covered my mouth with duct tape.

Then they wrapped my wrists together.

But what really sent fear coursing through my veins was when they pulled a pillowcase over my head, completely shrouding me in blackness. I was starting to panic, feeling claustrophobic. My breathing sped up, along with my heart rate. I struggled to take in enough oxygen through my nose. I felt like I was going to die of suffocation as I kicked and thrashed, trying to break free.

CHAPTER 21

Cory

The wind howled against the boat and panic welled within me as I watched the yacht drift away on the horizon. I counted out forty dollars into Pablo's outstretched hand, hoping he would understand that I needed the boat to go faster.

He watched with a curious expression as I gestured for him to pick up the speed. "Must go faster," I said, gesturing to Bellany's yacht.

Pablo nodded, but he didn't speed up the boat. He just stuffed the cash into his pocket.

"We're losing her!" Wade said, through gritted teeth.

I reached into my pocket, grabbing the rest of the money. Fifty dollars was all I had left. I waved it in front of his face. "I will give you this if you go faster!"

My mind flashed back to the last time I tipped someone to speed up. It was in Las Vegas and it was for the exact same reason: to catch Bellany. Except this time there were no roads, no security gates blocking our path, no red lights, just the wide open sea.

"Hold on!" Gemma gasped, wide-eyed. "I just remembered how to say please go faster in Spanish!" She stumbled over to Pablo and pointed at the yacht. "Rápido, por favor!"

"You know how to speak Spanish?" Charlotte gasped. "I thought you took French in high school."

"I learned a little on TikTok," Gemma replied, pushing her windblown hair out of her face.

The boat's motor revved, finally picking up speed.

After another hour, we still hadn't caught up to Bellany. The hot sun was beating down on us, and I was starting to lose hope.

Gemma came and sat down next to me. She sat so close that her leg was touching mine. I had gotten used to her flirting, but this was not the time to do this.

"I--uh, I have a confession... I--I've never been on a boat before." Gemma's voice shuddered. She sounded nervous. "What if we break down? We're in the middle of nowhere. Who's gonna come and save us?"

"The boat has a radio," I said, gesturing to it. "Pablo will call for help if he needs to."

"What if it doesn't work?" Gemma bit her bottom lip. I could feel her trembling beside me.

Charlotte nestled up to Wade. Her face looked kind of pale. I wondered if she was getting seasick.

"How much longer is this going to take?" Gemma raised a hand to shade her eyes from the sun. "It doesn't seem like we're catching up. It seems like we're falling further behind. Look at how small the yacht's getting. Maybe we should go back."

"You want to quit, after all we've been through?" Wade asked, his voice tense.

I wasn't ready to give up yet. There was still daylight. We had plenty of time. "Just be patient, Gemma. We'll catch up."

I kept my eyes peeled, searching for signs of a break in our luck as we crossed the choppy sea. By some miracle, it finally happened. The yacht came to a stop and cast its anchor, allowing us to catch up!

Pablo turned the boat and cut the engine. He said something in Spanish that I couldn't understand. I assumed he was telling us that he couldn't get any closer. We were going to have to jump overboard and swim.

Wade leaned over the side of the boat. "It's about the distance of a football field. We could easily swim it."

"The distance of a football field?" Gemma shook her head fiercely, sending her hair into a frenzy. "Nope. Not gonna do it.

That's way too far to swim."

"No, it's not!" Wade insisted.

I knew what was going on with Gemma. She wasn't upset about the distance--that wasn't the problem. It was her fear of sharks.

"Look," Charlotte said, pointing at a small ladder that hung from the stern of the yacht. "We can climb aboard there."

This was the only way. We had to swim.

Gemma stepped back from the edge of the boat, a look of terror on her face. "Can't Pablo get us any closer?"

Wade gritted his teeth like he was trying to restrain himself from saying what was really on his mind. "Listen, Gemma. Pablo can't get us any closer, not without possibly damaging his boat. This is it. This is how close we're gonna get. You have to swim."

I slipped the shoes off my feet, then reached inside my pocket and pulled out my phone. It was useless to me out here. There hadn't been a cell signal for hours, and there was no way my phone would keep working after being submerged in the ocean. I tossed it overboard.

"Cory, what are you doing?" Gemma gasped. "That's your phone!"

She knew our phones would be destroyed in water. She wasn't thinking rationally.

"Come on," I urged. "Get ready. We need to jump overboard. Take your shoes off. It'll be easier to swim without them."

She looked down at her sandals. "These are Micheal Kors. Do you know how expensive these are? I'm not just leaving them here. And I'm not ruining my phone either. I need it!"

"Gemma," Charlotte spoke in a soft, calming voice. "Take your shoes off. You need to get ready to swim."

I didn't know what to do with Gemma. She was refusing to comply. The only other option was to leave her on the boat with Pablo. But even that idea made me feel uneasy.

I placed my hands on Gemma's shoulders, looking into

her eyes, hoping she would see how serious I was. "You have to be brave, Gemma. You have to swim."

"No, I can't--I can't go in there! What if a shark gets me?"

"Don't worry." I squeezed her shoulders gently. "I'll stay right by your side the entire time. I won't let anything happen to you. I promise."

"I'm too afraid to go in there!" she cried, tears running down her face.

If I had only known how serious her phobia of sharks was, I never would have let her come. I wrapped her in my arms to comfort her and also to say goodbye.

"I'm so sorry that you're scared," I said. "I wish I could take the fear away from you, but only you can do that." I let go and looked down into her glossy eyes. "Stay here and ride back with Pablo."

"Okay. I--I'll just stay here," she agreed, grabbing hold of the railing.

I hated leaving Gemma behind and wished there was another alternative. Charlotte didn't seem interested in staying with her. She was determined to catch Bellany.

Wade helped Charlotte climb over the side of the boat, and they both jumped, plunging into the deep blue sea.

I was about to jump next, but then Gemma grabbed my arm. "Stay with me, Cory. Please! Let's go back together."

She should have begged for her best friend, Charlotte, to stay with her. What made her think that I would? "We've come this far, Gemma. We're almost there. I'm not going back now."

"Please stay with me!" she cried out, almost in hysterics.

I cast a glance at Charlotte and Wade. They had already started swimming. "Gemma, you've got to let go of me."

"No, Cory! Don't leave me!" Her fingernails dug into my arm.

This was getting ridiculous. I didn't want to have to physically pry her fingers off of my arm. "You can come with me or stay here by yourself. It's your choice."

"No. I can't go with you!" she cried.

"Okay, you've made your decision, and I've made mine," I said, calmly. I pointed over my shoulder. "I gotta go."

"Cory! Stay with me!"

Gemma's fingernails dug deeper into my arm. That was it for me--I'd had enough. I grabbed hold of her and picked her up as she kicked and screamed. I tossed her overboard, then dove in after her.

Gemma coughed and spit water out of her mouth, but she was okay. She was fine. All she had to do now was swim.

"Adios!" Pablo called as he started up his boat again.

I treaded water, waiting for Gemma to start swimming. I wanted to make sure she was okay.

"Help me, Cory! Help me!" she cried.

I couldn't believe it. She wasn't swimming toward the yacht. She remained in place, bobbing up and down on the choppy sea, freaking out!

"Cory!" she wailed.

I knew better than to go near her while she was in such a frantic state. She'd probably try to drown me.

A loud rattling sound filled the air, and a sense of dread ripped through me like lightning. I snapped my head around, my gaze landing on the bow of the yacht, only to confirm what I already knew. The anchor was being hoisted up!

Did Bellany know we were here? Has she spotted us? My eyes darted around, scanning the yacht. I caught sight of a figure on the top deck. Long hair blew in the wind. I strained to see her face, but she was too far away. Was it her? It had to be.

Anger stabbed my chest like a hot dagger. How could Bellany leave us stranded in the middle of the ocean? Was this her idea of revenge?

Didn't she realize that I had saved her life when we left Las Vegas? If it wasn't for me, she would have died from a gunshot wound to the head. I was the one who protected her and made sure she was left behind, unharmed. I made sure she had the means to escape. I left her with the keys to the minivan.

I continued to tread water, scanning my surroundings,

only to confirm my worst fears. There was no land in sight, and no other boats to rescue us. Our lives depended on making it to the yacht. I hoped we would get there before the engines engaged.

My eyes shifted to Wade and Charlotte. They were still swimming, about halfway there.

The clattering of the anchor's chain had stopped, and I knew time was running out.

My heart was thudding violently against the walls of my chest. "Come on!" I yelled at Gemma, my voice booming. "Let's go!"

"I can't!" she gasped, starting to slip underwater.

I couldn't leave her. We were either getting out of here together, or we were staying until our last breath.

My gaze fixed on a certain spot in the ocean behind Gemma, and I inhaled sharply. "Shark!" I shouted as loud as I could. "There's a shark behind you!"

CHAPTER 22

Cory

Gemma swam with a fury--desperate strokes against the ocean's surging current, water splashing everywhere. It was as if a fire had been lit under her.

I hoped she would keep up the pace. We had to catch the yacht while we still had the chance.

The muscles in my arms and legs ached as I tore through the cold, choppy water. My lungs burned from holding my breath.

I occasionally stopped to glance back and make sure Gemma was still there. She was lagging behind, the distance between us growing, but she hadn't stopped. She was swimming as fast as she could, desperate to outswim the shark.

But Gemma wasn't in danger of being attacked. I had lied. There was no shark behind her, at least none that I could see.

My arms and legs moved faster as I swam toward the yacht, and when I finally arrived, a hand grabbed hold of my wrist. I looked up and saw Wade staring down at me. As soon as I climbed aboard, I spun around, searching for Gemma.

Wade and Charlotte shouted, telling her to keep swimming. I figured she couldn't be that far behind me.

The yacht's engine rumbled to life, and my heart thundered in terror. Sweeping my gaze across the dark churning waters, I caught sight of Gemma. She wasn't moving fast enough.

I scanned my surroundings, searching for a lifesaver to throw overboard but couldn't find one. "Is there a rope somewhere? A pole? Anything?"

"I don't know!" Charlotte began searching the deck.

"Come on, Gemma!" Wade called on bended knee, hand stretched out, waiting for the chance to grab her.

Someone needed to stop the engines! My eyes shot up to the top deck, desperate for a sign of Bellany. But she was no longer there. I figured she couldn't have gone far. She had to be here somewhere.

My gaze continued to bounce around, searching for even a trace of her. But it was as if the yacht was completely abandoned--not even a hint of life to be seen.

This didn't make any sense. Where were all the people? There was no way Bellany could run this yacht on her own. A vessel of this size had to have a crew.

Hoping that maybe the crew was somewhere nearby, I thought of something that should grab their attention immediately. "Man overboard!" I shouted. "Stop the boat! Man overboard!"

Charlotte joined me, and we both continued to shout, "Man overboard!"

But nobody came, and the engines were still running.

Charlotte grabbed my arm, a look of panic on her face. "What are we going to do?"

I made a vow to myself that I was not going to leave Gemma behind. If she wasn't going to make it, then I wasn't going to either.

"She's almost here!" Wade's voice boomed.

My heart raced as I narrowed my eyes, searching the surface of the ocean for Gemma. He was right--she wasn't that far away.

"I found a rope!" Charlotte shouted, running toward us.

I knew a rope would be impossible for Gemma to find out there in the churning sea, unless something was tied to the end of it. I tied the rope around my waist.

Wade grabbed onto the other end. "Go for it, man--I got you!" He braced himself against the side of the yacht.

Charlotte grabbed onto the rope too, and I dove into the turbulent ocean, hoping that by some miracle the rope would be long enough for me to reach Gemma.

My arms and legs cut through the ocean water. I kicked and pulled as fast as I could. Craning my neck, I raised my head above the water, quickly sucking in air, then down I went again.

I hoped Wade and Charlotte would be able to pull both me and Gemma back to the yacht. But first I had to reach her.

Craning my neck again, my eyes swept the water. But the moment was too brief. I couldn't find her. I knew that if I didn't grab hold of Gemma soon, I would have to untie the rope.

My chest tightened at the thought of Gemma and I being lost at sea. But I pushed that fear aside and kept going.

I took another breath, then saw splashing. It was Gemma! Hope continued to swell inside me. I swam harder until I felt something bump against my hand, and my heart leapt in my chest.

"Cory!" Gemma cried.

I grabbed hold of her, fingers squeezing with a vice-like grip. I continued to cling to her as Wade and Charlotte pulled us back to the yacht. The rope was digging into my skin, and I gritted my teeth in pain, clinging to Gemma, until we were finally safely aboard the yacht.

Gemma laid on the deck, trembling and gasping for air. Her lips were blue, her wet hair matted to her head. I noticed her expensive sandals were missing from her feet. Either she had kicked them off or they fell off.

Charlotte sat next to her, holding her tight. "You're safe now. Everything's going to be fine."

I paced the deck, my entire body still pulsing with adrenaline. I couldn't believe we all made it. We were safe.

Wade clapped my shoulder. "Dude, I didn't think you'd be able to reach her!"

"I couldn't have done it without your help." I looked down at my hands. They were shaking.

"It's a good thing the engines weren't going any faster.

'Cause if they were, she'd have been lost at sea, and we'd never see her again."

I turned my gaze to the endless blue ocean. What I didn't want to admit was that if I hadn't rescued Gemma, then I would've joined her.

Charlotte noticed that Wade and I were about to begin searching the yacht and called for us to stop. "Wait until Gemma gets her strength back, so we can stay together."

Charlotte was exhausted and had rope burns on her hands. She needed extra time to recuperate too. Wade's hands weren't as bad as hers. I had a rope burn around my stomach, but my shirt covered it up.

Wade and I sat on some cushioned lounge chairs nearby, but I wasn't able to relax. I kept my eyes peeled for Bellany, wondering when she would show her face. She had to know we were on the yacht. It wasn't like she could hide from us forever or run away. It was time for her to come out and face us.

When Gemma finally regained her strength, she and Charlotte came to join us.

I moved my feet out of the way, allowing room for Gemma to get by. But instead of passing, Gemma stood directly in front of me, her narrowed eyes locked onto mine.

As I sat there observing the high level of rage and anger on her face, my instincts kicked in. I almost dodged what was coming, but then I decided not to. Gemma had every right to be angry with me. When her open hand made contact with the side of my face, the slap echoed off the exterior walls of the yacht.

"Ouch!" Wade covered his mouth with his fist, eyes wide.

"Gemma!" Charlotte gasped. "What is wrong with you? Why did you do that?"

Gemma pointed an accusatory finger at me, eyes wild with rage. "Cory threw me overboard, and then he told me that there was a shark!" Her head swiveled, eyes landing on mine. "You scared me half to death! I almost died of a heart attack! I almost drowned!"

Wade erupted in laughter, cutting through the tension.

"You told her there was a shark?"

Charlotte bit her lip, and I saw a hint of a smile on her face.

"It's not funny!" Gemma grabbed the nearest cushion and threw it at Wade.

But he caught it and kept laughing. When he finally regained his composure, he reached out and gave me a fist bump. "A shark!" He cracked a smile again. "That was genius!"

"Genius!" Gemma shrieked. "Are you crazy? What Cory did wasn't genius. It was irresponsible and totally uncalled for!"

"You're wrong, Gemma," Charlotte said, the amusement now gone from her face.

"Excuse me?" Gemma blinked in surprise.

"You gave Cory no other choice," Charlotte explained. "He did what he had to do in order to get you safely aboard this yacht. You should be thanking him."

Gemma's mouth fell open. "No, I shouldn't! What Cory did was cruel, and if you can't see that, then maybe you're cruel too."

Wade held his hands up. "All right, all right. Just hold on a minute... Let's think about this here." His eyes swung to me, then back to Gemma again. "In case you haven't realized it yet, this yacht is moving. And it's moving fast. If it weren't for Cory's quick thinking, you wouldn't even be here right now. You would've been left behind, stranded in the middle of the ocean by yourself." He leaned forward, eyebrows raised. "And then you really would've been shark meat."

Gemma gritted her teeth, hands balled into fists.

I had to stop this before it escalated any further. "Gemma." I paused, waiting until she made eye contact with me. "I want to apologize. I'm sorry that I scared you. I'm sorry that I lied." I rubbed the side of my face. "I deserved to be slapped--I had it coming."

Wade shot me a look, as if questioning my sanity. "Are you serious?"

"I don't want to argue anymore," I said, rising from my

chair. "I just want to find Bellany. She's the reason we're here."

Wade nodded in agreement. "Yeah, it's time to confront the psycho. Where's she at?"

"That's a good question." Charlotte turned in every direction, looking for Bellany. "Why hasn't she come out here yet? Why is she hiding?"

Wade arched an eyebrow. "Maybe she wants us to come find her. Maybe she wants to play a little game of hide and seek."

"So immature," Gemma grumbled.

I wasn't sure who she was referring to: Bellany or the rest of us. And honestly, I didn't care.

"Do you think Bellany's driving this thing?" Charlotte asked as we made our way toward the front of the yacht.

"I doubt it. She probably hired someone," I said, wondering how many other people there were on this thing. Where did they all go?

We found a door, which we assumed led to the helm station. But it was locked, and we couldn't break it down. Whoever was in there, steering and navigating this yacht, had to have heard us. And they were deliberately choosing to ignore us.

While the girls continued to pound on the door, trying to get someone to open it, Wade and I searched for another way in.

The windows of the helm station were tinted black, impossible to see through.

"She can't hide in there forever." Wade picked up a chair and hurled it at the window. It was a direct hit, but the glass didn't break. It didn't leave a scratch.

Wade and I continued to throw chairs and tables at the windows, anything we could get our hands on, in an attempt to smash the glass. Nothing worked. The glass was impenetrable.

When we returned to the girls, we found Gemma crying.

"What happened?" I asked.

Gemma began pacing, arms flailing. "I lost my phone. It must've fallen out of my pocket in the ocean."

"Even if you did still have your phone, it wouldn't work. It's not waterproof," I reminded her.

"I know!" she cried, still pacing. "I just want it. I want my phone! I need it!"

"You don't need your phone," Charlotte sighed.

"What about my sandals? What am I going to do without them?"

I leaned in close to Charlotte and kept my voice low. "Why is she acting like this?"

"I don't know. I tried to get her to stop, but she won't listen to me."

"She's lost it," Wade muttered, shaking his head. "I always knew she was emotionally unstable."

Gemma grabbed fistfulls of her own hair like she was trying to pull it out. "We're never getting off this yacht! We're gonna die out here!"

"Hey," I said, reaching for her. "We're not gonna die. We're gonna be just fine--I promise." Honestly, I wasn't sure if we would survive this either. But I wasn't going to admit it.

"No, we're not!" she cried, burying her face into my chest.

The yacht was amazingly big and beautiful. It obviously cost a fortune. But there was something off about it; something I couldn't quite put my finger on.

The uneasy feeling inside me continued to grow, and not just because we hadn't been able to find Bellany. I felt like something bigger was going on here, but I didn't know what it was.

Even in the broad daylight, with the sun shining brightly in the sky, there was a sense of darkness all around. The last thing I wanted to do was stay here tonight. I didn't want to find out where this evil feeling was coming from.

CHAPTER 23

Cory

Gemma was still having some kind of a nervous breakdown. She started pacing again. Her bare feet slapped against the hard wood deck as she continued to list every possible negative scenario she could come up with, which always resulted in our death.

We had been trying to talk her out of this downward spiral but so far we hadn't been successful.

"Why don't you smack her in the face," Wade said to me. He was totally frustrated, and I was too. "She did it to you. Go ahead and do it back."

"What?" Charlotte's jaw dropped open as a horrified gasp escaped her lips. "I can't believe you would even suggest such a thing. On what planet do you think it's okay for a man to hit a woman?"

"I don't mean smack her to hurt her," Wade explained, defensively. "I mean smack her to give her system a shock. She needs to snap out of this. Something has to jolt her to make her reset."

"No!" Charlotte shouted. "Nobody is smacking her."

"What if this yacht is on autopilot?" Gemma's voice shuddered. She looked like she had seen a ghost. "What if the autopilot malfunctions, and we slam into some rocks somewhere and start sinking?"

I couldn't take it anymore. I had to stop her. "Come on," I said, grabbing hold of her wrist. "We need to search the yacht. Bellany's here somewhere. We're gonna find her."

"No she isn't," Gemma replied, refusing to walk with me. "We're alone. Nobody else is here. It's just us."

"You can't possibly know that, Gemma," Wade said, his tone thick with irritation.

Charlotte nodded. "Yeah, Gemma. We haven't searched this place yet. We don't know who else is here."

An image of the girl I saw standing on the top deck entered my mind. "I know we're not alone. I saw Bellany earlier."

"You saw her?" Charlotte gasped, eyes wide. "When?"

I wasn't completely sure if it was Bellany, but who else could it be? This was her yacht. "When I was in the water swimming. She was watching us from up there." I pointed to the top deck.

Gemma was the first one to start climbing the stairs. The rest of us followed. Then we all split up, scouring every inch of the top deck. I discovered a helipad and wondered if Bellany had plans on using it. Would she try to escape? Would she leave us stranded here?

None of us ended up finding Bellany on the top deck, but we weren't done searching. We quickly came up with a list of things to look for, in addition to Bellany. Food and water was a top priority.

We agreed that finding a radio or some kind of communication device was another important thing to search for. We hoped we would discover life vests and possibly smaller boats or jet skis.

And lastly, we were going to search for anything that could be used as a weapon to defend ourselves.

Wade and Charlotte paired off, and I was stuck with Gemma. But thankfully exploring this place had distracted her from wallowing in the depths of despair.

She wrapped her arms around her stomach. "Let's find the kitchen. I'm hungry, and I'm so thirsty."

She wasn't the only one. I was dying of thirst, desperate for some water.

None of the faucets, toilets or showers worked. The hot

tub was empty. There was no ice in any of the freezers. The refrigerators were empty. The cupboards were bare. There was nothing on this entire yacht to eat, not even a random can of soup, or a jar of peanut butter to be found.

The longer our search stretched on, with nothing to show for it, the more I feared the worst--we were going to die out here! I didn't want to think about this, but I had to face reality.

Surviving without food for a while wasn't the biggest problem we were facing. It was the lack of drinking water. A human being could only last three days without water.

Gemma was becoming increasingly upset, complaining about being thirsty and hungry. I encouraged her to take a break and sit down and rest. "It's hot outside. Let's cool down in one of the rooms." Thankfully the air conditioner worked.

"I hate this place!" she groaned as she entered one of the sitting rooms.

I picked up the TV remote, hoping we could watch something to distract ourselves for at least a few minutes. The TV turned on, but that was all it did. I messed with the remote, trying to get something to appear on the screen. Then I searched for a computer, or a modem, or something that might be connected to the TV. But there was nothing. The cabinets and closets were empty.

"Of course the TV doesn't work," Gemma huffed, on the verge of tears. "Why would it? Why would anything on this yacht be the slightest bit enjoyable? This place is nothing but a floating house of horror."

I placed an arm around her shoulder to comfort her. I wanted to say something encouraging and optimistic, but I couldn't find the words. I was struggling too. The guilt had hit me hard. I was responsible for the mess we were in. This was all my fault.

I wished I had never contacted Gemma, or Wade, or Charlotte. I wished I had left them out of this and dealt with Bellany on my own. It was because of me that their lives were in danger. "I'm so sorry. This is all my fault."

Gemma looked into my eyes. "No, Cory. It's not your fault. It's Bellany's fault. She's pure evil. She's the worst human being on the planet…"

Bellany was on this yacht somewhere. She was hiding, but why? What was her end goal? Did she really want us to suffer and die? Was she ever going to show her face?

"It's a good thing you didn't bring Tasha," Gemma said, her words tearing through my thoughts.

"I know." I sighed, nodding in agreement. I was still deeply worried about her though. What if I never make it back home? What would happen to her? Would Victoria be able to take care of her?

"Cory, I don't want to die," Gemma said, resting her head on my shoulder.

"You're not going to die," I said, trying to convince myself as much as her that this was true. But we were sailing further and further away from home. And there was no sign of land anywhere.

CHAPTER 24

Cory

Charlotte and Wade had just returned from searching the yacht and were unable to locate any of the items we needed. They had also discovered more locked doors.

Wade's jaw clenched, eyebrows cinched together. "We banged on the doors and yelled. We tried to break them down, but nothing worked."

The four of us sat around the table on the top deck, the wind whipping through our hair. We all had the same desperate look in our eyes, probably wondering how much longer we could survive. We were faced with a future full of uncertainty, and we were afraid.

The blazing sun was about to set. I gazed at the sky, wondering how many more sunsets I would see before I died. Three? Maybe four?

"It feels like we're totally alone." Charlotte swept her long caramel locks behind one ear, trying to prevent the wind from whipping it back into her face. "The rooms that we were able to access hardly had anything in them." She drew her arms tightly around her stomach. "They were totally stripped down. There were no blankets or pillows, just mattresses on bed frames. There were no towels in the bathrooms. No clothes in the closets." She made a cringey face. "We couldn't find any toilet paper, either. There's no soap, no shampoo, no toothpaste."

"This yacht hasn't been stocked and prepared to go to sea," Wade said, a distant look in his eyes.

Gemma let out a sigh, tears spilling down her face. "This

is a total nightmare."

"I know things seem desperate right now," I said, trying to find something to hope for. "But who knows, we might be returning to land soon."

Charlotte, Wade, and Gemma cast their eyes at the expansive ocean stretched out before us. There were no other vessels in sight and no signs of land anywhere, not even a bird in the sky.

The sun had started to dip below the horizon, painting the sky in a deep blood-red. The air felt like an oven, drying out my mouth and throat. We were surrounded by so much water, yet we couldn't drink it.

The girls got up and headed to the bathroom, leaving Wade and I alone.

"Dude," Wade said. "I'm starting to wonder if Victoria played us."

The thought of Victoria betraying me made my stomach churn.

"Think about it," Wade said, tapping his finger on the table. "Victoria told us that Bellany was on this yacht and in the process of escaping. But in reality, Bellany wasn't escaping. She had set a trap. And Victoria led us straight to it."

The sickening feeling in my stomach continued to worsen. "But Victoria acted like she really wanted to come with us."

"That's right. She did, because it was just an act," Wade insisted. "She wanted us to believe her. And to trust her."

"If Victoria was acting, then she deserves an award. She definitely fooled me."

Wade arched an eyebrow. "She learned from an expert."

My stomach continued to twist and turn at the thought of Bellany coaching Victoria on what to do and say. "We gotta get out of here." I pushed my chair back, rising to my feet. I had to escape from this floating prison. Tasha's life depended on it. "Show me where those locked doors are."

We waited for the girls to return, then headed

downstairs.

"Here's one of them," Wade said, leading me to a door at the end of a hall.

I turned the doorknob, expecting it not to move, but there was no resistance at all. I pushed it open with ease.

"That door was locked," Wade insisted, staring at it in disbelief. "Someone must have opened it."

When I entered the room, I felt like I had just stepped into one of my nightmares.

"What is going on here?" Charlotte gasped, placing a hand over her mouth.

Gemma pushed past me, heading toward a cluster of safes lined up against the back wall.

I counted ten safes in total, of varying sizes. The smallest was the size of a shoe box. The largest was about four feet tall. Every single safe was bolted to the floor, except for the smallest one. We tried to open them. But they were all locked.

My heart sped up, sweat dripping down my face and neck. None of the locks on the safes were digital. They were the same kind of locks from my recurring nightmares; the same kind of locks I could never unlock--no matter how many times I tried.

In my nightmares, Tasha was always in danger and trapped on the other side of a door. The only thing stopping me from saving her was the lock!

Wade knelt down beside one of the safes and began spinning the number dial. "What do you suppose is inside here? Some kind of treasure? Maybe some gold bars? Cash?"

Gemma licked her lips. "I'm hoping for a large glass of ice cold water."

"Cory." Charlotte nudged my shoulder. "Remember that game we played with Victoria where we shared our three biggest fears. Aren't combination locks one of your biggest fears?"

Wade and Gemma both slowly pivoted in my direction, their eyes locked onto me, waiting for my response.

"Yeah," I said, wiping the sweat off my forehead. "These are the same locks from my nightmares."

Wade tipped his chin up and gave a firm nod. "Victoria must have told Bellany about our fears, and now she's using it against us."

There was no doubt in my mind anymore about how much Bellany hated me. She wanted me to suffer and then die.

Gemma's gaze darted from one person to the next. She had a wild look in her eyes again. "Bellany knew about my fear of sharks. She set this whole thing up so that I'd have to swim with sharks!"

Wade stroked his chin, a pained look on his face. "Bellany also knew that Tasha was afraid of boats. She knew that someone would have to stay behind with her. Someone she could trust. Victoria."

How could I have left Tasha behind with Victoria? What kind of brother am I? My heart pounded against my ribcage as I thought about all the bad things that could happen to her.

Charlotte stepped in front of me, studying my face. "You don't look so good, Cory. You look pale."

I leaned against the wall and slowly slid down to the floor. "I hope Tasha's okay," I said, taking a deep breath as a sick feeling continued to grow inside me. I buried my face in my hands, fighting off a wave of nausea. It wasn't seasickness making me feel this way. It was fear.

"If Victoria harms your sister in any way, I'll make her pay. I promise you that." Wade's voice shook as he spoke, the anger tangible in his words.

My mind was becoming consumed with terror. Was Tasha suffering? Was she scared? What was happening to her?

"Don't worry, Cory," Charlotte said. "I'm sure she's fine."

"Yes, of course she is," Gemma agreed quickly. "She's probably just chilling at the house, eating snacks and watching movies."

The room became silent for several minutes while I sat there, trying to overcome the nausea and thoughts of despair.

When I finally felt good enough to lift my head, I discovered why everyone was being so quiet. All three of them were busily spinning number dials, trying to crack open the safes. I had zero confidence they'd be successful. The odds were stacked against them so high, it was like trying to run on water. Impossible.

I surveyed the room, taking note of the high ceiling. It was strangely coated in black paint. Weren't ceilings usually painted white? Not only was the ceiling painted black, but so were the walls and the adjoining bathroom. There wasn't a single window to break up the darkness. The only sources of light came from the open door and the intense spotlights directed at the paintings of mermaids that hung on each wall.

My insides roiled with recognition as I studied the paintings. Every brushstroke called out to me, and I knew why they looked so familiar. They resembled Tasha's drawings. Except these paintings were much more elaborate and detailed. They had been professionally done.

Gemma sighed in frustration as she tugged on the door of one of the safes. It was still locked. Her number combination hadn't worked.

Charlotte tried to open the safe she had been working on. But again, no luck. She stepped away and turned toward the door. "I wonder if those other rooms are unlocked now too. Maybe we should go check."

Wade spun the number dial one last time then tugged on the safe. Another fail. He turned around, the frustration visible on his face. "Yeah," he said, raking his fingers through his hair. "We're not getting anywhere with these safes."

Gemma sat down next to me, hooking her arm through mine. "You guys go ahead without us. I'll stay with Cory until he feels better."

After Wade and Charlotte left, Gemma began petting my arm like I was a cat or something. "If you need to throw up, there's a bathroom right there. It's just a few feet away."

The last thing I wanted to do was vomit. That would only make me more dehydrated. "I'll be fine," I said, taking a deep breath. I unhooked my arm from Gemma's and laid down, pressing the side of my face against the cold wood floor and closing my eyes.

Gemma rubbed my back while she sang a medley of Disney songs. She actually had a nice voice and was pleasant to listen to. "Just don't sing any *Little Mermaid* songs, okay?"

"No problem," she agreed.

I was grateful for the distraction. It helped take my mind off of worrying about Tasha.

Gemma finished singing another song, then stopped to clear her throat. The door slammed shut, the bang reverberating in my ears, and my eyes snapped open. I sat up with a jolt. Gemma raced to the door, only to discover it was firmly locked.

"Who shut the door and locked it?" Gemma asked, her eyes darting around wildly as if there was someone else in this room.

I pushed myself up off the floor to see if I could open the door, wondering if it was just stuck. But it wouldn't budge. It was definitely locked.

I turned to the row of safes and a chill ran down my spine. Being trapped inside this room made me feel like I was trapped inside one of my nightmares.

Gemma began screaming and yelling for Wade and Charlotte to come rescue us.

I tried to break down the door. I kicked it and slammed my body into it repeatedly, until I was too sore to continue.

A single sheet of white paper rocketed out from beneath it and went sliding across the floor. Gemma stood there, transfixed by its eerie sight.

I picked it up, and when I realized it was a handwritten note, a feeling of dread washed over me. I read it out loud: "Ready to play a game? Bottles of water await in one of the safes. All you have to do is find the right number combination to access it. Count the pearls in each mermaid's necklace. Count the seashells scattered across the shores. Count the number of stars hanging in the skies. Then your thirst will be no more."

Gemma raced over to the nearest painting, too thirsty to

waste time complaining about the task at hand. "I'll count all the pearls and the stars. You count the seashells."

My throat was parched and screamed for hydration. I frantically tried to locate and count each little seashell, which wasn't easy. They were almost impossible to spot amongst the sea of sand and stones.

We managed to come up with what we hoped was the correct number combination. Now all we had to do was try it out on each safe, until one finally unlocked.

As I began to work the first lock, a familiar anxious feeling came over me. I knew it all too well from my nightmares. Sweat dripped down my face as my heart pounded in anticipation.

The first safe was a bust. The second safe was too. My hands were shaking and my thoughts were on Tasha again. I prayed she would be okay and that I would see her again soon.

"I got it!" Gemma squealed, ripping me from my concentration.

I took a deep breath, trying to relax as she reached inside the safe and retrieved two bottles of water. She handed me one. I had never realized just how small an eight ounce bottle of water was until that moment.

"There's a note," she said, reaching inside the safe again. She held up the small piece of paper, squinting at the words. "Don't drink it!" she shouted.

I quickly set the bottle of water down on top of the safe. "What does it say?"

"It might be poisoned!"

"Poisoned?" I repeated, hoping Gemma was just joking.

Then she began to read the note: "One of these bottles of water holds the promise of sweet relief, while the other contains a deadly poison that will leave you gasping for air, your stomach roiling in pain. With each sip, death will creep closer. Choose wisely. Your life depends on it."

I took the note from her and reread it.

"This isn't fair. I'm so thirsty, Cory." Tears sprang to

Gemma's eyes and her bottom lip began trembling.

"I know. I'm thirsty too. But we can't drink this. We can't take the risk."

"We counted all those stupid things in those stupid paintings for nothing!" She snatched the note from my hand and began tearing it into tiny pieces that fluttered to the floor, scattering in every direction.

I picked up the bottles of water, studying them, trying to determine which one was poisoned. Hopefully neither of us would become desperate enough to drink one of these. But I wanted to be prepared, just in case.

Gemma collapsed to the floor and screamed as if she was in agony. "I can't do this anymore!"

"Gemma, we're not gonna be stuck down here forever. We will get out." I was trying to be optimistic, hoping she would shut up.

My eyes shifted to the locked door. Why hadn't Wade and Charlotte come back yet? Where were they?

CHAPTER 25

Cory

Since Gemma and I were confined in this room together, with nothing else to do, I began working on the locks. I sometimes chose random number combinations, basically just whatever popped into my head. Other times, I chose important dates like birthdays, holidays, basically anything of significance I could think of.

My heart raced each time I pulled on the door of a safe to see if it had unlocked. But I was always met with disappointment. The doors were shut tight.

My back was starting to ache from being hunched over and my fingers were cramping from spinning the number dial, but I didn't stop. I couldn't.

Strangely, what had once been my biggest fear was now my only source of hope. There had to be some drinkable water in one of these safes, or maybe some food, or possibly something that would help us escape. I had to make it out of here alive and get back to Tasha.

Gemma had long since given up banging on the door and trying to break it down. She called for Wade and Charlotte, but they never came. She also tried to help me open up the safes but was unsuccessful.

Her frustration and anger continued to escalate. I had to listen to her constant complaining, which was starting to feel like torture. Why couldn't she go back to singing Disney songs?

"What's the use in opening another safe?" she asked, pacing the room. "It's just gonna be full of stuff we can't eat and drink. Bellany just wants to torment us. She wants to play games and make us suffer."

"There isn't anything else for me to do. I might as well try."

"There is something else you can do."

I gestured to the door. "I already tried to break it down. You saw how hard I tried. It won't budge."

Gemma shook her head. "I'm not talking about the door."

"Okay, then what?" I scanned the room, unsure what she was referring to. There was no way out. There were no windows. The air vents were too small to climb through. We were trapped.

"You could come and sit by me." She patted the floor next to her.

"I'm right here. I'm in the same room as you," I replied, shooting her a questioning look. "Why do I need to sit over there?"

Her bottom lip was jutting out. She looked like she was about to cry. Again. And honestly, I didn't think I could handle it. Hearing her cry was worse than listening to her complain.

I abandoned the safe I had been working on and sat next to her. The floor was uncomfortable, but my back felt better leaning against the wall. I opened and closed my fists a few times, stretching my aching fingers.

Gemma laced her arm around mine and rested her head on my shoulder. "Cory, I'm scared."

"I am too," I admitted. "I don't know how much longer we're going to be stuck here. But I'm not gonna give up hope."

She nuzzled in a little closer, melting against me.

My gaze shifted to the two bottles of water sitting on the floor, both unopened. I licked my lips, my mouth feeling incredibly dry. At what point would I be desperate enough to risk my life and drink one of them?

I had already examined both of the bottles closely. They were exactly alike, except one of them had a black dot on the label, about the size of a ladybug. But what did the black dot mean? Did it mean that it was safe to drink or that it was poisoned?

I was starting to feel drowsy, my eyelids heavy. Was it the middle of night or maybe early morning. There was no way to know how many hours we had been stuck here.

"Are you tired?" I asked Gemma, hoping she'd say yes. I wouldn't be able to sleep if she kept talking.

"I'm exhausted," she sighed. "I wish there was a couch or a bed to sleep on. This floor is so uncomfortable."

"Yeah it is… You can try to fall asleep on me if you want. Let me just adjust how I'm sitting." She lifted her head as I scooted back closer to the wall. Her arm was still laced through mine.

"How long has it been since you kissed a girl?"

Seriously? Why was she asking me this? My head dropped back against the wall. "I thought you said you were tired."

"It was Bellany, wasn't it? She was the last girl you kissed."

I wished I had never admitted that I kissed Bellany. "Yes, it was her." But thanks to my current situation, I have seen the error of my ways. I knew better now.

I no longer loved Bellany, nor did I feel bad about what I had done to her. I stole her money, but in no way did that come close to comparing to what she was putting me through now.

Holding us hostage without food and water, and ripping me apart from Tasha was much worse. I felt a deep sense of betrayal, unlike anything I had ever experienced in my life before.

"The last guy I kissed was Bellany's brother," Gemma sighed. "I spent years obsessing over Bridger. I thought he was everything. He was so perfect. After Bellany disappeared, we were together all the time. I helped him through his grief over losing her. We had been through so much together. I thought we were soulmates. Bridger made me feel like I was the only person on the earth that mattered to him. So you can imagine how shocked I was when he sent me a text, ending our relationship."

I had already heard all about Gemma and Bridger's breakup. She talked about him incessantly.

"Cory, I'm so glad you're here with me." Gemma snuggled closer, which I didn't think was even possible. It already felt like she was glued to my side. "I don't want Bridger to be the last guy I ever kiss, and I'm sure you don't want Bellany to be the last girl you ever kiss." She looked up at me, batting her eyes.

Great. This was the last thing I wanted to have to deal with. "I'm sure we're going to get out of here, Gemma. We're going to live our lives, move on, and leave our pasts behind."

"What do you think about us… moving on together?" Her fingers squeezed my arm.

This was not the time or place. And she definitely was not the girl for me. "Listen, Gemma… You're gonna meet someone else one day; someone who's going to love you and adore you. Someone who's going to treat you like a princess. The right guy is out there waiting for you."

There was no hint of sadness on her face. She seemed unfazed and undeterred, which shocked me.

"Cory, I don't want to be with someone else. I want to be with you. I think I've fallen in love with you."

"No, you haven't fallen in love with me. You're still getting over a breakup. You need time to heal."

She shook her head. "No, I don't. You're the only person I want to be with. I've just been too afraid to admit it."

"I'm sorry, but I don't feel the same way about you."

A strange look crossed her face. Her body stiffened, and she quickly pushed herself to her feet. "Oh my gosh," she said as she stumbled back. "You're still in love with her! You love Bellany!"

"No, I don't."

She pointed her finger at me, jabbing it in the air, her face contorting with anger. "You're a liar. You're in love with her!"

I bit the inside of my cheek, fighting back my own anger. But I just couldn't take it anymore. "You actually think I could love someone who is trying to kill me; someone who is making me and my friends suffer? Someone who has taken my sister away from me and done who-knows-what with her? You can't possibly be serious."

Gemma still had a snarky look on her face, her arms tightly folded across her chest.

I'd had enough of her! I got up and headed over to one of the safes. Spinning the number dial was a much better option than talking to her. I continued working on cracking the safe for probably over an hour. Never once did I turn around to look at Gemma. I heard her moving around the room and sighing loudly, but I didn't speak a word to her.

My thirst was almost unbearable, and my back and fingers were aching. I stood up and stretched, trying to ease the pain. Gemma was pouting, sitting against the wall, and glaring at me.

I picked up the two bottles of water and studied them under the light. I still couldn't detect a single difference in the color of the water.

I sat down on the floor and began unscrewing the caps.

"Are you gonna drink that?" Gemma asked, her voice cracking.

"I'm just going to smell it and see if I can detect a difference." She watched me intently as I placed each bottle under my nose.

"What does it smell like?"

I couldn't detect any difference. "Nothing," I said, screwing the lids back on.

Gemma's eyes bored through me from across the room. "Cory. Promise me you won't do something stupid like take a sip of one of these bottles."

"Don't worry. I won't." Not yet anyway, I thought to myself. But eventually one of us was going to get desperate enough to take the first sip and probably guzzle the whole thing down.

CHAPTER 26

Cory

Gemma and I jolted awake, her body pressed against mine, as a loud noise echoed through the room. Our heads swiveled in every direction, searching for the source. Nothing within our view had changed. We checked the bathroom then rushed to the door. It was still locked. The noise was coming from outside.

"What is that?" Gemma asked, pressing her ear to the door.

The sound pulsed rhythmically and constantly. "A helicopter," I said, looking up at the ceiling, wishing I could see it. Was someone being dropped off or was someone being picked up?

"Do you think we're gonna be rescued?"

"I can only hope." But how would they know we needed rescuing? Would they come look for us?

"I hope Wade and Charlotte can flag them down somehow," Gemma said, biting her fingernails.

The noise continued for at least a half hour, maybe more, while Gemma and I pounded on the door and yelled for help.

"Do you think they're dropping off supplies?" Gemma asked, staring up at the ceiling.

I doubt it, I thought to myself. "I don't know."

The noise from the helicopter eventually faded away, and nobody came to rescue us.

Gemma's body trembled with fear, her eyes darting around the room. She was becoming more frantic by the second. "Bellany didn't get on that helicopter and leave us here, did she?"

"No, of course not. She wouldn't do that. She's gonna let us out of here eventually." I didn't believe a single word I just said. I just wanted to stop Gemma from freaking out. "Everything's fine." I wrapped her in my arms as she melted into my chest.

We eventually fell asleep again, lying on the hard floor, and I had another nightmare. I dreamed I was swimming in the ocean, and I heard screaming. The screams were coming from Tasha. She was drowning, and no matter how far I swam, I couldn't get to her. The ocean current kept pulling me back.

I awoke with a startle, and I thought I heard Tasha scream. But it wasn't her. There was a phone in here somewhere, and it was ringing!

"What's going on?" Gemma wiped her eyes.

I got up and followed the sound. It was coming from behind one of the mermaid paintings. I ran my fingers along the edges of the frame and pulled. The painting swung open, revealing a small recess in the wall where a corded phone sat, and it was still ringing.

Gemma pressed the speaker button. "Hello?"

"Hello," an electronically altered voice replied, sending shivers down my spine.

I had expected to hear Bellany's high-pitched voice. Why was she disguising it? "Bellany, let us out of here! Unlock the door now! Come here and talk to me in person!"

"Yeah, stop being such a coward!" Gemma snapped. "We know you're here. We know you locked--

"Shut up and listen!" the voice shouted, interrupting Gemma. "It's time for another game. You both must choose a bottle of water and take a drink from it. Then after you both take a drink, you'll receive the combination to the next safe, which contains more water and food."

Gemma's eyes narrowed. "You mean more poisoned water. I don't think so!"

"Stop interrupting me!" the voice yelled. "This is a new game. The water in the next safe will be safe to drink."

"Neither of us is going to drink the water," I insisted. We weren't that desperate--not yet anyway. I still had hope that someone would come and rescue us. I wasn't ready to risk my life for a drink of water.

"I guarantee that you will drink it. Because if you don't, then one of your friends will be killed."

Bellany's words felt like daggers piercing my soul. I couldn't believe what I was hearing. She really did want to kill us!

"Bellany," I said calmly, "you've got to stop this. Please. Come and talk to me, okay? We can work this out--I know we can. Let's talk this through. You and I, together."

The voice let out a menacing, bone-chilling cackle that echoed through the room. There was nothing funny about what I had said. I was pleading for mercy.

"Bellany," I said calmly, forcing down the rage that was bubbling inside of me. "I don't know what Victoria told you or what your plans are, but I promise you that we never wanted to cause you any harm. I swear we didn't. We just wanted to talk to you and have an intervention. That's why I invited your brother to come to Mexico too, and I'm sorry he wasn't able to come. But I promise, all we wanted to do was help you and stop you from harming yourself and others."

Gemma's eyes flashed with a spark of desperate anticipation. She mouthed something, gesturing to the phone.

"What?" I whispered, unable to figure out what she wanted.

"Cory's telling you the truth," she said, leaning into the phone. "I swear! Here's how the whole thing went down. Originally, he only wanted Bridger to come to Mexico. But then Bridger told me, and I kind of invited myself. Then I told Charlotte and Wade, and they wanted to come too. I mean, can you blame us? Nobody knew where you were. You're like this mystic creature that's impossible to find. And I'll admit it, we wanted a chance to confront you. But we didn't want revenge. We wanted to get you help. You're sick, Bellany. There's something wrong in your brain. You've got some kind of mental illness..."

Searing heat flooded my veins as I shook my head in silent protest. What was Gemma thinking? Calling Bellany crazy was one of the worst things she could do!

"Enough!" the voice shouted, the echo whipping through the air. "It's been quite intriguing listening to all this nonsense, but I must stop you now and inform you that I am not Bellany. Who I am, is of no concern to you right now. Let's get back to the game...You both are desperate for water. Your thirst, I'm sure, is almost unbearable. I'm simply offering you a solution. Well, actually, it's more of a dilemma. You can choose not to drink the water and continue to go thirsty. But if you do, then you'll be sacrificing one of your friends. The question is simple. Do you value your life more than one of your friend's?"

I didn't want to take part in this sick game. This needed to stop! "If you're not Bellany, then who are you and why are you doing this to us?"

"If you don't drink, then either Wade or Charlotte will be killed."

Tears filled Gemma's eyes, her bottom lip trembling. "You're gonna kill one of them?"

"I see you've already made your choice, Gemma. You're not going to drink the water. You wish for one of your friends to die."

My heart leapt into my throat. "No! Wait! We haven't decided yet." I wanted to make sure that I understood what we were being asked to do. "So Gemma and I have to choose together. We both have to be in agreement. We both must drink the water. And if we don't, then one of our friends will be killed. Is that correct?"

"Yes," the voice replied.

Gemma shook her head rapidly, fear in her eyes, as if she was pleading for me not to agree.

"You will have two minutes to make your decision," the voice said, "and I'll let you know when that two minutes starts."

What? Was this person watching us? I scanned the ceiling, searching for a camera. "How will you know if we drink it?"

"I'm watching you," the voice replied. "Right now, Gemma is standing next to you biting her fingernails. And you, Cory, are nervously tapping your fingers on your leg."

A chill ran down my spine. The person on the phone had described exactly what Gemma and I were doing.

Now I knew why the ceiling was painted black and the lights hung so low. It was impossible to see the location of the cameras. The ceiling was much too high for me to reach. I couldn't even reach it if I jumped. I turned to my right, scanning the safes. If I climbed on the tallest one, maybe I could reach the ceiling, but I doubted a camera would be accessible from there. The person on the phone was too calculating to make that kind of mistake.

"Why are you doing this to us?" I asked, hoping to buy ourselves some time and convince whoever this was to stop playing this cruel game.

"I have my reasons."

"Bellany!" Gemma shouted. "Quit messing around and open up the door! You have no right to keep us here!"

I wished Gemma would stop calling this person Bellany. I no longer believed it was her. Bellany could be conniving, and vicious at times, but she wasn't a monster. "Who are you?" I demanded.

"Your two minutes start now!"

"No!" Gemma screamed, her throat raw with terror. "No, don't do this to us! Stop!"

I couldn't let my friends die. I picked up one of the bottles of water, my heart racing, and unscrewed the cap.

CHAPTER 27

Cory

I only had two minutes…

"I'm not about to sacrifice your life," I said to Gemma. "And I'm not going to sacrifice Wade or Charlotte's either. I'm the reason we're in this situation." I held onto the water bottle, knowing that I had to drink it. "None of you would have come here, if it weren't for me." I gripped it tightly, my heart racing. "If the water is poisoned, we'll find out soon. Then you can drink the other one."

Gemma's eyes widened in sheer terror. "Cory, don't! Don't do this!"

I had to. I knew it the moment I learned that either Charlotte or Wade could die. I checked the label on the water bottle. It had a black dot on it, which I hoped meant it was safe to drink. I placed it to my lips and poured it into my mouth.

After I swallowed, I tried to count the seconds that had passed in my head, wondering how much time remained. But my mind was spinning in every direction, and I couldn't focus.

I worried about Tasha. My heart ached for what might happen to her if I didn't survive. I hoped Gemma, Wade and Charlotte would find her and take care of her.

The emotional pain I felt over abandoning Tasha was suffocating. I couldn't control the rate of my breathing.

Gemma searched my face for signs of distress. "Cory! Are you okay? Do you think it was poisoned? Is it burning your mouth? What about your stomach?"

"I don't think it was poisoned." I didn't feel any physical

pain anywhere. I felt fine. "I'm okay--at least I'm okay right now. I don't know if I'll have a delayed reaction though. But Gemma, you don't have to drink the water if you don't want to. This whole situation is my fault, not yours."

"I'm afraid," she cried, picking up the open bottle of water. "I don't want to die!"

"Then don't drink it! Just leave it!"

"No," she shook her head. "I have to. I wouldn't be able to live with myself if I didn't. Are you sure you're not in any pain?" she asked, her voice shuddering.

"I feel fine," I insisted, wondering how much time we had left. I hoped the water was safe for her to drink. I didn't want her to die.

Gemma lifted the bottle to her lips, her hand shaking. She gulped down a few swallows, then started sobbing. I took the bottle from her and set it down out of the way so it wouldn't get knocked over. Then I wrapped her in my arms and held her tight.

"You two surprised me," the voice said with an eerie chuckle. "I thought you'd let one of your friends die."

"What?" Gemma snapped, pulling away from me with fury in her eyes. She began cursing at the person on the phone.

I couldn't allow Gemma to provoke whoever this was. Our lives were in danger. I grabbed hold of her, covering her mouth with my hand, until she finally stopped struggling.

"You have some temper, don't you," the voice chuckled.

Nothing about this was funny. "We did what you wanted," I said. "Now tell us the combination to the safe."

"Eight, thirteen, zero," the voice said. Then the phone clicked, and the call ended.

"Eight, thirteen, zero," I repeated, heading to the nearest safe.

Gemma tried to unlock the largest safe, but the combination didn't work. I was working on my second safe, hoping the person on the phone hadn't lied to us.

"I got it!" Gemma cried. She reached inside the safe and pulled out a single, eight ounce bottle of water and two granola bars. "Are you kidding me! This is it? This is all the food and water we get? I put my life on the line for two granola bars and one bottle of water!"

I wasn't surprised or upset. I hadn't been expecting much more than this. The person or persons holding us captive had no intention of making our lives any less miserable. They only wanted to prolong our suffering.

CHAPTER 28

Cory

Gemma and I shared one of the granola bars and set aside the other one for Wade and Charlotte. We saved the bottle of water for them too. Then we shared the bottle we had already started drinking and finished it off.

I didn't know if we would ever see Wade and Charlotte again, but saving some food and water for them felt like the right thing to do.

Gemma was lying on the floor, curled up into a ball. She had cried herself to sleep, despite my effort to comfort her.

Maybe she heard the doubt in my voice when I told her that we would get out of here. I tried to mask it. But how many times could a person say that *everything was going to be fine,* when they really didn't believe it, and still sound convincing?

I picked up the phone, wondering if I would hear a dial tone or that same unsettling, distorted voice again. Fortunately, it was a dial tone.

Gemma and I had already tried to call Bridger's phone number. Gemma knew it by heart. But the call wouldn't go through. Gemma had also tried calling some other phone numbers, like her mom's and some of her friends' back in North Carolina. Again, the calls wouldn't go through. I didn't have anybody to call, other than Tasha and Victoria, but I couldn't remember Victoria's phone number.

Tasha had a cell phone at home. She usually didn't carry it around with her. But I knew the number and I dialed it again, hoping the line would connect and she would answer, even though I knew it wouldn't.

After the call failed to go through, I dialed numbers at random, wondering if I would be able to reach someone who could help us. But again, the calls wouldn't go through.

I wondered if this phone was only set up for making calls on the yacht, from room to room. I tried one digit numbers, two digit numbers, three, and so forth, hoping I would possibly reach Wade and Charlotte, yet at the same time I wondered if the person on the phone had lied to us. What if Wade and Charlotte weren't even here? What if they were taken away on the helicopter?

After trying different numbers, with no success, I was so frustrated that I nearly ripped the phone out of the wall and threw it across the room.

I took a deep breath to calm down as I stared at the dial pad, then I noticed a button with the pound sign, and my heart thudded hard against my ribcage. What if I was supposed to press the pound sign after I dialed a number?

I tried three digit numbers, starting with one hundred, followed by the pound sign. I worked my way up to one hundred twenty-one, and then I heard it ring! My fingers squeezed the phone as I held it to my ear.

"Hello?" a high-pitched voice answered, and my knees almost gave out.

The voice didn't belong to Wade or Charlotte. It was Bellany!

"Hello?" she repeated.

How was this possible? Had I been wrong? Was Bellany keeping us here? Was she the one who disguised her voice?

"Hello?" she repeated, this time sounding more desperate, almost like she was afraid.

"Give me that," I heard someone say in the background. It sounded like Wade. "Hello? Who is this?"

There was no mistaking, it was Wade's voice.

"Whoever you are, answer me!" Wade demanded. "Why are you keeping us here? Why are you doing this to us?"

I heard more voices in the background. What was Wade doing and why was Bellany with him?

I cleared my throat. "It's me, Cory. Gemma's here with me too."

When Gemma heard me speak, her eyes popped open and she sat up. I put the phone on speaker, so she could be just as shocked as I was.

"Cory!" Wade said, his voice tense. "We're locked in one of the bedrooms on the yacht! Where are you guys at?"

I had a much more urgent question to ask him. "Is Bellany there with you?"

"Yeah, man. She's here. We're all here."

"Who?" Gemma jumped in. "Who's there with you?"

"Me, Charlotte, Bellany, Victoria, and Tasha."

My heart skipped a beat as hope swelled inside me. "Tasha's there? Is she okay? Let me talk to her!"

"Hold on…" he said, and I heard some commotion in the background. I heard what I thought was her voice. But how could this be possible? How was she on the yacht? Did the helicopter bring her?

"Hi, Cory. Where are you?" Tasha asked.

The happiness I felt was so overwhelming, it brought tears to my eyes. I thought I would never hear Tasha's voice again. She sounded like she was doing fine. "I'm in one of the other rooms on the yacht."

"Well, can you come and get me? Can you come open the door so we can get out of here? I'm tired of being locked in this room."

I wanted so badly to help her, and it tore at my heart that I couldn't. "I'm sorry, Tasha. But I can't. I'm locked in a room too, and I'm unable to get out. At least not yet anyway. But I will get out of here. I promise I will. Can you just be patient and wait for me?"

"Okay, well I guess so. But please hurry, Cory. I'm tired of staying here. I want to eat some dinner. I'm hungry."

My heart felt like it was being ripped out of my chest. I

was powerless, and I hated it! I felt like I was a kid again, back in our foster home, unable to help her. "I'm so sorry you're hungry, Tasha. I'm going to try my best to get out of this room and bring you something to eat." My eyes traveled over to the granola bar that was sitting on top of the safe. One granola bar wasn't enough to share with everyone.

"Can you get me something to drink too? I'm really thirsty."

My eyes shifted to the water bottle. "Yes, of course. I'll find you something to drink too. I promise." I was unsure if I'd be able to deliver on this promise. I felt like I was lying to her.

"Tasha," Gemma said, interrupting our conversation. "It's so good to hear your voice, sweetie. How did you get here? Who brought you?"

"Um, an old lady brought me here. She brought me, Victoria, and Bellany here on a helicopter. But I don't remember the helicopter ride. I was sleeping."

"Tasha," I said. "Can you give the phone to Wade again? I need to talk to him."

"Sure. One sec… But just so you know, Bellany didn't hurt me. She didn't do anything to me at all. She's been really nice. So you don't have anything to worry about. Okay, Cory? She's not a bad person. She's really pretty, and she's nice."

I had warned Tasha about Bellany many times before. She knew to be leery of her, but she couldn't fully comprehend the situation. Tasha was too innocent and kind. She trusted people and could easily be manipulated. Bellany had obviously already figured this out.

Gemma frowned. "Bellany's fooling you, sweetie--"

I shot her a look and held up my hand. Tasha was in enough distress already. Gemma did not need to add to it. "Tasha. I'm so glad that Bellany has been kind to you. Thank you for telling me. Now can you let Wade talk on the phone?"

"Sure. Hold on."

"Hey," Wade said.

"Tell me what's going on. Tell me everything."

He sighed heavily into the phone. "So I don't know if you heard the helicopter, but that's how your sister, Victoria, and Bellany were brought here. All three of them had been sedated. Victoria and Bellany vaguely remember starting to wake up as they were being carried out of the helicopter. Tasha doesn't remember anything. She was totally passed out."

"Was Tasha hurt?"

"No, nothing like that. She was just sedated, jabbed with a needle."

Gemma's eyes narrowed as she shook her head. "Bellany is lying, and so is Victoria. They weren't sedated. They're the ones doing this to us!"

Now was not the time to be jumping to conclusions. We didn't know what was going on or who was responsible. I rested a hand on Gemma's shoulder, and she jerked away from me.

"Cory, you know I'm right," Gemma insisted. "Bellany and Victoria are the ones who are responsible for what's happening to us! This is all their fault! None of us would be trapped here if it hadn't been for them! They're the reason--" Gemma's voice broke as she began to cry.

I held her in my arms to comfort her, since there was nothing else I could do. I hated feeling so helpless. I couldn't save Tasha--I couldn't save any of us!

"Is she okay?" Wade asked.

"Yeah, she's fine. We've been through a huge ordeal. You wouldn't believe what's happened..." I went on to explain how we were forced to drink water, not knowing if it had been poisoned. When Wade heard that he or Charlotte could have been killed, he muttered something under his breath that I couldn't make out.

I waited a few beats then asked him how they all ended up together in the same room.

"Charlotte and I were in this bedroom, searching it, and we found a bottle of water in one of the drawers," he explained. "We were so thirsty, we drank about half of it, and then the next thing we knew, we were waking up to the sound of a helicopter. We were still pretty out of it, super groggy. We were too weak to get up, but we saw some guys decked out in black from head to toe, masks covering their faces. They carried your sister, Victoria, and Bellany into the bedroom and laid them on the other bed. Then they walked out and locked the door behind them. That's how we all ended up here."

"Does Bellany know who the masked men were?" I asked.

As soon as I mentioned Bellany's name, Gemma tossed her hands up. "Of course she knows them. She hired them!" Gemma shouted. "They're working for her. This is all just a big game to her. She's messing with our heads. It's all her fault! And Victoria's helping her..."

"Wade," I said, raising my voice so he could hear me over Gemma's ranting. "What did Bellany say? Who were the masked men?"

"She said that she doesn't know who they are, and Victoria backed up her story. They both said they were abducted from your house and sedated. They don't remember anything that happened between the time they were abducted from your house and the time they arrived on the yacht. Tasha's abduction story was different though. She said some old lady kidnapped her from the beach and then stuck her with a needle, which put her to sleep."

Every muscle in my body tensed. "An old lady? What old lady?"

"Tasha said that she didn't know who she was. She had never seen her before. She described her as being a grandma, and..." Wade paused a couple beats. "Look, man," he said, his voice lower. "We're stuck in here. There are no windows. The door is locked. The walls are made of some kind of metal or something. All I know is that I can't break out of here. We're trapped."

"Join the club," Gemma sighed. "We're all going to die on this stupid yacht." She started pacing, arms folded across her chest. "I should have never got off of Pablo's boat. I should have gone back with him to shore."

The phone beeped with another call coming through and my stomach dropped. "Wade! I think the person holding us captive is calling again. They're on the other line. I'll have to call you back."

"Okay, man. Be safe!"

I switched to the other line, wondering what this psycho wanted now. "Hello?"

"How was the granola bar?" the voice asked.

Gemma came charging toward the phone, a look of rage on her face. "Do you think this is funny? Is this some kind of a sick joke to you?"

"My, aren't we feisty," the voice replied. "I thought it was the hunger that was making you grumpy, but obviously not."

Gemma's brows cinched together. "Are you nuts? Do you have a screw loose in your head? A half a granola bar isn't enough food. We're starving, and we're thirsty!"

"My, my, my, aren't we ungrateful," the voice chided.

I placed a hand on Gemma's shoulder to stop her before she said something we'd probably both regret.

"Why are you holding us captive?" I asked. "What do you want from us?"

"I didn't call to give you that kind of information. I called to offer you a chance to get some more food, since both of you are so incredibly hungry and ungrateful for what I have already given you."

"Ungrateful?" Gemma gasped.

"That's right, my dear. You are a spoiled brat. And because of that, I'm going to make this next game a little more unpleasant..." the voice chuckled. "You'll have five minutes to finish all of the food. You both must eat the exact same amount. If you manage to finish it in time, then I will reward you by providing your friends with some food and water. If you fail to finish the food, then your friends will get nothing."

Gemma and I exchanged looks. Just how much food was she talking about? Would we be able to finish it in time? "What's the catch?" I asked. "What if we can't finish it?"

"If you both fail to consume all of the food, then your friends will get nothing. Oh and another thing... One of your friends will be killed. Are you willing to take the risk?"

I didn't want to wager anyone's life, but I also knew that they were starving and they needed something to drink. My fists clenched. I wanted so badly to punch something. "How much food?" I asked through gritted teeth. "What is it?"

Gemma looked at me wide-eyed. "I'm starving, Cory. We have to do this."

"What if it's too much food to finish in time? What if it's rotten and totally inedible?"

"It's not rotten," the voice replied. "It's quite fresh and edible."

It was probably too much food then, or something else unpleasant I just hadn't thought of yet. I felt uneasy about this. "Gemma, the risk is too big. We can't wager someone's life!"

"I'm starving, Cory! I promise I'll eat all the food. That granola bar didn't fill me up at all. If anything, it made me more hungry."

"We still have the other granola bar we're saving. If we get desperate enough, we can eat it." I picked it up and held it out to her. "In fact, you can have it right now. You can have all of it."

She refused to take it from me. "You want me to give up having a full stomach of food for one measly granola bar?" Her lips pressed into a straight line. "No. I'm sorry. I won't." She shook her head. "Think about it, Cory. If we do this, then your sister will get food and water too. All of our friends will."

Or one of them might die. I wasn't willing to risk Tasha's life, or anybody else's. While I felt confident that I could finish the food, no matter what, I wasn't sure I could count on Gemma. She was a small person. I doubted she would be able to consume a large amount of food in a short period of time. I didn't think she could physically handle it.

"Please, Cory."

"You have to finish the food though, Gemma," I said, staring deeply into her eyes. "If you don't, one of them will die."

"I know! I get it!" Her attention shifted to the phone. "Yes! We accept. Give us the food!"

"My, my, my..." the voice said. "Your mother must not have taught you any manners. Say please."

"Please!" Gemma replied, a frown on her face.

"Cory," the voice said. "You both have to agree. Do you accept my terms?"

Gemma clasped her hands together, pleading for me to agree. "We can do this," she said. "And we'll also be feeding Tasha. You don't want her to starve, do you?"

I didn't want her to possibly die either. I felt like we were making a deal with the devil. Something wasn't right. "What kind of food?" I asked. "How much food?"

"It's a simple yes or no question, Cory," the voice replied. "You have ten seconds to decide."

Gemma grabbed my arm. "Say, yes!"

"Five seconds..."

Gemma's fingernails dug into my skin. "Cory! Please!"

"Yes," I agreed. But I feared I was making a monumental mistake.

CHAPTER 29

Cory

The voice on the phone gave us a combination to another safe. Problem was, we weren't told which safe it would open and the five minute time clock had already started.

"Hurry!" I pleaded with Gemma, hoping she would move through the safes quickly.

"I am!" she replied, defensively. "I'm hurrying!"

I tried the first safe. It didn't work. Then I moved to the next, glancing over my shoulder. Gemma was attempting to open the largest safe. What in the world was she thinking? That thing could hold enough food to last us for weeks. It was about four feet tall.

My hands shook as I worked the combination to the next safe. What if we didn't finish in time? What if Tasha died?

"Got it!" Gemma shrieked, having successfully opened the largest safe.

I was terrified of what we might find inside. Even if it was full of my favorite foods, too much of it would be impossible to finish in time.

We found a large box of saltine crackers that could probably feed thirty people. Gemma screamed louder than I had ever heard her scream before. "No! I can't!"

I remembered that one of her biggest fears was saltine crackers, because she almost choked to death while eating some. I grabbed Gemma by the shoulders, my eyes locked onto hers. "You promised you would do this! You have to eat the crackers!"

I ripped open the box and dumped out four sleeves of

crackers, giving her two of them. Gemma and I began stuffing our mouths. I managed to consume the entire first sleeve of crackers before Gemma had finished half of hers.

"My mouth is so dry," she said, tears in her eyes. "I have to drink something."

I stuffed another handful of crackers into my mouth and grabbed the bottle of water we had been saving for the others. "Drink this!"

Gemma swallowed down some of the water, then continued eating.

I felt like I had cement in my mouth. As much as I didn't want to consume all the water, I knew I had to drink some.

"You have one minute remaining," the voice announced.

I had two crackers left, but Gemma was only a third of the way through her last sleeve of crackers. "Come on, Gemma. You can do this!"

I stuffed the last two crackers into my mouth as I watched her struggle to swallow, crumbs all over her shirt. "Take another drink!" I held out the water.

She strained to swallow more crackers, then the water. She had already consumed more water than me, but I didn't care. She needed to finish all the crackers! "Gemma, hurry! Don't chew so much. Just swallow!"

I wished I knew how much time remained. Was it ten seconds? Was it five? "Hurry, Gemma! Eat!"

Her eyes widened, and she started coughing.

Oh no! Please don't choke! I held out the bottle of water again. "Here. Drink!"

The coughing continued.

What if she vomited? Would the psycho on the phone still honor our deal?

I patted Gemma on the back, hoping it would help. She elbowed me, took another gulp of water, then began stuffing crackers into her mouth again.

But I worried she wasn't eating fast enough. "How much time does she have left?"

"Five seconds," the voice replied and my stomach dropped.

Gemma stuffed the last handful of crackers into her mouth, chewing furiously.

My heart raced as I watched. "Swallow it! Gemma! Swallow!"

She gulped down the rest of the water as she tried to finish consuming the crackers, but most of the water ran down her chin. She swallowed hard, then opened her mouth and stuck out her tongue. All of the crackers were gone!

"You did it!" I picked her up and spun her around.

CHAPTER 30

Bellany

This bedroom was way too crowded and stuffy. There was nowhere to sit, other than on the floor or on one of the queen size mattresses, but there were only two. And right now, Wade and Charlotte were occupying one and Tasha was splayed out on the other. Victoria was hovering over me, while I sat on the floor with my sandwich.

I hadn't eaten a peanut butter and jelly sandwich since I was a child. Normally I stayed away from carbs like bread, and I certainly never touched jelly. It had way too much sugar in it. But I had to make an exception this time, which I wasn't happy about.

Everybody else had already scarfed down their sandwiches like animals. Victoria had somehow forgotten everything I had taught her about being a lady, and I doubted Charlotte had ever been taught any manners by her trashy mother.

Tasha, on the other hand, was a special case. She was a child in a big person's body, and I knew that children were easily influenced and manipulated by others. She was only mirroring what she saw the other girls do.

Wade had practically stuffed his entire sandwich into his mouth with one bite. He was a rugged and outdoorsy guy. He was quite delicious to look at.

I was taking my time and eating like I normally would, with manners. And it wasn't like I had anywhere to go. We were all locked in this room.

When Charlotte noticed that I still had half of my sandwich left, she gave me a dirty look and whispered something into Wade's ear. She had been doing this kind of thing ever since I got here, and it was really getting old. She was lucky she had Wade to protect her.

I picked up the other half of my sandwich, and Wade's eyes locked onto it, along with everybody else's. They all wanted it. I could tell by their ravenous stares.

"Are you gonna eat that?" Victoria asked, her eyes fixed intently on my sandwich.

There was no way I was going to give it to her.

I walked over to Tasha with a friendly smile on my face. She was the perfect pawn. "Tasha," I said, holding out my sandwich. "You can have the rest of mine."

She snatched it out of my hand, but then she hesitated before taking a bite. "I can have all of it?"

"Yes. All of it," I assured her, knowing everybody was watching.

Tasha took a couple bites and licked some of the peanut butter off her finger. "You're the best, Bellany. Thank you so much!"

Yes, I am the best, I thought to myself. Nobody else bothered to share their sandwich with her. They weren't as thoughtful and generous as me. Tasha had better remember this.

After she finished eating, she was so full and satisfied that she laid down and closed her eyes to take a nap.

I sat back down on the floor with my back against the wall. Victoria sat next to me. This room was already cramped enough as it was. I didn't need her making things worse by sitting so close.

Find your own wall, I thought to myself. Then she leaned in, her shoulder touching mine, and I gritted my teeth, about ready to punch her in the face.

"What do you think Wade and Charlotte are saying to each other?" she whispered in my ear.

This was probably one of the dumbest questions she had ever asked me. "I don't know. Why don't you ask them?" I whispered back, curious if she would do it.

"Really?"

"Yes. Really," I replied.

"Uh..." she hesitated, biting her lip. "Okay."

I couldn't wait to see this.

Victoria's head swiveled in their direction, her eyes wide and unblinking. She swallowed hard. "What are you guys talking about?"

Charlotte shot her a dirty look, which wasn't a surprise. "You want to know what we're talking about?" she asked.

"Yeah," Victoria replied, her voice cracking, which irritated me. There was no reason for Victoria to be nervous around Charlotte. Charlotte was a loser, plain and simple.

Charlotte sat forward, glaring at us. "If we wanted you to know what we were talking about, then we'd say it out loud so you could hear."

I couldn't take it anymore. Victoria was irritatingly way too insecure, and Charlotte was way too confident. She needed to be put in her place. "There's really no need to be rude, Charlotte," I chided.

I almost smiled when I saw the fury ignite in her eyes. What was she going to say, I wondered. Just how big of a fit was she going to throw?

Charlotte cocked her head. "That whole sharing your sandwich thing you did with Tasha was pretty pathetic. If you think that's gonna make us change our minds about you, think again. We all know who you really are. You're not fooling us."

Victoria shrugged. "I thought what Bellany did was really nice."

"Of course you did," Charlotte said, her tone thick with sarcasm.

Victoria didn't need to defend me. I could do that on my own. "I would rather have tried to break out of here, than eat a sandwich," I said, reminding Charlotte and Wade about what had happened earlier.

The person on the phone had instructed us all to sit against the farthest wall from the bathroom and to remain there while they delivered the food. We were warned that if we didn't comply, we wouldn't get any.

Needless to say, these idiots weren't brave enough to fight for their freedom. They passed up a perfect opportunity to escape, and instead settled for a peanut butter and jelly sandwich and a sip of water. So dumb.

When the masked man stepped inside the room to set the tray of sandwiches and water down on the floor, I wanted to spring to my feet and tackle him. I almost did. But Charlotte grabbed my arm to stop me. She ruined our chance to escape.

I was surprised that Wade didn't follow through with what I was trying to do. Although I suspected that he may have intended to do the same thing, only he couldn't after Charlotte drew the masked man's attention.

"I stopped you from ruining our chances of getting some food," Charlotte shouted, her voice booming.

Tasha opened her eyes as she rolled to her other side. "I wish I had some water to drink," she moaned, then quickly fell back asleep.

The tray of sandwiches the man brought had five paper cups on it, each filled with an inch of water, and that was all we had to drink. Everybody's mouth was dry after eating peanut butter.

Charlotte got up and walked across the room, heading straight toward me. She was trying to act tough, just like she used to do in high school.

"This is all your fault," she said, her voice lowered so she wouldn't wake up Tasha.

"My fault," I repeated, eyebrows raised. She was lucky Wade was here to protect her, otherwise she would be lying on the floor unconscious right now.

"Of course it's your fault. You've traveled back and forth across the country, wreaking havoc, and ruining people's lives everywhere you go. Well, congratulations Bellany, because apparently you've finally crossed the wrong person, and now they're taking revenge on all of us for something you've done. Yet you haven't bothered to apologize to us. Not even once!"

Charlotte jabbed her finger at me, which wasn't intimidating at all since she was standing four feet away. "You sit there acting like you're a victim and you're innocent. Well, nobody believes that. So stop fooling yourself, Bellany. You're delusional."

Did I ask her to come to Mexico? No, I didn't. Did I ask her to board this yacht? No. She did that all on her own. None of this was my fault, and I wasn't about to apologize.

Victoria shook her head. "You can't blame Bellany for this. She doesn't know who these people are--none of us do. We don't know why they're doing this to us or what they want."

"Wake up, Victoria!" Charlotte snapped. "It's time that you face reality. We weren't targeted for no reason. Bellany's the reason."

"Bellany is my friend," Victoria said, defensively. "She's my best friend, actually. And I don't appreciate you blaming her for something she didn't do. This isn't her fault."

Charlotte's mouth gaped open. "I don't know why you're still friends with her. Have you forgotten that she ditched you? Or was that a lie?"

"Well, uh, you see..." Victoria's cheeks reddened as she smoothed her hair back. "It turns out that she didn't ditch me at all. I was mistaken."

Charlotte turned to Wade. "Did you hear what she just said?"

Of course he heard. It wasn't like he was distracted doing something else. There was nothing else to do. The bedroom was completely bare.

"Yeah, I heard," he said, getting up to move closer. He sat on the edge of the bed Tasha was sleeping on, but was careful not to disturb her. He chose that spot, because it was directly in front of Victoria. He leaned forward, eyes fixed on her. "You told us that Bellany left you penniless. You said that she totally ghosted you."

Was I surprised to find out that Victoria had lied to me? No. Victoria would tell anybody what they wanted to hear in order to save herself. I looked directly at her, but she wouldn't look at me. "You told them that?"

Victoria smoothed down her hair again. "Yeah, I um... I'm sorry I lied to you, Bellany. I just--I didn't know what else to say. I didn't want you to be mad at me."

Oh, I was definitely mad, and she was lucky I couldn't do anything about it right now.

Wade leaned forward, elbows on his knees. "What did you lie about exactly?"

Charlotte sat down next to Wade, glaring at Victoria.

She bowed her head, her gaze on the floor. "I told Bellany that you guys showed up at our house on your own and that I had nothing to do with it." A tear spilled down her cheek.

Charlotte let out a humorless laugh. "Yeah right. You invited us."

My supposed best friend had invited my enemies over to my house! I wanted to strangle Victoria!

"I didn't know Bellany was coming back," Victoria explained, her voice small. "I thought she had left me."

I understood how Victoria could think that. All my stuff was gone from the house. The bank account password had been changed, and she couldn't reach me by phone. But that was still no excuse for what she had done. She should have been patient! She should have shown me a little loyalty!

"Victoria," I said calmly, even though inside I was full of rage. "When I left the house that morning, you were still in bed asleep. I wasn't even gone for that long. Maybe like two hours." I turned my attention to Wade. "I never ditched her. I was going to surprise her and tell her that I had bought a yacht. I planned on leaving that morning with her."

Wade's eyebrows cinched together. "I see."

"Well, Bellany..." Charlotte smirked. "Looks like your

155

surprise backfired, didn't it?"

I felt a hand on my arm and turned to look at Victoria. She really shouldn't touch me right now.

"Bellany, I'm sorry I lied to you." Tears poured down her face. "I was scared. I thought you left me."

"Don't worry about it," I said, casually moving my arm away from her, exercising the utmost restraint. "It was just a misunderstanding. I should have told you that I bought the yacht. It was my fault."

"You mean it? You're not mad?" Victoria asked, wiping the tears off her face.

"No. I'm not mad," I lied, forcing a soft smile.

She threw her arms around me and hugged me, which made my skin crawl. I hugged her back, playing along, pretending like all was forgiven.

"I'm so sorry," she sniffed. "I really am. I never meant to hurt you. You're my best friend."

Wade's eyes shifted between Victoria and I, a scowl on his face. "I don't believe either of you. I think you're both lying."

Charlotte nodded in agreement.

I wasn't upset or surprised to hear that they didn't believe us. Earning their trust would take a lot of time and effort.

Victoria had a huge frown on her face. "What part don't you believe?" she asked them. "I told you guys the truth. I thought Bellany left me, but in reality she didn't. She was coming back, only I didn't know it."

Tasha moaned as she rolled to her other side, but managed to stay asleep.

Wade was studying me, his suspicious eyes scanning my face. But I didn't feel anxious under his scrutiny. He could stare at me all he wanted.

He cocked his head, narrowing his eyes, and I couldn't wait to hear what he was about to say. "I don't think you were kidnapped," he said. "You planned this. The men working on this yacht are working for you. They're following your orders."

Victoria's head swiveled in my direction, her mouth

agape. "Did you plan this Bellany?"

I couldn't believe she just asked me that. Just a minute ago she was begging for my forgiveness. I seriously wanted to smack her across the face. "I didn't plan this," I replied.

"She's lying," Charlotte sneered, arms folded tightly. "She's just trying to manipulate us."

"If I had planned this, I wouldn't be sitting here in this room with you guys right now. I'd be out on the deck, soaking up the sun with an ice cold drink in my hand, and a platter of fresh vegetables on a table next to me."

Wade shifted forward, his eyes narrowing. "Bellany, if you want us to trust you, then tell us something that we don't know. Give us some useful information."

I did have some useful information and had been waiting for the right opportunity to share it, which was now. "When our captors brought us here, I told you how I was still groggy, and it was dark, and I didn't get a good look around."

"Yeah," Wade said, shrugging his shoulders. "What about it?"

"Well, since I didn't see the outside of the yacht, I can only tell you about what I've seen inside this bedroom and the adjoining bathroom. What I can tell you is that I have never seen this bedroom or bathroom before." I shook my head. "I didn't buy this yacht. It belongs to someone else."

"Are you serious?" Victoria shouted in my ear.

Oh, this girl. I gritted my teeth, pausing a moment. "I'm dead serious." I scanned their faces. "This isn't my yacht."

Wade fixed his gaze on Victoria, inhaling sharply. "You said this was Bellany's yacht."

"I--I thought it was. I--I could've sworn..." she stumbled over her words. "It looked exactly like the pictures." Her eyes blinked rapidly. "Bellany, are you sure this isn't the same yacht? Are you positive?"

It didn't matter how many times she asked me. The answer was still the same. "This is not my yacht."

Victoria's face twisted, and her breathing quickened. She

got up off the floor, backing away from me. "But the yacht you bought is named Jenny. I saw the picture. That's what this yacht is named. It's written on the side in big letters." She turned to Wade and Charlotte. "You guys saw it too."

Charlotte tilted her head slightly, eyebrows creased. "So there are two yachts with the same name. Two yachts that look almost exactly alike on the outside."

"The wrong yacht!" Wade glared at Victoria.

She shook her head. "I swear I had no idea. I thought this was Bellany's yacht. It looked like the pictures. It had the same name."

Victoria's mistake had unleashed a powerful tsunami of consequences that couldn't be stopped or reversed. This was her fault.

Wade's searing gaze remained tacked onto her. "I don't believe you. I think you did exactly what you were supposed to do--lead us here to this prison on water." He got in Victoria's face. "Who put you up to this? Who's keeping us here?"

Victoria's bottom lip quivered as tears spilled down her face. "I don't know--I swear! I don't know anything. I'm not involved."

"You're lying!" Wade shouted.

"I swear," she cried. "I'm telling you the truth. I thought this was Bellany's yacht. It had the same name. It looked like it too. It looked like the pictures."

Wade paced the floor, muscles tense, grumbling under his breath.

Charlotte was giving me a strange look. "Why should we believe you, Bellany?"

"I didn't buy a yacht on a budget," I explained. "I have plenty of money. I would never have settled for something subpar like this place, which obviously could use a complete renovation."

Charlotte rolled her eyes. "Oh, you're so rich, are you? Funny how that happens when you steal other people's money."

She had always been jealous of me. Charlotte was

consumed with envy from the moment I first met her. She wanted what I had: my beauty, my popularity, my family. She wanted my life. Nothing about her had changed over these past couple years. She was still obsessed with me.

"So whose yacht is this?" Charlotte asked, her voice rising. "If it's not yours, Bellany, then whose is it?"

Wade stopped pacing and turned to look at me, waiting for an answer.

"As you all know, I have many enemies--"

"No, really?" Charlotte interrupted, her tone full of sarcasm.

I wondered what Wade thought about his fiancé's childish behavior. It certainly wasn't flattering.

"Who do you think did this to us?" Victoria asked, wiping tears off her face.

"I'm hoping you guys can help me figure that out," I replied. "Have you noticed anybody lingering around Cory's house, or have you had any strange encounters with people? Does anything stand out in your mind?"

As soon as I asked the question, a weird look crossed Victoria's face. I waited for her to say something, but she didn't. She kept her mouth shut. I felt certain she was hiding something.

Wade and Charlotte claimed they hadn't had any strange experiences with people. Victoria said the same thing. But I knew she was lying, and I wanted to find out why.

Tasha awoke, which abruptly ended the conversation. The tension in the room dissipated as Wade and Charlotte turned their focus to her.

I got up from the floor and approached Victoria. "Would you mind coming with me to the bathroom?" I asked politely, pointing over my shoulder.

Her brows furrowed. "Why?"

I narrowed my eyes in response, and she immediately began walking toward the bathroom.

CHAPTER 31

Victoria

I was afraid to go into the bathroom alone with Bellany. I knew she was furious with me for lying.

Wade, Charlotte, and Tasha watched us walk across the room. I hoped one of them would intervene if things got out of hand and Bellany started attacking me or something.

She followed me inside the bathroom and shut the door. Then she turned on the fan, the humming noise filling the air.

The yacht was rocking back and forth. I leaned against the counter to steady myself, my knees feeling weak.

The pleasant expression on Bellany's face fell. Her lips pressed into a tight line, jaw tensed.

"Uh, what's up?" I asked, trying to hold it together and not panic. I didn't feel safe being alone with her, and I didn't like being in tight spaces.

"You tell me," she hissed.

Nervous butterflies swirled in my stomach, and my heart thumped wildly in my chest. "I don't know what you mean." I shrugged. "What are you talking about?"

"Listen carefully," she said in a low voice. "You need to remember where your loyalty resides." She pointed to herself. "It resides with me." Then she pointed toward the door. "Not with Wade and Charlotte." She stepped forward and I flinched, fearing she was about to hit me. "Stop taking their side." Her face was inches away from mine. "Stop ganging up on me with them."

I had learned that when dealing with Bellany, it was

always best to just agree and apologize. "Okay, I promise. I won't. I'm sorry."

"You and I are a united front--from here on out. Understand?"

I was just grateful she hadn't tried to hurt me. If my loyalty was all she wanted, I was going to make her believe that she had it. "I promise. You can count on me." I wasn't really sure I could deliver on that promise though.

Bellany stepped back, giving me some space. But I still felt anxious. This bathroom was small, and I felt like I couldn't breathe. The air was too thick, and Bellany was blocking the door.

"I need you to focus and think," Bellany said.

I took a deep breath, trying to calm down. "Okay."

"We need to figure out how to get off this yacht, which means that we need to find out who's keeping us here."

Why couldn't she talk to me about this in the bedroom? Why in here? The bathroom was too small.

"Did you notice any strange or suspicious people lingering around our house?" she asked. "Did you talk to anyone?"

I hadn't spent much time at the house. I was too busy hanging out with Cory, Tasha, and the rest of his friends. "No, not really. Not that I can think of."

"Are you sure there isn't someone who stands out in your mind? Anyone at all?"

"Nope." I shook my head. I wanted to get out of here. I couldn't breathe.

Bellany's face hardened as she stepped closer. "Don't answer me so quickly. I want you to put some thought into it. Think back through your memories. Think about everybody you've come in contact with since we arrived in Mexico. Did anyone give you a strange vibe? Did you ever feel like someone was watching you?"

A memory surfaced in my mind that I was trying to suppress. The old lady.

"What is it?" Bellany asked, studying my face.

"Nothing," I insisted, trying to act casual. But I was failing miserably. My heart was beating too fast.

Bellany pointed at me. "I've seen that look on your face before, Victoria."

I wiped the sweat off my forehead. "What look?"

"That look!" she snapped. "You're hiding something."

My cheeks felt hot, and I couldn't slow down my breathing.

"You remember someone, don't you!"

I spread apart my hands. "Sorry. I don't," I lied, anxious for this conversation to end. I had to get out of this bathroom.

Bellany locked the door, and sweat started rolling down my back.

She pushed the toilet lid down. "Sit!"

I couldn't control my claustrophobia any longer. "I can't," I said, gasping for air. I started toward the door, and she jumped in front of me.

"You're not leaving."

My chest felt constricted. "I can't breathe! This place is too small. I'm feeling claustrophobic!"

Bellany shook her head. "I'm not letting you leave until you tell me what you're hiding."

"Help!" I shouted, tears filling my eyes. "Help me!"

The door pounded. "What's going on?" Wade's voice boomed from the other side.

Bellany quickly unlocked the door and opened it. I was right on her heels, pushing to get out. I ran past Wade, gasping for air. The bedroom was much bigger than the bathroom, but I still felt trapped--I was trapped!

"I've got to get out of here!" I ran from door to door, banging on them with my fists, unsure which one would get me out of here. They were both locked.

I didn't want to freak out, but I couldn't stop. I couldn't calm down! The only thing on my mind was escaping from here!

I twisted and pulled on the doorknob of each door, but

they wouldn't budge. "Help me break down one of these doors!" I gasped, trying to wedge my fingers into the small crack between the door and the wall.

"Why isn't anybody helping me?" I cried out in desperation and began punching and kicking the doors. "Help me! Please! I've got to get out of here!"

I could hear them talking behind me, but I couldn't focus on what they were saying.

"Why isn't anybody helping me?" I screamed.

The air was too thick. My chest constricted as I continued to gasp. The walls felt like they were closing in on me.

"Victoria. You need to stop!" Wade grabbed me, but I pulled away.

"I gotta get outta here!" I ran to the other door and pounded on it again.

"Stop, you're hurting yourself," Wade said, pulling me back.

"Let go!" I screamed, struggling to break free.

"Calm down!" Charlotte shouted. "Wade's not going to hurt you! He's trying to help you!" She grabbed hold of my wrist. "Look what you've done to yourself! Look at your hands!"

When I looked down, I saw red, and the room started spinning. Everything went black.

CHAPTER 32

Victoria

I opened my eyes, wondering if I had passed out--it was the only explanation that made sense. I was lying on one of the beds, but I couldn't remember how I got here. There was a gap in my memory. The last thing I remembered was Wade restraining me and Charlotte screaming in my face.

Dread washed over me as I rolled onto my back and saw the familiar black ceiling hanging above and the black walls surrounding me. I ran my hands along the mattress. No sheets. No blankets. No pillow under my head. Nothing had changed. I was still trapped in the bedroom with everybody else, and they were all staring at me like I had grown a second head.

"Hi," Tasha said, plopping down on the mattress next to me. "Do your hands hurt?"

They did hurt, especially my knuckles. I looked down at them and saw blood.

"I wish I had a Band-Aid to give you," Tasha said, frowning. "You need lots of Band-Aids."

Charlotte came over and sat next to me too. She rested a hand on my shoulder. "Victoria, are you okay?"

I folded my arms, tucking my hands out of sight. "I'm fine." I wasn't fine. My hands were throbbing.

A ringing sound blared in my ears, startling me. It was the phone! Bellany got to it first and picked up the receiver. "Hello?"

Wade pressed the speaker button and an eerie, robotic voice filled the air. "It's time to play a game. Choose a letter in the alphabet. If you choose correctly, you will receive some food and water. You have ten minutes. Choose wisely." The call ended, and the room fell silent.

"A letter?" Charlotte sighed. "We have to guess a letter in order to get something to eat and drink?"

"How are we supposed to know which one?" I asked, hoping that someone else had an idea, because I sure didn't.

Wade's eyes slid to Bellany. "Do you have any clue what this fool is talking about?"

She shrugged. "I have no idea."

"I'm starving, and I'm dying of thirst," Charlotte said, holding her stomach. "We've gotta figure this out!"

"My favorite letter is T," Tasha reported happily. "Tasha starts with T."

"That's a good guess," Charlotte said. "But let's keep thinking."

Bellany stared off, deep in thought, just like everybody else, except for Tasha. She was singing the ABC song. She sang it through twice. On the third time, she stopped when she got to the letter S.

"The old lady that kidnapped me was wearing a necklace with the letter S on it. She said her name was Jenny. But Jenny doesn't start with an S. It starts with a J."

"That's correct," Bellany replied. "Jenny does start with a J."

"Then why was the old lady wearing an S on her necklace?" Tasha asked, wrinkling her nose.

I was almost positive I had met the same old lady. I wondered if this was my chance to come clean and tell Bellany. But I was afraid. She was going to be furious with me for not telling her sooner.

"What did the old lady look like?" Bellany asked Tasha.

"She was old, but not super old. Her gray hair was wavy," Tasha replied, swaying her hands in the air.

Bellany sat down next to Tasha on the bed. "Was there anything else unique or unusual about her appearance?"

Tasha thought about her question for a moment. "Her

neck…" she paused, placing a hand on her neck, just under her chin. "The skin jiggled like a turkey."

My heart raced as the image of the old lady Tasha described penetrated my mind. It was her--the same old lady I had met at the beach. I had also seen her at the hospital, and again in front of the rental house.

Admitting I had met her meant that we could possibly get something to eat and drink. I had to do it. "I think I met that same lady," I said, avoiding making eye contact with Bellany. "She had a necklace with an S on it. She had gray hair and a jiggly neck like Tasha described."

Bellany sighed loudly. "When did you see her?" she asked. "Where?"

"I saw her on the beach, not far from Cory's house, the day Tasha almost drowned. I just thought she was a lonely old lady, desperate for someone to talk to."

I thought it was strange that only Tasha and I had met Jenny. Why was that, I wondered. Maybe there was no reason at all. Maybe Jenny just took advantage of an opportunity that had presented itself.

"The old lady is named Jenny…" Wade's eyebrows drew together and the muscles tightened along his jawline. "This is her yacht."

Charlotte dropped her hands to her sides, slapping her legs. "If her name is Jenny, then why does she wear a necklace with an S on it? Why not a J?"

The phone rang, startling me. I hated feeling so on edge all the time.

Wade pressed the speaker button.

"What letter have you chosen?" the robotic voice asked.

Wade quickly scanned our faces. "S. The letter is S."

"That is correct," the robotic voice replied. Then the call ended.

"Yeah! We did it!" Tasha clapped her hands, bouncing on her toes. "I hope we get a big glass of water. And I hope we get some pizza too."

A click sounded. It came from the door at the far end of the bedroom. My heart leapt into my throat. Were we getting out of here?

CHAPTER 33

Victoria

Wade made it to the door first. When he turned the knob, it opened! We all followed him through the doorway and found ourselves in another bedroom. Wade tried to open the next door, but it wouldn't budge. "It's locked," he said, slamming his fist against it.

I tried to open it too, hoping that somehow it would magically work for me. But again, the door wouldn't budge. I tried to wedge my fingers into the crack and pry it open. "Ouch!" I groaned in pain, quickly giving up on that idea. My fingers were too sore.

This bedroom also had an adjoining bathroom with no windows. I checked the faucets in the sink and the shower. There wasn't any water. I opened the cupboard. It was empty.

Back in the bedroom, I saw a phone sitting on a shelf. It was exactly like the phone in the other bedroom. The walls and ceiling were also painted black. But the furniture was different.

There was a twin bunk bed with no pillows or blankets, a vanity with a circular mirror and a stool in front of it, a small square table with four chairs, a chest of drawers, a shelf, and lastly a rug on the floor. The furniture was made of wood. It was bulky and painted brown. It looked like it belonged in a log cabin or a child's bedroom, definitely not on a yacht.

Tasha began climbing up the ladder to the top bunk. It squeaked with every move she made, and I wondered if it was safe for her to climb on.

A smile spread across her face as she dangled her feet over

the edge. "I want to sleep up here tonight."

When was it going to be night? Was it night right now? If only we had a window to see the sky outside.

Charlotte searched the chest of drawers. "Empty," she groaned, slamming a drawer shut. "There's nothing in here."

Wade inspected the vanity. "There's nothing in here either."

The person on the phone promised us something to eat and drink, so where was it?

I looked over at Bellany. For some strange reason, she was standing in the middle of the bedroom, her eyes on the bottom bunk.

Charlotte collapsed onto a chair and laid her head down on the table. "I can't do this anymore!"

"Yes, you can," Wade said, rubbing her back. "We're gonna get through this. Together."

"Don't cry, Charlotte." Tasha patted the spot next to her on the bed. "You can come sit by me if you want. It's fun up here."

Charlotte's shoulders shook as she cried.

I guessed it was her turn to have a breakdown. At least she wasn't hurting herself like I did. I looked down and my hands. There was dried blood under my fingernails and scabs on my knuckles.

Wade wrapped his arms around Charlotte. He kept telling her that everything was going to be okay and that he loved her.

Witnessing this made me feel so lonely. I wished I had Cory here to comfort me.

Bellany kneeled down next to the bottom bunk and began searching along the side of the mattress. I wondered what she was looking for. Was there something stuffed inside it?

"Unbelievable!" Bellany said.

I walked over to see what she had found. It was just a small tear in the mattress. "Is something in there?"

"No, nothing's in there," Bellany replied. "But I've seen this mattress before. I've slept on this exact same bed." She placed a hand on the ladder and shook it, a squeaking noise filling the air again.

Charlotte pulled away from Wade, wiping tears off her face. "The same bed? What are you talking about?"

Bellany headed over to the vanity and sat down, her eyes meeting us through the reflection in the mirror. She looked like she had seen a ghost. "I've seen all of this furniture before. It was in my cabin when I stayed on Catalina Island." She spun around to face us. "I know who's holding us captive."

CHAPTER 34

Bellany

Everybody was eagerly waiting for me to explain why the furniture in this bedroom was so familiar to me. I planned on telling them the truth, knowing they were going to be furious.

But in an effort to deflect some of their anger and rage, I turned to Victoria, hoping she would help tell the story. "Remember that old woman I told you about named Shandy?"

"Who?" she replied, a blank look on her face.

How could Victoria not remember the stories about Shandy? Had she not been listening to me? "Shandy owned a summer camp on Catalina Island," I reminded her.

"That sounds kind of familiar."

"Victoria," I said, frustrated. "I told you how I barely managed to escape the island, because Shandy sent her men after me. You do remember that, don't you?"

Victoria tilted her head, brows furrowed. "You were a camp counselor... is that right?"

Finally that little brain of hers was starting to work.

"A camp counselor," Charlotte repeated, eyes wide. "I feel so bad for those kids."

I ignored her insult and continued with the story. "I was originally hired to work as a summer camp counselor, but it turned out Shandy canceled camp, because she had something else in mind. She gathered all the camp counselors together and offered us a chance to compete in a series of games. The prize for winning was ownership of Camp Sunshine and a substantial amount of money. But unfortunately, the team I was assigned to compete with wasn't very good. So in order to increase our chance of winning, we had to cheat."

"Cheating is bad," Tasha said, shaking her head, curls flying.

I gritted my teeth and forced a smile. "Yes, Tasha. Cheating is bad, and I'm really sorry that I did it."

"Yeah, right," Charlotte grumbled as she climbed up the squeaky bunk bed to sit next to Tasha.

"What else happened," Wade asked, placing his foot on the rung of the ladder and leaning against it.

"Shandy found out that I was the brains behind the whole operation."

"The brains?" Charlotte scoffed, rolling her eyes.

She was trying my patience. Again, I wished Wade wasn't here to protect her.

Wade's back stiffened, his eyes glued to me. "What happened after Shandy found out?"

I wasn't going to explain every little detail, just the main highlights. "Shandy threatened me. So I had to threaten her back."

Charlotte let out a loud sigh. "Of course you did."

I gritted my teeth, struggling to keep my temper under control. "Yes, I did. I was trying to save my life."

"Shandy was going to kill you?" Tasha asked, wide-eyed.

"Yes. She was mad at me for cheating, and ruining her games."

"What did you threaten her with?" Wade asked.

I lowered my gaze to the floor, acting like I was ashamed. "I threatened to blackmail her. I--"

"That's right," Victoria interrupted. "You discovered that Shandy murdered her husband. So you threatened to tell the police."

Wade let out a heavy sigh. "Are you still blackmailing her?"

"No, and I never did. But apparently she still thinks that I'm going to. And she's probably still mad that I ruined her games. She spent a lot of time, money, and effort on the whole thing."

"I remember you said that Shandy was a huge fan of the show, *Survivor*," Victoria said, finally contributing something worthwhile to the conversation. "The games were kind of her own version of that reality series, right?"

"Yes. She loves *Survivor*, and she loves playing games." I gestured around the bedroom. "I think we're stuck in another one of her games right now."

"Great..." Wade raked his fingers through his hair, grumbling. "We're all contenders in this psycho's elaborate game."

"A game?" Tasha asked. "What do we get if we win? A trip to Disney World?"

"Yeah, maybe," Charlotte replied, but her tone was unconvincing.

Silence filled the room like a thick fog as everybody digested this information. I was kind of surprised they weren't yelling and screaming at me.

CHAPTER 35

Victoria

Wade, Charlotte, Bellany, and I were huddled around the table, talking about Shandy. We kept our voices low so that Tasha couldn't hear us. She was on the top bunk pulling threads out of the mattress and singing to herself.

Wade and Charlotte wanted to know the kinds of games and challenges that Shandy had come up with in the past. After listening to Bellany's description, it was clear that our experience was much worse. Shandy was depriving us of food and water, and she was holding us against our will.

We had been so busy talking that we hadn't noticed Tasha climb down from the top bunk. When I turned around to check on her, she was gone. I jumped out of my chair, my heart racing. "Tasha! Where are you?"

"Here I am," she said as she walked back into the bedroom, holding a box of Cheerios.

"Where did that come from?" Charlotte gasped.

Tasha bounced on her toes, a smile on her face. "It was sitting on the bed in the other bedroom, and there's some milk too!"

We all raced into the other bedroom. I was hoping there would be more food than that. What I wanted most was some water, but I would gladly accept milk as a substitute--I was dying of thirst.

Wade didn't seem interested in the food. He went straight to the door and checked to see if it was unlocked. It wasn't.

"Someone must have delivered this while we were

distracted in the other bedroom," Charlotte said, taking the box of Cheerios from Tasha. She gave it a shake, and it sounded full.

There was a gallon of milk sitting on the bed, along with five bowls and spoons. I grabbed hold of the milk and ripped off the lid. Then a terrible odor filled the air, making me gag. I quickly capped the milk again. "It's spoiled!" I covered my mouth with my hand, fighting back the urge to throw up. Shandy promised to give us something to drink. But we couldn't drink spoiled milk!

Tasha screamed, and I thought maybe she was hurt. But there wasn't any blood. She hadn't fallen. What was wrong with her?

"Spoiled milk is one of her biggest fears," Charlotte said, wrapping her arms around her, but Tasha didn't want to be touched. She pushed her away.

I didn't know what to do to help her calm down, but I felt like I had to do something. She wouldn't stop screaming and crying.

"Look, Tasha." I picked up one of the bowls. "I'll pour you some cereal. You can eat it dry. It's still good that way." For some reason, telling her this only made her cry harder.

Wade grabbed the gallon of milk and headed to the other bedroom. When he returned, he no longer had it with him. I hoped he hadn't poured it down the drain. There was no water to wash it down with. It would stink up the entire bathroom and probably the bedroom too.

Wade and Charlotte tried to comfort Tasha and assure her that the milk was gone now. Bellany sat on the edge of the bed and did nothing to help. I wondered what was going on in that head of hers. Sometimes she seemed so detached from the rest of the world.

Tasha ran into the other bedroom. "It's still there!" I heard her scream. She came racing back to us, tears rolling down her face.

Charlotte turned to Wade. "Where did you put it?"

"In the shower."

"The shower? That's not a very good hiding place," Charlotte snapped.

"What did you want me to do with it? Pour it down the toilet without any water to flush it with? Do you know how bad that would stink?"

"Stop yelling at me!" Charlotte shouted, her face turning red. "You're making Tasha more upset!"

Wade stormed off, heading to the other bedroom. He slammed the door behind him. Loud bangs and crashes erupted, followed by a spray of glass shattering, then more crashes and bangs.

Tasha hugged the box of Cheerios to her chest and sat on the bed. She looked scared, but at least she wasn't crying anymore.

"He's acting just like his step brother," Charlotte said, irritated. "He needs to learn to control his temper."

I couldn't blame Wade for acting out. He had reached his breaking point, and we had all been there. Charlotte too. "I don't think anybody's thinking rationally right now," I said, in his defense. "We're all hungry and thirsty."

"Wade's behavior has nothing to do with that," she snapped. "He just can't be cooped up like this. He's used to driving all over the country, hunting down fugitives for his mom and stepfather."

"Wade!" Tasha called. "I'm gonna pour you some Cheerios. Come and get some!" She reached into the box and scooped out a handful, placing it into a bowl. I was so hungry, I didn't care that she was touching the food. I would gladly eat it anyway.

Bellany got up from the bed and walked over to the door. She knocked as she opened it. "Wade, can I come in?" Then she disappeared into the bedroom, pulling the door shut behind her.

The crashing and smashing stopped. I looked at Charlotte, wondering if she was going to go in there too. But Charlotte was busy helping Tasha divide up the Cheerios equally.

My stomach grumbled. I was so hungry and wanted to

gorge myself, but I also wanted to know what was going on in the other bedroom. What was Bellany doing with Wade? What was she saying to him?

I headed for the door. "I'll be right back."

When I walked into the bedroom, I couldn't believe my eyes. The chest of drawers had been completely demolished. A handle was lying on the floor next to my shoe. Pieces of wood were scattered everywhere.

The vanity was upside down. The table no longer had legs, and the chairs were now just a pile of wood. The mirror had been shattered into a thousand pieces. Remnants were scattered everywhere, reflecting off the light like diamonds.

Wade hadn't touched the phone though. It was still completely intact, plugged into the wall, and sitting on the shelf.

After a quick survey of the destruction, I shifted my attention to Wade and Bellany. Instinctively, I pulled the door shut behind me.

Bellany and Wade were sitting on the bottom bunk together, and Wade wasn't wearing a shirt anymore. Upon closer inspection, I discovered why. His hands were cut up and bleeding. Bellany had ripped his shirt into shreds and was using them as bandages.

The wounds on my hands were nowhere near as bad as his. Wade was bleeding a lot. The blood had already soaked through the fabric. Did he need stitches?

I headed over to the bed, grateful I had tennis shoes on to protect the bottoms of my feet. "Is there anything I can do to help?" I asked, and then I noticed the bottom of Wade's feet. He wasn't wearing shoes and his feet were all cut up.

The door banged. "Hey! Unlock the door!" Charlotte called from the other side.

"It's not locked," I replied, heading back to the door. I turned the knob to pull it open, but it wouldn't budge. I kept pulling and twisting. "Something's wrong. I can't open it."

Wade appeared at my side and tried to open the door. He punched it with his fist, right by my face. "You locked the door!"

he shouted at me.

I was so scared, I thought I might pee my pants. But my bladder was completely empty. "I swear, I didn't! I don't know how this happened. I didn't lock it!"

Charlotte was freaking out on the other side of the door, crying hysterically.

Wade tried to open it again, but it was no use. Then he took a deep breath to calm down. "Babe, we can make it through this," he said, both hands pressed against the door. "We're not that far apart from each other. You're gonna be okay."

"I can't do this anymore!" Charlotte cried from the other side.

She wasn't the only one. I couldn't do this either. I laid down on the bottom bunk, placing my hands over my ears to block out the noise. Then suddenly it all stopped. Everything went eerily silent, except for a distant ringing. It wasn't coming from our phone. It was from the phone in the other bedroom. Was Shandy calling, or was it Cory?

CHAPTER 36

Victoria

Wade, Bellany, and I hovered at the door, trying to listen to what was going on in the other bedroom. But Charlotte's voice was too muffled. We couldn't hear anything she was saying.

Wade banged on the door. "Tasha!" he called.

"What?" she asked from the other side.

"Who's on the phone?" he asked.

"It's Cory and Gemma," she replied.

"What are they saying?" Wade asked, pressing his ear to the door.

"Charlotte told them about Shandy, and now she's telling them about how we got separated. She said she thinks Bellany and Victoria are big meanies, because they locked the door on purpose. She thinks they're working for Shandy."

I always hated it when people accused me of things they had no proof of. I ran away from home for this exact reason.

Chantel had written horrible things about me in her diary, calling me a psycho and a stalker. She accused me of sending her death threats. But she couldn't prove it, and neither could the cops.

So when the cops accused me of killing Chantel, I was shocked. I asked them what kind of proof they had. All they had were the death threats on Chantel's phone and the stuff she had written in her diary.

But there's a huge difference between threatening to kill someone and actually going through with it. People made death threats all the time out of anger, jealousy, or whatever. That didn't make them murderers.

All I wanted was for Chantel to break up with Xavier. The threats I sent made that perfectly clear. If Chantel wanted to live, then she would have to dump him. I knew that Xavier liked me. I felt confident he and I would be together if Chantel would just get out of our way.

Wade tapped me on the shoulder, ripping me from my thoughts. What was he going to do? Hit me?

"Wade, I'm just like you," I said with pleading eyes, my heart racing. "I'm a prisoner here too. Why would I lock the door? It makes no sense."

He stared at me a few beats, then his eyes shifted to Bellany.

She threw her hands up. "I was with you on the bed, bandaging your cuts. I didn't touch the door."

His shoulders relaxed. "Yeah. I know. Sorry I overreacted."

He began cleaning up the mess, piling all the pieces of broken furniture in the corner of the room. Bellany and I helped. I didn't really want to, but I felt like I should.

I couldn't believe the amount of destruction he had caused. It was like a tornado had torn through here.

My energy was super low, and I had to sit down on the bottom bunk to rest. It kind of irritated me that there were no chairs to sit on anymore, thanks to Wade's angry outburst.

I didn't care how cute he was with his bare chest and bulging muscles. I thought he was a jerk for destroying the furniture. It was all we had. We were stuck here.

As I sat on the bed watching them clean, I noticed that Bellany couldn't keep her eyes off of him. I suspected she was doing it on purpose. She wanted Wade to know that she was admiring him. This was her attempt at flirting. I had seen her do it many times before.

Bellany bent down right in front of him to pick up a piece of glass.

"Don't!" Wade said. "You might cut yourself." He raised his bandaged hands.

"Oh, right. Thanks," Bellany said with a half-smile, leaving the glass on the floor.

The corner of his mouth turned up, and I immediately began to worry that maybe Bellany's flirting was having an affect on him. I could not let this happen! If the two of them got together, I'd be the odd person out. And I knew from experience that this was not the desirable position to be in.

The longer Bellany's flirting continued, the angrier I got, until I just couldn't keep my mouth shut anymore. "Bellany, he's engaged to Charlotte."

She shot me a look. "I'm aware of that."

"Then stop flirting."

"Hold on," Wade said, interrupting us, his eyes on the door. "Why can't I hear them anymore?" He pounded on the door. "Hey! Charlotte. Are you there? Tasha? Why are you so quiet over there? What's going on?"

Several seconds of silence passed without a reply. I couldn't hear any muffled voices either. There was no noise at all.

"Are they asleep?" Bellany asked.

I got up from the bed and headed to the door. I pressed my ear against it. Silence. I didn't know how long it had been like this. I hadn't been paying attention.

Wade pounded on the door again, this time harder. "Charlotte! Are you all right? Tasha! Somebody answer me!"

Nobody answered.

CHAPTER 37

Victoria

The three of us banged on the door, calling for Tasha and Charlotte. We were at it for a while, but we never heard a word from them. It was deathly silent in there, and Wade was really starting to lose it.

Every ounce of strength and energy that Wade had inside him was being utilized to try to break down the door. Bellany and I backed away, giving him space, as he repeatedly kicked it. When that didn't work, he tried slamming his body against it. But the door was impenetrable. He needed to stop before he hurt himself.

I leaned into Bellany's ear. "How much longer do you think he's going to do this?"

She shrugged.

"He's not going to be able to break down that door," I whispered. "It's impossible."

"I'm aware of that," she replied in a snarky tone. "Just like I'm aware he's engaged."

I moved to the other end of the room, giving her space since she was mad at me. I stood there watching Wade pick up every heavy broken piece of furniture and slam it against the door.

Eventually Bellany came over to stand next to me, which kind of surprised me. I thought she was going to keep holding a grudge. "He's afraid they're dead," she whispered.

"They couldn't be dead," I said, refusing to believe it. "They probably just accidentally got locked in the bathroom or something."

Bellany made a face. "If they were in the bathroom, they'd be banging on the door, and we'd be able to hear them."

She was probably right. The only other possibility I could think of was that maybe they got out. But then I realized that couldn't be true. If they got out, then they would have banged on the door to let us know. They wouldn't just leave without saying something to us. Unless... "Maybe Shandy had her henchmen move them to another room."

"Or maybe they're dead," Bellany whispered again. She narrowed her eyes, staring at the locked door, deep in thought.

Wade finally took a break from trying to break down the door and began shouting Tasha and Charlotte's name over and over again.

Bellany approached him cautiously. "Hey, Wade..."

"What?" he asked, catching his breath. His entire body was glistening with sweat, even his hair was wet. The bandages on his hands were completely soaked with blood.

"I wonder if Shandy moved Charlotte and Tasha to another room," Bellany said.

What? That's what I said and she totally dismissed me. How could she pretend like it was her idea?

The phone started ringing, ripping through the air like thunder. And this time, it was the phone in our room.

Wade raced to pick it up. "Where's Charlotte--where is she? Where's Tasha? What did you do to them?"

Bellany pressed the speaker button.

"It's time to play another game," the eerie robotic voice said, making me shudder. I wished Shandy would just speak in her normal voice, because this one was freaking me out. "Spin the bottle," the robotic voice continued. "This is a game that Bellany is quite familiar with. But this time we're going to play by my rules."

CHAPTER 38

Bellany

Spin the bottle. I knew the game all too well. But I usually played it by my own set of rules.

"Listen carefully," the robotic voice announced as Wade, Victoria, and I crowded around the phone. "I can see everything you do. I'm watching you. So I'll know if you fail to follow my directions."

I scanned the ceiling, searching for cameras. The black paint made it impossible to see them. Plus the ceilings were high and the lighting was dim. If I were to stand on the top bunk, I could touch the ceiling, but only right above it.

"I have Charlotte and Tasha with me," the robotic voice said. "If you fail to follow my directions, then both of them will be killed."

Victoria and I exchanged looks.

"You better not hurt them!" Wade shouted, the vein on the side of his head bulging.

"You are in no position to threaten me!" the robotic voice chided him.

Wade's face twisted with rage. He picked up a scrap piece of furniture and snapped it in half. Splinters flew in every direction as he continued ripping the wood apart with his bare hands, shredding it into pieces. I stepped aside, giving him some space.

"You must do everything I tell you," the robotic voice said. "Understand?"

"Yes, we understand. We'll do what you say," Victoria

replied, her voice shaking.

Speak for yourself, Victoria.

Wade picked up another scrap piece of furniture and threw it across the room, smashing it against the wall.

"Before we start playing spin the bottle," the robotic voice announced, "all three of you must step inside the bathroom and close the door. You must stay there until you count to three hundred. Then you may come back out, and I will provide you with further instructions."

My mind was only focused on one thing--getting out of here! And I already had a plan to do it. But I was going to need Wade and Victoria's help.

"What are you waiting for?" the robotic voice asked. "You heard me. Get into the bathroom. Now!"

I was the last one to enter the bathroom. Wade shut the door behind me and sat down in front of it. He clasped his hands together like he was praying. His lips moved, but he didn't speak out loud. As I watched his mouth, I realized he was counting.

"Wade," I whispered with urgency, bending down to look him in the eye. "We should barge into the bedroom and attack whoever's in there. We have to escape while we still have the chance."

Wade shook his head, eyes narrowing as he continued to count.

"Bellany," Victoria whispered, arms folded tightly across her chest. "Have you forgotten that Charlotte and Tasha's lives are at stake? We can't risk losing them."

Apparently Victoria had forgotten that she wasn't supposed to gang up on me anymore. She was supposed to be on my side.

I took a breath to calm down. "We can do this," I said, hoping they would listen to me. "Whoever's in there right now opened the door, which means we can escape."

"No, it's too risky..." Victoria said.

Wade glared at me as he muttered each number between gritted teeth. He was blocking the door, and there was no other way out.

"This might be our only chance," I said, my eyes bouncing between him and Victoria. "It's now or never."

"What if they have guns?" Victoria asked, wide-eyed. "What if they shoot us?"

The gun argument was a good one, but I had something better. "Shandy can't be trusted. If we stay, our lives will be in danger. For all we know, Tasha and Charlotte might already be dead. And we're going to be next if we don't escape now!"

The corners of Wade's mouth turned down. "They're not dead. They're still alive."

We hadn't heard a shred of evidence to back that up. We hadn't heard their voices. We hadn't seen them. But if Wade wanted to believe that they were still alive, then fine. I wasn't going to argue with him. "Wade, once we get out of here, then we'll search the yacht. We'll find them and rescue them. But we have to break out of here now, before it's too late!"

"No!" he hissed, his voice low. "I don't want Charlotte and Tasha to die. And if you open this door, that's exactly what's going to happen. They'll see us on the cameras, and they'll kill them!"

Wade and Victoria were making a huge mistake. But once they realized this, it would be too late. I stood there watching them count, growing angrier by the second.

Victoria cleared her throat. "Time's up. I counted to three hundred."

"Me too," Wade said, finally moving out of the way.

When we entered the bedroom again, I ran to the door and turned the knob. It wouldn't budge. I checked the other door too. It was also locked.

A mixture of frustration and anger was boiling inside me. I wanted to yell and scream at Wade and Victoria. They had passed up the perfect opportunity to break out of here. They should have listened to me!

"What's this?" Wade asked, standing over a cardboard box. He bent down and opened it. "There's water in here!" He reached inside and pulled out six water bottles. The last thing he pulled out of the box was an empty wine bottle.

Spin the bottle was the game I had played with the other camp counselors when I was on Catalina Island. I used this game to manipulate my team members into cheating.

"I'm so thirsty!" Victoria ripped the lid off of one of the water bottles.

"I wouldn't do that if I were you," warned the robotic voice.

"Why not?" she asked, her eyes darting around, looking up at the ceiling.

"Those are for the game. You must sit in a circle first and place the empty wine bottle in the center. It's time to play, spin the bottle."

The three of us sat down, and Wade placed the wine bottle on the floor.

"Why don't you go first, Wade," the robotic voice said. "Go ahead. Give the bottle a spin."

"And then what?" he asked, staring at it like it was a grenade about to go off.

We had already heard about the twisted games Cory and Gemma were forced to play. They were lucky to still be alive. What was going to happen to us? Wade and Victoria had to be wondering this.

"The rules are simple. Whoever the wine bottle ends up pointing to gets to choose one of the bottles of water to drink," the robotic voice said.

The game couldn't be that simple. There had to be a catch.

Wade placed a hand on the wine bottle. "Is that it?"

"Why can't we just drink some of the water now?" Victoria asked, staring at the glistening bottles of water, licking her lips.

"Because, my dear, it might be poisoned," the robotic voice chuckled.

And there it is, I thought to myself. The catch. I rose to my feet and backed away.

The color drained from Wade's face. He looked like he was going to be sick. "You're gonna make us play this game until one of us drinks poison?"

"Sit down, Bellany!" the robotic voice shouted.

I returned to the circle, or rather the triangle, and sat down. But I was not going to drink any of the water.

"Now listen to me closely," the robotic voice said. "After you choose a water bottle, you must drink all of it--every single drop. The game will continue until at least one of the poisoned water bottles has been consumed."

Or one of us quits, I thought to myself. "How many are poisoned?" I asked, scanning the bottles.

"I'm not going to answer that question," the robotic voice responded.

"What will happen to us if we drink the poison?" Victoria asked, hugging her knees to her chest.

"Your mouth and throat will burn, then your stomach, followed by a rather unpleasant death."

Victoria gasped, cupping a hand over her mouth. "I don't want to die!"

You should have thought of that sooner, Victoria. You should have listened to me!

"If you don't want to die, then don't play, my dear," the robotic voice replied. "But if that's the choice you're going to make, then I'm going to have to kill Tasha and Charlotte. Is that what you want, Victoria? Do you want me to kill them?"

"No! Please don't!"

"As you wish. Let the game begin!" the robotic voice announced. "Wade, you can go first."

Wade immediately gave the wine bottle a spin. He didn't even hesitate.

Victoria whimpered and cried as the wine bottle started to slow. It almost landed on her, but the yacht was rocking, providing it with a little more momentum. It made another full turn and finally came to a stop.

I gritted my teeth. The wine bottle was pointing between

me and Victoria. It hadn't landed on anyone. "What exactly are the rules when this kind of thing happens?" I asked.

"Victoria," the robotic voice said, making her jump.

Tears filled her eyes. "It didn't land on me!" she insisted, shaking her head. "It's closer to Bellany!"

I glared at her, surprised by her audacity. She knew she was lying--we all knew it. The evidence was right in front of our faces.

The yacht rocked again, and the bottle rolled across the floor to Wade.

"Victoria," the robotic voice said. "I do not tolerate cheaters. If you try something like that again, you will suffer the consequences."

"I'm sorry," she cried.

"It's your turn to spin, Victoria," the robotic voice announced.

Wade passed the wine bottle, and she reached for it with a shaky hand.

"I have a question," I said, scanning the ceiling. "What if Victoria spins the bottle and it lands on herself? Does that mean that she drinks the water?" My gaze returned to Victoria. She should quit while she still has the chance.

"Yes, that's correct," came the reply. "Victoria, it's your turn."

"Please don't make me do this!" she begged.

She didn't have to play. She could choose to quit right now and let Charlotte and Tasha die. The choice was an easy one to make.

"Spin it!" Wade slammed his fist on the floor. "Spin the bottle, Victoria!"

She held the wine bottle in her lap, staring down at it.

"If you're quitting, then Charlotte and Tasha will die," the robotic voice warned. "You have thirty seconds to decide."

"Victoria!" Wade slammed his fist again. "Spin it! Spin it now!"

Quit the game, I thought to myself, eager to see what she

would choose.

"Spin it!" he shouted, face turning red. His entire body was rigid. He looked like he was about to attack her.

Be brave and stand up to him, Victoria. Your life depends on it.

She set the wine bottle down and gave it a spin, her eyes glued to it.

My gaze shifted to Wade. He wasn't looking at the wine bottle. He was looking at me. Did he know that I would refuse to play? Had he figured that out?

Victoria let out a whimper when the wine bottle finally stopped spinning. It pointed directly at Wade and remained stationary for at least three seconds. Then the yacht rocked, shifting the bottle again, and it rolled across the floor.

Too bad it hadn't pointed to Victoria.

"Looks like we have a winner!" the robotic voice announced.

"I'm so sorry, Wade," Victoria cried, reaching for him.

The robotic voice chuckled. "It's time to quench your thirst, Wade. I'm sure you're just dying to drink some of the water, aren't you?"

He immediately got up and walked over to the bunk bed, muttering under his breath. He sat down next to the water bottles, trying to decide which one to choose. I couldn't believe he was actually going to go through with this. He didn't have to do it. He didn't have to die.

"I'm so sorry!" Victoria cried.

"It's not your fault," he said, selecting one of the bottles.

He was right. It wasn't Victoria's fault. It was his for playing the game. "You don't have to drink it," I said, curious to hear his response.

"Yes, I do. If I don't survive, tell Charlotte that I love her." Wade unscrewed the lid, tossed it onto the floor, and started gulping down the water.

Victoria and I sat there watching him drink the entire bottle in a matter of seconds.

How long would it take before the poison kicked in? Was his mouth burning? Was he in pain?

Wade shifted his eyes, looking directly at me. The corner of his mouth twitched, and I waited for him to say something. But he didn't. He just kept staring at me.

"It's your turn, Bellany," the robotic voice announced.

"I'm not playing." I picked up the wine bottle and threw it as hard as I could, smashing it against the wall. The glass shattered, spraying everywhere.

Wade groaned, clutching his throat. He fell heavily, hitting the floor with a bone-jarring thud. Then laid on his side, writhing in pain. The question had been answered. His water bottle was poisoned.

"Help him, Bellany!" Victoria cried. "Save him!"

"What makes you think that I can save him?" Had she lost her mind?

Wade groaned, breathing heavily as the poison continued to suck the life out of him. His skin grew cold and clammy. He foamed at the mouth, until he finally stopped moving.

Victoria's cries filled the air. I didn't know why she was so upset. Wade meant nothing to her. She barely knew him.

"Victoria!" I finally snapped at her. "He's dead, and there's nothing we can do about it. Stop crying!"

She buried her face in her hands, shoulders shaking.

"Why are you so upset? Did you not understand how this game worked? The rules were explained to you. One of us was going to die. You're lucky it wasn't you."

Victoria laid on the bottom bunk, sobbing. "But what if I die next? If I die, then I'll never get the chance to see my parents again. I'll never get to apologize for running away. They're probably worried sick about me. They'll never know what happened to me--"

"Shut up!" I shouted. "That's enough, Victoria! I'm tired of listening to your whiny voice!"

Her tears kept flowing. "What if I never see Cory again?"

Cory? What was she talking about? "Why are you worried

about Cory?"

"I love him."

My mouth dropped open. "You love him?"

"Yes. He's my soulmate."

"Your soulmate?"

"Yes!" she insisted. "He's always so sweet and kind to me. He's the man of my dreams, and I know he feels the same way about me."

I couldn't believe what I was hearing. "Has Cory told you that he likes you? Has he kissed you, held your hand, professed his love for you, anything like that?"

She hugged her knees to her chest, shaking her head. "Not yet. He just hasn't had the right opportunity."

Under normal circumstances, I doubted Victoria would have admitted her true feelings about Cory to me. But she had just seen Wade die. She was completely delirious.

Victoria's eyes widened. "Did you hear that?"

"Hear what?" I shrugged.

"I thought I heard a noise." She headed straight towards the door that connected the two bedrooms. She turned the doorknob. "Bellany! It's unlocked!"

As soon as Victoria walked through the door, it slammed shut behind her. When I tried to open it and go in after her, I couldn't. It was locked. I pounded my fist against the door. "Victoria! The door's locked! I can't get in!"

She didn't respond. There was absolutely no noise coming from the other side of the door. A chill crept up my spine as I slowly turned around. Wade's lifeless body lying on the floor about ten feet away from me.

CHAPTER 39

Victoria

When I woke up, I felt groggy and disoriented. As I looked around the room, my memory slowly started to come back to me. I remembered Wade drinking poison. I remembered watching him die. My eyes searched the bedroom, and I realized I was alone. Where's Bellany?

I walked over to the connecting door. When I twisted the doorknob, it opened.

Bellany sat up when she saw me. "Where have you been?" she asked, and she sounded irritated. Then she pushed past me, heading through the doorway.

I didn't follow her. I stood there frozen, staring at Wade's dead body lying on the floor. How I wished it had just been a nightmare. I wished it wasn't real.

I felt a hand on my arm. "Come on," Bellany said, pulling me back into the bedroom.

My head felt foggy, like I couldn't think straight. I sat on the bed, hoping the sensation would go away.

"What happened to you?" Bellany asked.

"I don't know. The last thing I remember was walking in here, the door slamming shut, and then everything went black. I must have passed out or something."

She shot me a look. "You passed out?"

"Yeah, I guess I must have. When I woke up I was lying on the bed."

Bellany bent down and looked under the beds. Then she checked inside the bathroom. "The box of Cheerios is gone," she said through gritted teeth.

Was she accusing me of eating it?

The connecting door slammed shut, a loud bang echoing off the walls. "Who did that?" I gasped, holding my hand over my heart as it hammered in my chest.

Bellany tried to open it, but she couldn't. She kicked it, grumbling something under her breath, breathing hard. She walked across the room and sat down on the other bed, her hands balled into fists. She looked furious.

"Should we call Cory?" I asked, unsure what else we could do. It had been a while since we talked to him.

"Why, so you can profess your love to him?"

My mouth dropped open. Then I remembered what I had said to Bellany, and my cheeks started to burn. "Nevermind, we don't know his number anyway."

"It can't be that hard to figure out. Go ahead and try if you want to," she said, her eyes narrowing. "I know you're dying to talk to him."

Bellany was already angry, and I didn't want to make things worse. "No. No, I'm good. I'm sure he'll eventually call when he wants to."

"He'll call to talk to his soulmate," she said, mockingly.

I wished I had never said anything about Cory to her. Why did I open my big mouth?

We both sat in silence for a long time. My lips were chapped, and it hurt to swallow. I was so thirsty. My stomach was empty. I wanted to distract myself from the pain and discomfort. I wondered if Bellany would talk to me, or if she was too mad. "What do you think Shandy's going to do with Wade's body?" I asked.

Bellany shrugged. "No idea."

"Are you sad that he died?" I asked, wondering how she felt about it. Did she miss him?

"Of course I'm sad."

But was she, I wondered. Bellany hadn't shed a single tear. She didn't seem upset at all when it happened, which I thought was super strange, especially since she had been flirting with him. "If you're so sad, then why didn't you cry?"

She looked at me, her expression blank. "There are five stages of grief, Victoria."

"Oh really? What stage are you in?"

"Denial," she said, flippantly.

"Denial? How could you be in denial? We both saw what happened. Wade's dead."

She lifted a shoulder. "I'm just not ready to accept it yet."

Her lack of emotion was bizarre. "I thought you liked him. I mean... you flirted with him."

Bellany's mouth dropped open. "You thought I liked Wade? Please," she said, rolling her eyes. "He's not my type."

"I know what I saw," I insisted, wondering why she wouldn't admit it. "You flirted with him."

She shook her head slowly, her eyes never leaving mine. "I was just being friendly."

I wished she would quit gaslighting me. "No, you weren't just being friendly. You liked him--I know you did!"

"I was only trying to manipulate him, Victoria. I can't believe you really thought I liked him. You're so gullible."

My heart pounded faster as my aggravation continued to grow. I was tired of her treating me like I was stupid. I wasn't going to let her get away with it anymore. "I hate you!"

Her upper lip curled. "You hate me? Are you in third grade or something? Grow up."

I couldn't stand her condescending attitude anymore. Every word out of her mouth was either an insult or a lie, and I was sick of it. "You don't care about anybody except for yourself."

Her eyebrows shot up. "You think I don't care?"

I knew for a fact she didn't care. She was the most selfish person I had ever met. "You don't have normal feelings like everybody else. You pretend like you do, but you don't. And that's because you're a sociopath!"

A line formed between Bellany's eyebrows, her gaze cold and menacing. "What about you, Victoria? Do you have feelings like everybody else?"

"What kind of question is that? Of course I do!"

She smirked. "Then why is it that every time you talk about your friend, Chantel, you never seem upset. You never once shed a tear." Bellany propped her chin on her fist, eyes drilling through me. "Is that because you don't feel sad about her being gone?"

"Of course I feel sad--I feel horrible!" I said, defensively. "You don't know how many times I've cried over losing her. She was my best friend."

"That's doubtful." Bellany chuckled, a grin on her face. "You sent her death threats. You wanted her to die, and your wish came true."

My fingers curled into shaking fists. "Why are you bringing this up now? This has nothing to do with--"

"Yes, it does," she interrupted me. "You think I'm a sociopath? Well, I think you better look in the mirror, Victoria. Only a sociopath would send their best friend death threats."

I glared at her, wishing I could smack that grin off her face. "So what? I sent her death threats. That doesn't mean anything. You know why I did it."

Bellany's wicked smile grew wider. "Let's review, shall we?" She laced her fingers together, over her lap. "You sent Chantel death threats, because you were jealous of her relationship with her boyfriend. You wanted Xavier to be with you, not her."

She unlaced her fingers and scooted to the edge of the bed, placing both feet on the floor. "I know what you did, Victoria." Bellany walked across the room, closing the distance between us. But I wasn't afraid of her--not anymore! If she was going to attack me, I was ready. I was going to fight back.

Bellany took another step closer, but I didn't move. I kept my feet firmly planted. "Here's what I think really happened." Bellany jabbed a finger in my face. "You shot Chantel on purpose."

"No, I didn't. It was an accident." I had already explained

this to Bellany, many times before.

I had told her how I was just trying to scare Chantel. I was trying to bully her into breaking up with Xavier. But she refused. Chantel wasn't intimidated by me. She thought I wouldn't pull the trigger. So I decided I was only going to fire one shot, just to scare her. But Chantel moved right when I pulled the trigger. It wasn't my fault. She should have held still like I told her to.

Bellany stood eye to eye with me, her hot breath on my face. "I know you better than you know yourself, Victoria. Which is why I know you killed Chantel on purpose. Just admit it!"

My chest tightened, and it was getting hard for me to breathe. I wished Bellany would back away and give me some space. "Stop saying that! It's not true!"

As I stood there staring into Bellany's eyes, I couldn't help but notice how dull and empty they were, just like her soul.

"You killed your best friend so that you could be with her boyfriend."

My fingernails dug into my palms. "I already told you what happened. I aimed at Chantel to miss. I just wanted to scare her."

Bellany shook her head slowly, never taking her ice cold eyes off of me. "I know what a good shot you are, Victoria. I've witnessed it. You took out Lane with a single bullet from a distance of at least a hundred feet away. Remember?"

"Of course I remember. He was pointing an arrow at you, about to shoot you with it, because he found out that you stole his money."

"Exactly. And you killed him with one bullet. You are an excellent shot, Victoria."

Why wasn't she grateful for what I had done for her? Why was she treating me like this? "I shot him to save your life. You're welcome!" I said through gritted teeth.

"A hundred feet. One bullet," Bellany said, angling her chin. "How far away were you when you shot Chantel? Ten feet? Five? Less? You told me you were in the same room as her, so you had to be close. And you expect me to believe that you shot her by accident?"

My fingernails dug deeper into the palms of my hands, but I didn't feel any pain. I was too angry.

"Admit it, Victoria!" Bellany hissed. "Deep down inside, you wanted to end Chantel's life. And that desire kept festering inside you until you couldn't ignore it anymore. You planned everything out ahead of time. Her murder wasn't an accident. It was premeditated!"

"No, It wasn't! She was my best friend!"

"If Xavier really wanted to be with you, then he would have broken up with Chantel. You do realize that, don't you?"

I balled up my fist, trying to decide if I should hit her. "Shut up!"

"You killed your best friend over a guy. A guy who didn't even like you."

I turned to walk away, because I knew if I didn't, I'd punch Bellany right in the face. But then I felt fingers wrap around my arm, squeezing tight, and I couldn't hold back any longer. I spun around, throwing a hard right, aiming at her nose. But she moved too fast, and I made contact with her forearm instead. The next thing I knew, I was flat on my back, my head landing on the floor with a loud crack. The pain was so intense, I couldn't breathe.

Bellany's eyes bored through me like hot knives. "You want to know what I was doing during the day while you were hanging out at Cory's house, stuffing your fat face, and gossiping about me? I was at the gym, learning how to fight, and I guess those lessons paid off, didn't they!"

I rolled onto my side and removed my hand from the back of my head, expecting to see blood. Luckily there wasn't any, but the pain wouldn't relent. I slowly pushed myself up off the floor, feeling light-headed, and climbed onto the bed.

I must have fallen asleep, or passed out again--I wasn't sure which. But when I woke up, I felt a huge bump on the back of my head. It hurt so bad, I wanted to cry.

"You've been out for a long time," Bellany said from across the room. She was sitting on the other bed, watching me.

"What do you want?"

"I need to tell you something." She got up and started walking toward me.

If she was going to try to attack me again, I wasn't going to just sit here and let her do it. I moved to the opposite side of the bed, about to jump to my feet.

"Victoria, I'm not going to hurt you. I need to tell you something. It's important."

I wondered if something had happened while I was unconscious. I glanced around the bedroom. But everything looked the same. "Don't come any closer," I said, holding up my hand.

"I need to whisper it in your ear." She glanced up at the ceiling. "So nobody else can hear."

My curiosity was piqued. I had to know what this was about.

CHAPTER 40

Victoria

Bellany sat down next to me and leaned into my ear. "I found a listening device on the floor, underneath the bed. It's really small, you can hardly see it."

My stomach dropped, and I instinctively stuck a finger in my own ear. But there was nothing there. I checked the other ear too. Nothing.

She pushed her hair back, tucking it behind her ear to show me.

As I leaned in and saw the tiny device wedged inside her ear, my heart skipped a beat. She was telling me the truth! "Holy crap!" I blurted out.

I scanned the ceiling, wondering if Shandy was watching and listening to us. Had she figured out what was going on? Did she know what Bellany had in her possession?

She leaned into my ear again. "I'm hearing men speak in Spanish," she whispered. "I have no idea what they're saying, but I figure I'll eventually hear someone say something in English. And I know I'll hear Shandy's voice soon. I just haven't heard it yet."

I held out my hand, eager to hear this for myself. "Let me listen?"

She shot me a look, shaking her head. "No!"

I wished that I spoke Spanish, then she would have had no choice but to give it to me. "I just want to listen for a minute," I said, hoping she'd reconsider.

"Why?" She cocked her head. "Because it's yours. Did it fall out of your ear when I tackled you to the ground?"

My stomach dipped. "What? Of course not!"

"I think it's kind of strange how this just magically appeared on the floor, don't you?" She scanned my face, looking for signs of deception, which made me even more nervous.

"Maybe it was there the whole time and you just didn't see it."

"It wasn't," Bellany hissed. "I know, because I checked every inch of this bedroom."

I felt like the very air around me had been sucked out of existence. How could I convince her to believe me? "Well, I don't know how it got there. It wasn't from me! I've never seen that before in my life."

"Shh!" She placed a finger to her lips, making me flinch. I thought she was going to hit me.

I followed her gaze to the wall. What was she looking at? There was nothing there.

"What's going on?" she whispered, still staring at the same spot for some strange reason.

"What?" I whispered, my heart speeding up in anticipation.

Her brows furrowed. "The voices stopped."

I wanted to hear this for myself. "Let me listen to it."

"No!"

The phone rang, cutting through the tension. Bellany and I hopped off the bed, racing to answer it. I got to it first and picked up the receiver, surprised I had beaten her. But then she pressed the speaker button, immediately deflating my victory.

"Hello," Bellany said.

"Bellany?"

A wave of relief washed over me. It was Gemma. Was Cory still with her?

"Yes, it's me?" Bellany replied.

"I'm here too," I said. "Is Cory there?"

"Yes, he's here," Gemma replied.

"Are you guys okay?" Bellany asked.

"We're fine. The person on the phone told us to call you. They're going to move us to your room. We're all going to be together."

The corners of my mouth turned up, and I realized I was smiling. I hadn't smiled in the longest time. "That's great news!"

"Let me talk to Tasha," Cory said. "Tasha, can you hear me?"

The smile fell from my face. I didn't want to be the one to tell him. I knew it would break his heart.

"Cory..." Bellany said, hesitating. "Tasha isn't here anymore. We don't know where she is."

"What?" he gasped. "What do you mean, you don't know where she is? What happened to her?"

I knew how much Cory loved his sister. It must have been killing him to be separated from her. I wished I had the answers he was looking for. "We got separated into a different bedroom from her and Charlotte," I explained. "It happened a while ago."

"Yeah, but you're in the same room as them again," Cory replied. "I dialed the same number. So where are they?"

"We don't know," Bellany replied. "They disappeared shortly after we got separated."

"But at least Tasha is with Charlotte, so she's not alone," I added, hoping that would comfort him.

Several beats of silence passed, and I wondered if the call had been disconnected.

"Did you hear any screaming?" Cory asked, his voice low. "Were there any sounds of distress?"

"No, nothing like that," I replied. "We didn't hear any commotion at all."

"Where's Wade?" Gemma asked, and I looked at Bellany, unsure what to say.

"Is he there, or did he disappear too?" Cory asked.

I didn't want to be the one to tell them. I hoped Bellany would do it. I looked at her with pleading eyes.

She nodded. "He's not with us anymore."

"He disappeared?" Gemma asked.

My stomach felt like it was being tied into knots. I bit my lip and stared at Bellany, wondering what she was going to say.

"He's in the other bedroom. We got separated from him."

I wished Bellany would just tell them the truth and get it over with.

"So he's by himself?" Cory asked.

I nudged her shoulder, eyes wide.

Bellany took a deep breath. "I have some bad news…" She went on to explain everything that happened.

I expected Gemma and Cory to call her a liar or to blame her for what had happened. But surprisingly they didn't. Not once did they question the validity of Bellany's story. Not once did they ask me to verify it either.

Instead, they reminded us about how they had already taken part in Shandy's crazy games. They knew from experience how serious they were. They could've died too.

"We should probably hang up now," Cory said. He sounded exhausted. "But before we go, there's something you both have to do." He cleared his throat. "The person on the phone said that you both have to go into the bathroom and shut the door. You're supposed to stay in there and wait until we knock on the bathroom door to let you know that we're there. Then you can come out."

"How long will that take?" I asked, already feeling anxious. I didn't want to be stuck in that bathroom again with Bellany. I feared I would have a panic attack.

"I don't know," Cory replied. "I assume it will be quick."

"Yeah, so don't open the door until we get there and knock," Gemma said, her voice tense. "If you come out of the bathroom before we knock, they won't let us be together. They'll separate us again. And keep us that way. It's really important that you do this."

I chewed on my fingernail as I gazed toward the bathroom. I wished small spaces didn't bother me so much.

Bellany rested a hand on my shoulder. "It's gonna be okay, Victoria."

"See you soon," Cory said, and he sounded nervous.

"We'll be waiting in the bathroom," Bellany replied.

After we hung up, Bellany headed straight to the bathroom. But I didn't follow. My feet wouldn't move. My heart was slamming against my ribs. I didn't know if I could go in there again.

"Victoria, come on."

"I feel like I'm gonna freak out. I feel like I'm gonna lose it!"

"Close your eyes," Bellany said, calmly. "Keep them closed, and I'll lead you into the bathroom. Just don't open them. Got it?"

I closed my eyes as she took me by the hand, then I heard the bathroom door close. I tried to focus my mind on Cory, instead of the small space. *You're going to see him again*, I kept thinking to myself, imagining his arms around me, holding me close.

"I have to tell you something," Bellany said, cutting through my thoughts.

She let go of my hand, but I kept my eyes shut. "What?"

"Don't worry, Victoria. What I'm going to tell you is good news. You're gonna want to hear this. I promise."

Good news? I could use some good news. "Okay," I said, wondering what it was.

"I'm going to whisper it to you."

I felt her push my hair back, and my eyes popped open. I took a couple steps back, distancing myself from her.

"Don't be afraid," Bellany said, calmly. "I promise it's good news."

She leaned in close, and this time I didn't back away.

"I heard something on the ear piece," she whispered. "I heard a man speaking in English. He said that we'll be playing another game."

My heart rate spiked. Another game? How could Bellany think this was good news? Had she lost her mind? "I don't want to play any more games."

She grabbed me by my arm. "Wait. There's more."

I took a deep breath, trying to calm down. "Okay."

She leaned into my ear again. "The winner of the game will be set free," she whispered.

"Are you serious?" She better not be lying.

"We'll be able to get off this yacht," she whispered. "We'll be free again, just like before. Then you and I can go wherever we want--anywhere in the world. We still have loads of money. We can start over again somewhere. And this time it won't be temporary. We'll buy a house..."

Bellany continued telling me about her future plans, which surprisingly included me. Although I wasn't sure if she really meant it. It was hard for me to figure out if she was lying. She was so good at it.

She stepped away from me, a smile on her face. "We'll buy a mansion," she said with a gleam in her eyes. "We'll buy luxurious cars. We'll be the envy of the town."

I tried to focus on her words, instead of how small and confined the bathroom was and how much my head and my hands hurt. I tried to envision the future she was describing. I wanted all of it, except I didn't want to have that kind of life with her. I wanted to have it with Cory. I had fallen deeply in love with him. My heart ached for him.

"We'll tell everybody in town that we're sisters," Bellany said, her smile growing wider.

I knew she expected me to smile back at her, but I couldn't do it. My cheeks were heavy. My face felt like it was frozen.

"What's wrong?" Bellany asked, studying my face.

I didn't dare tell her what I was really thinking. "I'm claustrophobic," I reminded her.

Minutes of uncomfortable silence passed, and I was on the verge of panicking again. How much longer were we going to be stuck in here?

"Are you still mad about me tackling you to the ground and bumping your head?" Bellany asked, breaking the silence.

Was that supposed to be an apology?

"I never wanted to hurt you, Victoria. But you gave me no choice. You tried to punch me in the face. Did you think I wouldn't defend myself?"

I had every right to punch her in the face--she knew it as well as I did. But I wasn't going to argue with her. I had something else more important to talk to her about. "If you really meant what you said about us starting over somewhere together, then I need you to prove it."

Bellany didn't even flinch. She didn't react at all. "What do you want, Victoria?"

"The money is supposed to be ours to share. But I don't have access to it anymore."

Her jaw tightened, lips pressing into a straight line. "You can access the bank account on my phone. The username and password will autofill. I left my phone at Cory's house. It's buried under the swing in the backyard. All you need is the pin number to unlock the screen."

Was she being serious? "What's the pin number?"

"It's 4444." She cocked her head. "I'm sure you'll be able to remember that."

I nodded once, wondering if she was lying. "Why did you bury your phone at Cory's house?"

"It's my backup phone. I always stash a backup phone somewhere. Plus I was being followed, so I knew I couldn't keep it with me."

"Do you have any other backup phones or just that one?"

"That's the only one."

"With such a simple pin code, aren't you afraid someone will access the bank account and take all the money?"

"No," she replied without hesitation. "They'll never guess a pin code like that. It's too easy."

Now that I had access to the money again, I felt a lot more relaxed. I didn't need Bellany anymore. Did she realize that?

CHAPTER 41

Cory

Armed men escorted Gemma and I out of our room. Leaving behind all of those safes was a huge relief. I never wanted to open another combination lock ever again in my life.

It was dark out, the sky pitch black. The armed men pointed their flashlights in the direction they wanted us to go. I kept my eyes and ears open for any signs of Tasha and Charlotte. But every door we passed was shut, and all I could hear were our own footsteps, the wind whipping through the air, and the ocean waves thrashing. I never heard calls for help, and I wasn't sure if that was a good sign, or if it was bad.

I had convinced myself that Tasha was still alive and that we would be reunited again soon. I had to keep hoping that everything would turn out all right, because the alternative was too daunting to even think about.

When we entered the bedroom, the door slammed shut behind us. I was relieved to see two beds. Sleeping on the hard floor had been brutal on my back. I noticed two other doors. I wasn't sure which one led to the bathroom. I headed to the one on the left, and Gemma headed to the one on the right. We both knocked. My door was locked. Gemma had found the bathroom.

Victoria plowed through the bathroom door, stumbling awkwardly into the bedroom. Her hair was a ragged mess, her clothes disheveled. There were dark circles under her eyes, and she looked like she had been crying.

When Bellany appeared, she glided across the floor with grace. Her long, dark hair flowing behind her. There was an air of deep sadness about her though, and that was different.

I could feel Gemma's stare from across the room. I knew she was watching me with a critical eye. She hated Bellany and had tried to convince me to hate her too.

I figured I should jump right into things with Bellany, instead of being cordial. "Those roses you sent me... they had thorns on them." Bellany had sent me roses when I first moved into my house. Tasha pricked her finger on one of the thorns and started bleeding. It was really cruel of Bellany to send those.

Her eyelashes fluttered, mouth hanging open. "Really? Wow. I'm so sorry about that. I ordered the roses over the phone. I had no idea they were prepared incorrectly. I just wanted to congratulate you on your new home."

I had a hard time believing her. She had a long history of lying. "I saw you at the hospital," I said, remembering how she had slipped into the elevator before I could catch up to her. She was deliberately running away from me.

Bellany tucked a strand of hair behind her ear. "Yeah, I'm sorry about running off like that. I didn't think it was the right time to... you know, catch up with each other... I'm glad Tasha recovered. I was really worried about her."

Was she? Again, I had a hard time believing her. "Yeah, well, I'm really worried about Tasha right now. I hope nothing bad has happened to her."

Bellany crossed her arms. The sadness in her eyes looked real. She was so convincing. I wanted to believe it was real.

Gemma cleared her throat, interrupting us. She glared at Bellany. "There are so many things I want to say to you right now. Let me start by saying, this is all your fault!"

"I know. You're right," Bellany replied without a moment's hesitation. "This is my fault, and I feel awful about what has happened to everybody. If there was anything I could do to stop Shandy from keeping us here and making us suffer, I'd do it--I promise you, I would."

Gemma held up a hand. "You know what? I don't want to hear it. All you do is lie all the time. So don't even bother."

Gemma scowled at Victoria next. "You're to blame too. You do realize that, don't you?"

Victoria was sitting on the bed. She looked like she might be feeling seasick or maybe she was just lacking energy. "I know," she sighed. "You have no idea how much I regret getting involved."

She wasn't the only one with regrets. I should have never invited Victoria into my home or into my life. I should have known something was up with her. She gave me a bad vibe right from the start, but I pushed that feeling aside and ignored it, because I was in the middle of a crisis with Tasha.

The phone rang and the knots in my stomach tightened. I knew whatever game Shandy had in store for us could potentially end in disaster, like it did for Wade. I just hoped we'd all make it through this alive.

The voice on the phone informed us that the game was an easy one. But only three of us would play.

"Who's gonna play?" I asked, wondering why she was leaving one of us out."

"Don't interrupt!" the voice shouted. "A box has been placed underneath the bed. You may retrieve it, but don't open it. Don't pick it up either. Just slide it across the floor."

"Great, another box," Victoria sighed, about to cry.

I reached under the bed and pulled out a large shoe box, but I doubted it contained a pair of shoes. I could feel that it was heavy, just from sliding it across the floor.

Bellany sat next to me, her eyes on the box. She whispered something, but I was unable to hear what she had said.

"Like I mentioned before," the voice on the phone continued, "only three of you will be playing. It's up to you to decide who sits out. You have five minutes to make your decision, starting now."

"Wait!" Gemma gasped, staring at the phone. "Aren't you going to tell us what the game is or what's in the box first?"

"Time's ticking," the voice replied.

"What if we don't want to play your game," Gemma said,

eyes wild. "What if we refuse?"

"Hey..." Bellany placed a hand on her arm. "Take a deep breath. Calm down."

Gemma jerked away from her. "Don't you dare touch me! This is all your fault, Bellany! So you're going to have to play the game--that's for sure."

I agreed with Gemma. Bellany couldn't sit out. She had to participate.

Gemma's eyes slid to Victoria next. "You're playing too. You're one of the reasons we're in this mess."

Victoria's shoulders hunched forward, her gaze lowering to the floor. "I know. I'll play," she said in a small voice.

"I'll play too," I said. "Gemma, you can sit out."

She sighed heavily, leaning back against the bed. "Thanks, Cory."

"Okay then..." the voice on the phone said. "Gemma, you must go through the connecting door, into the other bedroom. That's where you will wait until the game is over."

"You want me to go in there by myself?" The color drained from Gemma's face. "Is Wade's dead body still in there?"

"You have twenty seconds to comply. If you don't, I will kill both Charlotte and Tasha. The clock starts now."

I heard the lock on the door disengage, and my heart leapt into my throat. "Gemma! You have to hurry! Please! Tasha and Charlotte's lives depend on it."

Gemma scrambled to her feet with tears in her eyes. "This isn't fair!" she cried as she raced through the door and slammed it shut.

We could hear her sobbing, and I wondered if Wade's dead body was still in there.

"You may take the lid off the box," the voice announced, "but don't touch the item inside. If you fail to follow my rules, I will kill Tasha, Charlotte, and Gemma too."

Bellany lifted the lid, and my heart stopped when I saw what was inside. A revolver!

Victoria started crying hard, her entire body shaking.

Bellany looked like she was in shock. She just sat there staring at it.

"You're about to play a game of Russian roulette," the voice announced, "only you're not going to spin the cylinder on the revolver. That part has already been done for you."

Victoria wiped the tears from her eyes. "My dad's friend has a revolver just like that. It can hold six bullets."

"How many bullets are inside it?" I asked.

"There's only one bullet," the voice replied. "One of you is going to die."

"But what's the prize?" Victoria cried, hugging her knees into her chest. "What do we get if we survive this? Do we get to go free?"

"Victoria," the voice replied with a chuckle. "The prize is survival. I'm not going to set you free."

I wondered which one of us was going to die. What if it was me?

"But I don't want to play, unless two of us can go free!" Victoria shouted, her eyes scanning the ceiling. "It's only fair!"

The voice on the phone laughed. "If you don't play, then Tasha, Charlotte and Gemma will die. Is that what you want, Victoria?"

Oh, she was going to play all right--I was going to make certain of it! "Victoria, you're playing!"

"Yes, Cory, I know. I'm playing," she assured me, resting a hand on my arm. "I just wanted to see if there was a possibility we could get out of here, that's all."

It didn't seem like that to me. It seemed like she was willing to sacrifice Tasha's life.

"If there are no further questions, then let's begin," the voice said. "Who's going first?"

Victoria squeezed my arm, latching onto me.

"I'll go first," Bellany said, and when she looked up at me, a tear rolled down her cheek. "Cory, if I die, I want you to know that I truly am sorry. I also want you to know the reason why I came to Mexico." She paused, running a finger under her eye.

"I was hoping we could reconcile our differences, move on from the past, and start over again... Together. I truly am sorry for everything."

Victoria let go of me, placing her arms at her sides, her entire body rigid. She was glaring at Bellany.

"I hope you can forgive me, Cory," Bellany said, fighting back more tears.

It was impossible for me to know if Bellany truly meant what she said, or if she was just lying like she always did. But given the gravity of the situation, I gave her the benefit of the doubt. "I'm sorry too," I said. And I was. That was the truth. These were possibly our last moments together, and I didn't want to have any regrets.

"Thank you, Cory," Bellany said as more tears rolled down her face. She reached her arms around me and melted into my chest. I could feel her body trembling against mine. She whispered something in my ear, but her voice was so low, I could barely make it out. Did she just say, *I love you?* Bellany kissed my cheek before pulling away.

"Pick up the gun, Bellany," the voice said, sternly. "It's time to start the game."

Bellany turned to the box, but I couldn't watch. I lowered my gaze to the floor. My chest constricted as I braced for her to pull the trigger, wondering if these were her last moments.

CHAPTER 42

Victoria

I grabbed the revolver before Bellany could reach it, but I didn't point it at myself. I pointed it at her. She seemed shocked, but she shouldn't have been. She should've known this was coming, especially after what she had just done.

When faced with the possibility of death, what did Bellany do? She turned to Cory and threw her arms around him. But she couldn't have him. He was mine!

"What are you doing?" Bellany gasped in horror, as I pointed the revolver at her.

Cory stepped toward me, and I swung the revolver, pointing it in his direction. "Don't even think about it!" I wasn't going to shoot him. I just needed him to stay out of this.

He held up his hands and remained in place.

I pointed the revolver at Bellany again. She fixed her cold, hard stare on me. But I wasn't intimidated. I had the revolver, she didn't. And she was going to end up dead, just like all of my other former best friends. I killed them, because they tried to take away the people that I loved; just like Bellany was trying to take away Cory.

"Victoria," Bellany said, holding completely still. "Put the revolver down."

"Why? You were going to point at yourself anyway, right? What difference does it make if I pull the trigger, or if you do?"

"It makes a huge difference," she said.

I couldn't help but smile. I knew what she was really worried about. "You're afraid I'll keep pulling the trigger until I finally shoot you, aren't you?"

"Victoria." Cory's voice was calm and cool. His hands were still in the air. "Put the revolver down."

I chuckled at his ridiculous request. "Bellany doesn't love you, Cory. I hope you know that."

"I never thought that she did," he replied.

"Do you know why I'm doing this?" I asked, hoping he would understand.

"No. Why?"

"Because Bellany wouldn't have killed herself. She would have killed me." I kept my eyes and the revolver fixed on her. "Right, Bellany?"

"No, you're wrong. I wasn't going to do that."

"Yes, you were! Quit lying!" I widened my stance and focused on my target, which was right between her eyes.

Bellany froze. She hardly even blinked, which was wise of her. But I was surprised that she hadn't started begging for me to spare her life yet. Did she think I wouldn't pull the trigger? "You remember what happened to Chantel, right?" I asked her.

The corners of her mouth turned down, so I didn't have to say it out loud. Bellany already knew the truth.

"I'm a good shot. I never miss," I reminded Bellany, pointing the revolver directly at her face. Was she too prideful to beg for her life? Yes. But it didn't matter. I was going to kill her anyway.

Cory was mine, and there was nothing she could do about it. Plus, I had access to all the money. There was no need to keep her around anymore.

Just when I was about to pull the trigger, an alarming thought entered my mind. What if Bellany lied about her backup phone? "The stashed cell phone..." I said, watching Bellany's face, trying to read her expression. "Is it really where you said it is?"

"Yes," she replied, her eyes welling with tears.

Her answer surprised me. I had expected her to use the money as a means of negotiation. Why hadn't she done that?

"Any last words," I asked, adjusting my grip on the revolver. Bellany's eyes shifted, and I turned to look. Cory came rushing toward me, tackling me to the floor, knocking the air out of my lungs. He was on top of me, trying to pry the revolver out of my fingers. A loud bang ripped through the air, ringing in my ears, and he finally let go.

I stared into his beautiful blue eyes for the last time, knowing I would never see them again.

CHAPTER 43

Cory

Victoria was lying on the floor in a pool of her own blood, and my mind was spinning with the realization of what I had just done. I killed her! I murdered her in cold blood!

"Are you okay?" Bellany's voice was a distant echo in my mind as I stared blankly at my blood-soaked hands.

A feeling of dread settled in the pit of my stomach. We hadn't followed Shandy's rules for playing Russian roulette. But we did have a casualty. Was that enough bloodshed for Shandy? Or was she still going to kill Tasha, Charlotte and Gemma too?

"Well played, you two!" the voice on the phone announced. "It's time to move on to the next game."

"What?" Did that mean Tasha, Charlotte and Gemma were going to live?

The door swung open, slamming against the wall, and Bellany jumped into my arms. Four men with guns came storming in, ordering us to exit the room. A barrel of a gun was pressed against my back. Bellany was beside me, a gun pointed at her head.

"Move it!" the man shouted, jabbing his gun into my spine.

They led us to the rear of the yacht--the exact same place where we had originally climbed aboard. It was dark outside, but the moon hung brightly in the sky.

Bellany and I stood with our backs to the ocean, our heels uncomfortably close to the deck's edge. I could hear the waves lapping against the side of the yacht. The wind ripped through the air so violently, I felt like it might push me overboard.

My mind raced as I tried to figure out what to do. But the situation seemed impossible. I was outnumbered. I was unarmed. I had no plan!

"Cory!"

I turned to look, my heart racing. It was Gemma! Two men were leading her toward us at gunpoint. I scanned the deck behind her, searching for Tasha and Charlotte, but there was no sign of them. Where were they?

Gemma was forced to stand next to Bellany.

"Are you okay?" Bellany asked her.

Gemma nodded, her eyes on me. She looked terrified.

The armed men stood watch, guns at the ready. Were they going to shoot us and dump our bodies in the ocean?

"Is that her?" Gemma's voice cut through my thoughts.

I followed her gaze to the top deck. An older woman with gray hair was standing at the railing, looking down at us.

"Is that Shandy?" I asked Bellany.

"Yes. That's her," she said through gritted teeth.

"What kind of a sick woman are you?" Gemma shouted. "Let us go!"

One of the armed men raised his gun, pointing it at Gemma's face, and she immediately closed her mouth.

Shandy leaned onto the railing. "Cory," she said, her voice projecting loudly. "It's up to you to decide what happens next. You have two options. Option one, you can save yourself, Gemma, Tasha, and Charlotte, but you'll have to sacrifice Bellany."

"What do you mean, sacrifice Bellany?" My heart pounded as I looked into Bellany's eyes and saw an expression of sheer terror etched onto her face. I wanted to stand in front of her and shield her, but I knew I couldn't make any sudden movements, unless I wanted to risk getting shot.

"I mean, sacrifice her life. She will be shot and thrown overboard. Everybody else will be set free."

I felt a heavy ache in my chest. Again I looked at Bellany,

wondering if this would be the last time I saw her.

"Option two," Shandy announced, pointing at us. "You, Bellany and Gemma will be thrown overboard. You may survive, or you may not." She shrugged. "That's the risk you're going to have to take."

"What about Tasha and Charlotte?" I asked, my heart racing. "What will happen to them?"

"Tasha and Charlotte will be returned to your house, unharmed." Shandy leaned onto her elbows, fingers laced together. "But I must warn you about something, if you choose option two. We're miles away from land. And the ocean, well it's quite cold. Not to mention, there are plenty of ravenous creatures swimming around just waiting for a nice meal." She chuckled.

"Cory!" Gemma shrieked. "You can't possibly be considering option two! Don't be a fool! Take option one and save our lives! Bellany doesn't deserve to live. She deserves to die! She's the reason we're here. This is all her fault!"

Logically, I knew which option I should take. But my gut was telling me not to do it. I didn't want to be responsible for Bellany's death. I already knew what it felt like to kill someone. I couldn't get the image of Victoria's lifeless body out of my mind. I still had her blood on my hands.

I looked up at Shandy. "Would you consider altering option two and let Gemma go free with Tasha and Charlotte?"

She cocked her head. "I will accept that offer, but with one condition. Bellany's hands and feet will be tied together before she's pushed overboard. She's going to sink, right to the bottom of the ocean, unless you can find her and save her in time."

I knew I wouldn't be able to find Bellany using sight. It was too dark. I'd have to completely rely on touch. But was it even possible?

"Don't do it--don't risk your life for her!" Gemma cried.

"You've got to save yourself, Cory," Bellany said, tears streaming down her cheeks. "Tasha needs you. You've gotta be there to take care of her." Bellany's tears continued to flow.

I couldn't believe she wanted me to do this. She was giving up. She was sacrificing her life. "But I think I can save you," I said.

"Choose option one," Bellany cried. "Please! Just do it!"

"Listen to her, Cory!" Gemma pleaded. "You won't be able to save her. She's going to die and there's nothing you can do about it. Her death will not be your fault!"

It would be my fault. But I knew that even if I did manage to save Bellany from plunging into the depths of the ocean, there was no guarantee we'd survive beyond that. "I'm so sorry, Bellany," I said as tears filled my eyes, blurring my vision of her.

"You must make your decision now," Shandy demanded, pounding her fist on the railing.

I swallowed a lump in my throat. "I choose option one," I said, and my chest constricted.

"You heard him!" Shandy shouted. "Do it!"

The man standing directly in front of Bellany raised his gun. Three quick, loud bangs filled the air, ringing through my ears. Bellany stumbled backward, falling overboard. Droplets of water sprayed onto my face, or was it blood?

I stood there in shock, my ears still ringing. Then I heard a distant noise and saw lights appear in the sky. A helicopter!

CHAPTER 44

Tasha

Three Months Later.

Cory was helping me build a sandcastle, but he wasn't doing a very good job. He was way too slow. He kept getting distracted, staring out at the ocean. I knew why he did that. I remembered when Gemma explained it to me. She said, "He's grieving."

I didn't know what that word meant, so I asked her.

She said, "Grieving means that he's missing someone who died."

I asked Cory, "Are you grieving because you miss Wade, Victoria, and Bellany?"

Those three never made it onto the helicopter when we escaped from Shandy. They couldn't, because they were already dead.

Cory looked at me funny when I said the word, grieving. He was probably surprised that I knew such a big word. He said, "I'm not grieving. I'm fine--don't worry."

But then later, Gemma told me that he lied. She said he was grieving. Which confused me. Cory always told me never to lie. He said it was really, really bad to lie to people.

So I asked Cory why he lied since it was against the rules. Then he got mad at Gemma for telling me that he lied. They got into this huge argument--I mean huge!

Gemma yelled at him and said some really mean stuff. She called him "an idiot," and "a fool," and some other bad words I'm not allowed to repeat.

She yelled and said, "Bellany deserved to die, and so did Victoria!"

Well, that made Cory really mad. He said, "I want you to leave my house!" And he pointed at the door.

Gemma pulled the TV off the wall, and it crashed onto the floor. She totally broke it! Then she stomped down the hall, really loud. Stomp, stomp, stomp!

When she came back out of the bedroom, she had her suitcase. She screamed and yelled at Cory, called him some more bad words, then stormed out of the house and slammed the door really hard.

She didn't even say goodbye to me. She just ignored me, which I thought was really mean and rude.

The next day, I asked Cory if he was glad that Gemma was gone, because I sure was.

He said he wasn't glad, but he didn't want to be her friend anymore. So I guessed that meant that he kind of hated her.

I scooped some sand into the bucket, then looked back at our house. Cory said he might sell it. He wants to move to another house, because he doesn't like this one anymore. I asked him if we could move to another beach house, and he said, "No." He said it really sternly, so I knew he meant it.

Then I asked if we could move to North Carolina and live by Charlotte, because I missed her. She was a good friend.

But Cory said, "No." Except this time he wasn't stern, so I thought maybe he might change his mind.

I said, "If we live by Charlotte, then we can help cheer her up, so she won't be missing Wade so much."

But Cory still said, "No." And then he reminded me why we couldn't live in the United States. He said my mean foster parents might find me. That was when I changed my mind with lightning speed. I didn't want to live by Charlotte anymore. I wanted to stay far, far away from her and stay in Mexico.

Cory finally stopped looking at the ocean and turned to me. I handed him a shovel, hoping he would help me build my sandcastle.

"Tasha, did you dig a hole under the swing in the backyard?" he asked.

"Why would I dig a hole in the backyard when I have all this sand out here on the beach?" I asked, spreading my arms wide.

"Do you know how the hole got there?" he asked, raising an eyebrow, which meant that he was really serious. He wasn't joking at all.

"I don't know." Then I thought to myself, what could make a hole in the ground? A rabbit? A gopher? But those holes would be small. It had to think of a bigger animal. "Maybe a dog did it," I said. "Maybe there was a bone buried under the ground." I saw dogs in cartoons digging up bones all the time. But I had never seen one do it in real life.

"Yeah, maybe," he said as he turned to look at the ocean again.

This time I didn't interrupt him. I knew he was grieving.

CHAPTER 45

Bellany

The bullets were blanks, but they sure sounded real. My ears were ringing for several minutes after they were fired. After I fell into the ocean, I quickly grabbed hold of the ladder and waited until Cory and Gemma were ushered away.

The old woman with gray hair wasn't Shandy. Her name's Gloria. She was a desperate, out of work actress who also happened to have a criminal history. I hired her--and paid her quite well--for the acting job she did. She was worth every penny.

The first thing I had her do was meet Victoria. I had to find out if I could really trust Victoria, and I quickly learned that I couldn't. Victoria never mentioned the encounter she had with Gloria. She kept it a secret, so I knew she wasn't loyal to me.

I had vowed to get revenge on Cory, which was why I came to Mexico in the first place. Keeping Victoria around to help me do it was necessary. And she proved to be useful, especially when she found out what everybody's biggest fears were. That was a tremendous help.

When the big day I had been planning for finally arrived, I was ready. I left the rental house early with all of my stuff. I changed the password on the bank account, and then waited for Victoria to freak out like I knew she would.

When Cory and his friends showed up at the rental house, I was able to listen to everything they said. I had bugged the place. So when they set out to find the yacht, I already had my men ready.

There weren't two yachts. There was only one--the Jenny. And contrary to what I told everybody, the truth was I never bought it. I only chartered it.

I purposely let Victoria snoop on my phone, like I knew she would. The text messages were meant for her to read, and the look on her face was priceless when she thought I caught her snooping. I had to force myself not to laugh.

Chartering a yacht was a little tricky. I convinced the owner to let me hire my own crew, which wasn't easy. I had to pay extra for that. But luckily finding a new crew was a rather quick process. All it took was a little searching online and voilà.

I hired a group of men and one woman to navigate it. The woman was young and had long hair just like me. She proved to make a good body double from a distance. She stood on the top deck while Cory and the other losers were swimming toward the yacht. I knew they would think she was me.

I also hired some construction workers to make modifications to the yacht. And I hired an artist to create the mermaid paintings.

Then I hired another group of men to be my muscle. They came with their own guns and a thirst for blood, which was a nice perk. They also didn't cost me very much. I promised them a lot of beer and a party at sea, upon completion of the job. They were thrilled.

A couple of my men spiked the Diet Pepsi in Cory's fridge with a strong sedative, which knocked Victoria right out. I knew she would guzzle it down. She lived on that stuff. While she was knocked out on the couch, Gloria abducted Tasha.

When I arrived at Cory's house later that day, I had my men waiting in the garage. I warned them ahead of time that Victoria would likely have a gun, but they weren't intimidated. They seemed eager for the challenge.

It blew my mind that Victoria never figured out I was the mastermind behind all of this. If she was a little smarter, maybe she would have. But I didn't keep her around for her brains. She was easy to manipulate, right up until the point where she pointed the revolver at me. That was when I regretted not taking her out sooner. She was lucky she had a quick death. If I had been given the opportunity, I would have made her suffer.

The earpiece that I claimed to have found on the floor, had actually been in my ear the entire time. It wasn't just a receiver. It was a transmitter too, enabling me to remain in constant contact with my men.

When Wade, Victoria, and I played spin the bottle, I knew which bottles of water were poisoned. There was a small black dot on the bottles that were safe to drink. I thought the black dot was such a good idea that I had the dot placed on the bottles of water that were given to Cory and Gemma too, except none of those bottles were actually poisoned. I just wanted them to think they were to mess with their heads a little bit.

It was never my intention to kill Cory. I just wanted to make him suffer. After I broke him emotionally, I wanted to see if he could be reformed, reshaped and molded into the man I hoped he would be. But due to our sorted past, I had to provide him with some incentive first and make him believe that I loved him--which was yet another lie. I didn't love him. I saw potential in him, and that's all.

Since human behavior has always been hard to predict, I had to prepare a few contingency plans while on the yacht. Several rooms were set up as potential traps. I had tried to convince the others to attempt an escape a couple times. I knew that my men were prepared for such a situation. If we had tried to escape, they would have taken us to another room, where more surprises were in store. Unfortunately, we never got a chance to experience any of it.

While everybody else was starving and dying of thirst, I was just fine. I kept a few energy gel packs hidden in my pocket and sucked those down whenever I got the chance.

When Victoria got locked in the bedroom by herself, I had my men bring me some water and a protein bar.

Then when it came time to play Russian roulette, I was supposed to point the revolver at myself and pull the trigger first. The bullet wasn't in the first chamber. It was in the second chamber, so I knew I would be unharmed.

I had planned on handing the revolver to Victoria next. She was supposed to die of a self-inflicted gunshot wound to the head. That was my original plan, but like I said, human behavior was hard to predict.

My men should have barged in and stopped Victoria from pointing the revolver at me, but they couldn't find the key to the door. They had misplaced it! I docked their pay severely because of this. I could have died!

Fortunately Cory managed to stop Victoria before she shot me. If Victoria had been better nourished and hydrated, she probably would have shot Cory when he jumped her.

Cory's act of heroism impressed me, and I started to believe that maybe he could be reformed. All he had to do was pass one more test to prove it. But he ended up failing. He chose to sacrifice my life.

He should have chosen option two. I would have made it easy for him to save me. If I had been tied up and thrown overboard, I wouldn't have sunk to the bottom of the ocean. I had trained my men to tie me up loosely, so that I could break free.

Cory and I would have been rescued within minutes. I had another boat waiting nearby. I also had an underwater diver, just in case I needed some extra assistance.

But in the end, I felt satisfied with how things turned out. I got revenge, just like I wanted. Cory, Charlotte and Gemma lost the people they loved.

Cory lost me. Charlotte lost Wade. And Gemma lost Bridger.

When I first learned that Bridger was planning on coming to Mexico and that Gemma was his girlfriend, I immediately called him. Bridger hadn't heard from me since I ran away from home. So he had loads to say. He yelled at me. And I just let him. I apologized and promised to remain in contact with him, which seemed to cheer him up.

Then I lectured him about being in a relationship with Gemma. I told him she was a loser and he could do so much better. I didn't have to pressure him too much before he agreed to break up with her. He claimed he had been planning on doing it anyway. But I wasn't completely convinced. I sensed he really cared about her, which was disappointing. He seemed to have lost some of his self-confidence.

I recently mailed him a letter, reminding him to remain focused on his goals and to stay away from Gemma. I didn't sign it with my real name. I used our mother's middle name, Martha. Bridger would know it was from me. He used to call me Martha whenever we played house as kids.

The last thing I did before leaving Mexico was stop at Cory's house to retrieve my backup cell phone. Then I got in my car and headed back to the United States.

I planned on settling down in Montana, where I would be looking for a new man... Maybe I would meet a cowboy, or a construction worker, or a doctor. I didn't care what occupation my future Mr. Right had, as long as he wasn't a true crime podcaster--that had already been crossed off my list.

CHAPTER 46

Tasha

I felt bad for lying to Cory. I knew who dug the hole in the ground under the swing, and it wasn't a dog. I watched the person do it through my bedroom window late at night.

At first I didn't know who it was. But then the person walked under the light, and I saw their face. It was Bellany. She was carrying a shovel and a flashlight.

I had never seen a ghost before. And since Bellany was supposed to be dead, I thought she was a ghost. But then I decided that she couldn't be a ghost, because ghosts were supposed to glow and hover over the ground.

Bellany didn't glow. She didn't look bright at all. She looked dark. She didn't float or hover either. Bellany walked like a normal person.

So I thought really hard about what was going on. I remembered that Cory said a bad man killed Bellany, and she fell into the ocean. But then I remembered something else Cory had told me. He said that Bellany lied a lot. He said that one time she faked her death and ran away. That was when I figured it out! Bellany must have faked her death again!

After she dug the hole under the swing, I watched her walk out the back gate. Then I laid down in bed, but it was hard for me to fall asleep. I kept worrying she might come back and break into our house or something.

So I looked out the back window again, but this time I didn't see Bellany. I saw an opossum! Its eyes were shining under the light.

Cory had taught me how to spell opossums. It didn't start with a P. It started with an O, and the O was silent. Anyway, he taught me that opossums faked their deaths when they felt threatened. He said they couldn't help it. Their bodies just did it on their own. It was a survival instinct.

When I saw the opossum in the backyard, my brain clicked. It all made sense! Bellany was like an opossum! She felt threatened so she faked her death again!

Once I figured this out, I knew Bellany wouldn't be coming back around here anymore. She wanted to run and be free, just like an opossum!

Maybe one day I would tell Cory the truth about the hole under the swing and how it got there. But for now, I planned on keeping it a secret!

CHAPTER 47

Gemma

Bridger had been avoiding me ever since I got back from Mexico. He rarely texted me, and he wouldn't answer any of my phone calls.

I felt like I had no other choice but to confront him in person. I parked my car in front of his house and planned on waiting for him to come home. I wanted to know why he broke up with me. I also wanted to tell him all about everything that had happened in Mexico. He was lucky he didn't go.

While I was sitting in my car waiting, the mailman delivered Bridger's mail. As soon as he drove away, I opened the mail box and sifted through it, because I'm nosey like that.

I came across a pink envelope, which I assumed was from a girl, based on the color. There was no return address, which made me even more curious. Was Bridger seeing someone?

I took the letter with me and headed back home, where I carefully steamed it open. Inside, I found a postcard from Mexico with a handwritten note on it. At first I wondered if it was from Cory. But then I saw that it was signed by a girl named Martha. Who's Martha?

The note said: **Talking to you brought back so many memories from the past. I only wish I had reached out to you sooner. Promise me you'll stay on track with college. If Gemma tries to get in your way, all you have to do is offer her some saltine crackers. Believe me, she'll get all choked up over that. Anyway, I promise we'll talk again soon. Love, Martha.**

Saltine crackers! My mind flooded with memories of all

the trauma I had experienced on the yacht. There were only a few people still alive who knew about my fear of saltine crackers. Could Shandy have written this note? But she didn't know Bridger. She didn't have memories of him from the past.

This couldn't have been written by Cory. He didn't have a past with Bridger either. And this definitely wasn't written by Tasha. There weren't any spelling errors.

I texted Charlotte and asked her if she had sent it. She texted back and said that she hadn't.

It couldn't have been from Victoria, Wade, or Bellany. They were all dead.

Who could have sent this, I wondered.

Over the next couple days, I couldn't stop thinking about the letter. I had to figure out who wrote it. For some reason, the same name kept coming to my mind. Bellany.

She never wanted Bridger and I to be together. She forbade him from seeing me. She definitely had a past with Bridger--she was his twin sister. They grew up in the same house. She knew about my fear of saltine crackers, and she was living in Mexico. This couldn't all be just a coincidence, could it?

As I struggled to make sense of everything, I began looking through some old text messages between me and Bridger:

Bridger: **I'm going to focus on school and having a relationship with you will only distract me from that.**

Me: **What makes you think a relationship with me will distract you?**

Bridger: **It just will. OK!**

Me: **No it won't! Again, what makes you think that?**

Bridger: **Someone gave me some good advice, and I'm going to take it.**

Me: **Who gave you advice? Some other girl? Because if it's another girl, I can guarantee you she has an ulterior motive. She wants you to be single so she can have you.**

Bridger: **There's no chance of that.**

Me: **No chance? That's a laugh. Whoever this girl is, she's** manipulating you. **She wants you.**

Bridger: **She's not interested in me that way!**

Me: **You're being naive. Of course she's interested in you!**

Bridger: **That's impossible! You have no idea what you're talking about!**

As I studied the string of texts, I kept wondering why it was impossible for Bridger to fall in love with this unknown girl.

I checked the postmark date on the envelope just to make sure it had been sent recently. Once I confirmed this, my mind started racing. I didn't want to believe it, but there was no other explanation.

Bellany told Bridger to break up with me!

She wrote the letter!

She was Martha!

She was still alive!

I jumped into my car, my heart slamming against my ribs. I weaved in and out of traffic, speeding through yellow lights. As I raced down the road, one question kept running through my mind: Could a person be charged with murder for killing someone who's supposedly already dead?

Honestly, I didn't care. I was going to kill Bellany anyway!

ACKNOWLEDGEMENT

Special thanks to Denise for being the ravenous reader that you are and for your invaluable advice! It means the world to me!

Dear Reader,

I'm incredibly grateful that you chose to read my book, when I know you have so many other options. Thank you! I'd love for you to rate/review it!

Sincerely,
Michele Leathers

ABOUT THE AUTHOR

Michele Leathers

Michele Leathers's books have climbed to the top of Amazon bestseller lists. Her novels are fast-paced and full of jaw-dropping twists that will keep readers guessing till the end. Michele Leathers received a Bachelor's degree in Philosophy from North Carolina State University and is a full time writer. She's not ashamed to admit that she's addicted to Diet Pepsi, chocolate, and writing. She's a shrewd observer of people, always looking for ideas and inspiration for her books. Follow Michele Leathers's Amazon author page to keep up with her latest releases! www.MicheleLeathers.com

BOOKS IN THIS SERIES

They All Had A Reason

They All Had A Reason: A Rumor. A Secret. A Lie. A Murder. (They All Had A Reason. Book 1)

They All Had A Secret: A Betrayal. A Deception. A Tragedy. A Murder. (They All Had A Reason. Book 2)

They All Had A Fear: A Past. A Debt. A Reckoning. A Murder. (They All Had A Reason. Book 3)

They All Had A Chance: A Pact. A Test. A Dilemma. A Murder. (They All Had A Reason. Book 4)

They All Had A Plan: A Passion. A Hatred. A Jealousy. A Murder. (They All Had A Reason. Book 5)

They All Had A Grudge: A Reason. A Secret. A

Fear. A Murder. (They All Had A Reason. Book 6)

BOOKS BY THIS AUTHOR

Shadow Copy: Exit Darkness (The Shadow Copy Series Book 1)

Shadow Copy: Enter Light (The Shadow Copy Series Book 2)

Made in the USA
Las Vegas, NV
16 December 2023

82980860R00138